C000195746

FAIRCHILD

JAIMA FIXSEN

Copyright © 2013 by Jaima Fixsen

All rights reserved.

No part of this book may be reproduced in any form or by any electronic or mechanical means, including information storage and retrieval systems, without written permission from the author, except for the use of brief quotations in a book review.

To Jeff
Thanks for supporting me as writer in residence

CHAPTER 1
FATHERLESS

T he day Sophy let Mrs. Upton's pig into the laundry, her mother died.

Snuffling contentedly, the pig took to rooting through the snowy linens just like a happy baby, which was fitting, since Mrs. Upton cherished her spotted prizewinner like it was her only child. Satisfied with her revenge, Sophy vaulted over the fence and pelted down the lane to safety. Though small, she was spry and fast.

Served the old cow right.

"Ooof!" she grunted, stumbling headfirst into the dusty road.

"Watch yourself!" snapped Mr. Lynchem, the minister, righting himself just in time. His books were not so fortunate; they tumbled to the ground. "Slow down and look where you are going!"

"Beg pardon, sir!" On her feet again, Sophy ignored the dust on her pinafore, her stinging palms and her bashed knee, diving to retrieve Mr. Lynchem's books. She swiftly brushed the covers with the clean edge of her pinafore before thrusting each volume into his hands. He was piecing together his torn dignity, his enormous chest swelling with outrage under his black coat. She could not linger, for any moment Mrs. Upton would—

"AAieeee!"

Too late.

"What have you done?" Mr. Lynchem's caterpillar eyebrows inched closer. He glared at Sophy for a mere second before deciding she was guilty. Ignoring her protests, he tucked his books under one arm and seized her ear with the other. She swallowed a yelp of pain and lifted on to her toes, struggling to match his long strides as he marched her back to Mrs. Upton's.

She was waiting in the garden between the cabbages, her insulted linen strewn about her. Her eyes were as round as marbles, her flabby cheeks quivering with outrage. She lit into Sophy, her voice rising and falling through at least two octaves, carrying through the entire village.

" . . . no good rascal!"

" . . . soiling all my linen!"

" . . . not to be borne!"

At length, she sputtered to a halt, breathless, having used nearly every word in her vocabulary.

"She will launder everything again," Mr. Lynchem pronounced. "Immediately."

With identical dagger glares, the two of them herded Sophy to the washtub and set her to work hauling and heating water. Sophy spent what remained of the afternoon hunched over the tub in a cloud of steam and indignation, growing sweaty and sore. When the sheets and Mrs. Upton's gigantic undergarments were at last hanging on the line, she ached like she'd been through the wringer too.

"Finished, are you?" Mrs. Upton sniffed. "Get along then."

Curtsying stiffly, Sophy turned and stalked through the gate, muttering under her breath. Next time she wouldn't get caught. If Mrs. Upton dared to say things again about her mother—

"You're not a bastard," she told herself. Her voice was sure, but inside she was unconvinced. Mother had moved to the village of Bottom End, already widowed, before Sophy was born. She called herself Mrs. Prescott. Until recently, Sophy hadn't questioned this story, accepting that she and her mother were like those stalwarts of so many stories: people without any relatives at all. Now, at ten years, Sophy was a realist. Fairies didn't exist, and neither did the shaggy beast she imagined lurking in the cellar.

She'd become conscious of the villagers' speculating looks, but hadn't understood them until yesterday, when she overheard Mrs. Upton saying with her usual complacence, "I don't know if there ever really was a husband, for I cannot convince Mrs. Prescott to tell me anything about him. She just smiles—smiles! Don't I, who have mourned my dear Francis for twenty-two years, know just what a true widow must feel? That girl of hers could very well be . . ." Here Mrs. Upton's voice dropped to a whisper. The tea circle ladies were listening so intently their cups didn't even clink.

Sophy might have ignored this, had she been alone, but two of the village girls were with her, crouching like rabbits on the other side of the fence, under the raspberry canes.

"She's lying," Sophy insisted. They only giggled behind pink stained fingers.

Hoping to prove Mrs. Upton wrong, Sophy loped off to the rectory so she could sneak into Mr. Lynchem's book room. It was easy enough, with everyone leaving their windows open in the late summer heat. Tiptoeing through the dim, silent room, she located Mr. Lynchem's volumes of the Naval Gazette without any trouble, but found only an Oliver Prescott in the casualty lists. His death was two months after her birthday, and Mother always said her father had died before she was born.

Stymied, her thoughts had turned to revenge. Letting the pig into the laundry had seemed an excellent idea—until she'd been caught.

Halfway down the High Street Sophy spied Fred, her occasional friend, cleaning the windows of his father's apothecary. He turned in response to her greeting, taking in her damp dress and limp curls. "Said you'd get caught, didn't I?"

Sophy nodded glumly.

"Well, you're wet already. May as well give me a hand." Fred proffered his bucket. Sophy reached inside for a rag. Her fingers were still pruney, and she would rather wash windows with Fred than confess to her mother just yet.

"Was Mrs. Upton mad?" he asked, climbing a stool to reach the panes at the top, the ones with gold lettering painted on the inside.

Sophy couldn't hide a smile. The final victory had gone to Mrs. Upton, but she had scored a point or two first.

Fred laughed. "Must have been a sight. Mind you get the dirt in the corners." Sophy rolled her eyes. Though half a year younger, Fred's estimation of his own importance had multiplied since becoming his father's helper in the shop.

As she wiped away the grime from the square panes, the wares inside became bright and new. Sophy peered through each clean pane, taking inventory: packets of hairpins wrapped in yellow paper, patent medicines in tall bottles, the expensive Denmark Lotion only Miss Sikes bought, hoping to coax a proposal from widowed Farmer Briggs.

"Thanks, Sophy," Fred said when they were finished, circling his arms and making his shoulders pop. She allowed Fred to invite her inside so his father could send her home with a peppermint. Sucking her candy, she made her way home, weary and thoughtful.

Her mother's cottage was a little way out of the village at the end of a lane, a pretty, square house with white walls and black shutters. The thatched roof was grey as a pigeon's wing. It was a fine house for a mere school teacher. Her mother's salary was meager, yet compared to other widows in the village, they lived well. Mother never had to turn her dresses over and Sophy never wore second hand shoes. They had Bertha, for the cooking and cleaning and even a spinet in the parlor, which her mother had insisted she learn to play. Was such affluence really a result of her faceless father's legacy? Sophy did not know, but she was very nearly certain the good people of Bottom End would not allow a woman of doubtful morals to continue teaching their small boys. Waving absently to Jim, who came once a week for the heavy gardening, Sophy let herself in the kitchen door.

"Sophy?" Mother's voice floated from the parlor. "Wherever were you all day?" Sophy trudged into the room. Immediately, her mother took in her water-spotted dress and unkempt hair.

"Sophy, what happened?"

She confessed about the pig, leaving out her motives. Mrs. Prescott's mouth stiffened, resisting a smile.

"That was wicked of you, darling," she said. "You deserved to get caught. Come here." Drawing a small comb from her work-box, she tidied Sophy's hair with gentle fingers, coaxing the bright red curls back into shape. She turned away to hide a grin, saying in a choked voice, "Was Mrs. Upton very upset?"

Sophy recognized that she was forgiven. Her lips slid into a grin as she regaled her mother with a vivid account of Mrs. Upton's diatribe and the redness of her face, earning a hearty laugh.

"That old busybody," Mrs. Prescott sighed, wiping her eyes. "Whatever did she do to deserve such a prank?"

Sophy didn't feel like explaining.

"Never mind," her mother said, seeing her reluctance. "Oh, you were naughty, but I wish I could have seen it. Just don't ever try it again."

Sophy considered asking her mother for the truth. Was she a bastard? But she felt all the warmth of her mother's affection and shrank from spoiling the companionship of the moment. If she asked about her father, her mother would only spin her a fairy story. She had heard so many. Her father had been a lion tamer, a general and a pirate captain. In every story he had a different first name, each more outlandish than the last—Raoul Prescott, Fight-the-good-fight-of-faith Prescott, Sophocles Prescott. Sophy had learned not to press her mother for real answers. Did she really want to know the sordid reality? Not today, she decided. Her questions would keep for another time. Instead she asked to see her mother's latest sketches: a landscape of green mountains and a picture of a ruin set in a formal garden. Both were drawn with such ethereal beauty they looked like they were about to float off the paper.

"Do they need anything?" Mrs. Prescott asked.

"Maybe . . ." Sophy hesitated. "That cloud doesn't feel heavy enough. If you put some indigo along the bottom . . ."

"That's just what it needs. I'll add some in tomorrow."

The nights were getting longer. Dark settled early over the house, bringing a wind with the smell of rain in it. Mrs. Prescott lit a fire—the first one since summer began—and they toasted bread and cheese for supper, finishing with roasted chestnuts from the tree in front of the house. Sophy couldn't wait for them to cool. Sucking a burned finger, she struggled to peel them one handed.

"Spare my fingers and peel one for me, love," her mother asked.

"Open wide, then," Sophy said.

Mrs. Prescott laughed, but played along. She bobbed her head, missing the chestnut Sophy tossed. It rolled down her skirts and onto the floor.

"Try again, Mother," Sophy commanded.

"Throw it straight this time."

Mouth gaping, Mrs. Prescott made a noise indicating her readiness. Taking careful aim, Sophy lobbed the nut at her mother's mouth, crowing with triumph when it disappeared down her throat with a pop. Her mother's lips stayed open, frozen in a perfect pink circle. She lifted a hand to her throat, curling forward strangely.

"Mother!" Sophy leaped across the room, seizing her by the

shoulders to look at her face. Mrs. Prescott's eyes bulged with terror, her lips fading blue, her fingers clawing at her throat.

"Bertha! Help me!" Sophy dropped to the ground, pulling her mother with her, pounding her back and listening for a cough that refused to come. *This isn't working*, she thought, terrified by the way her mother had gone limp. She seized her mother's dress, planted an elbow on her back and pulled, ripping the dress open, revealing the tightly laced stays. Sophy's fingers didn't shake, but the knots and lacings were taking too long to loosen. Bertha's pudgy hands fluttered beside her.

"Get out of my way!" Sophy shouted, springing up to rifle through her mother's painting box for the palate knife. She sliced through the laces, yanked open the stays, and pounded her mother's back again and again. And again.

"It's not working dearie." Bertha's voice quavered, stopping Sophy's arm mid swing.

"There's still time," Sophy said, glancing wide-eyed around the room. "Run and get help. We can send for the doctor—"

"Jim's gone for him already. It's too—"

"It is not." Sophy's eyes flashed, but she could see the grey skin of her mother's hands. "It is not too late."

"Come with me."

"No. I'm not leaving."

"Sophy, love. You've done everything a body can do. Don't stay around for the rest. I'll speak to the doctor."

Sophy clung to her mother's limp arm and set her teeth, but Bertha had decided. "Come now," she said, scooping Sophy up by her arms. Sophy pummeled Bertha with angry fists, but Bertha's arms were strong. She hauled Sophy to the kitchen and wrapped her in a blanket, rocking and crooning, but she was beyond comfort.

Still determined, Bertha poured out a dose of laudanum and held Sophy's nose until she swallowed it. For the rest of her life, the smell of sweet, strong alcohol would turn her stomach.

CHAPTER 2
SPECULATION

There was a funeral, which Sophy was not allowed to attend.

"Heavens, child! That isn't done!" Bertha explained.

So Sophy sat in the parlor, brooding on her fate and watching a trapped fly bat against the windowpane. Remembering ghastly orphan stories from Mr. Lynchem's repertoire of cautionary tales was easier than coping with the overwhelming panic that came when she tried to imagine life alone, without her mother. Sophy, desperately practical even in grief, believed these stories would harden her to face her inevitable future. If she imagined the worst, she would be prepared for the desolate years stretching before her.

After the funeral, there were visitors: Mr. Lynchem, Mrs. Upton and all the well-meaning women of the parish Sophy despised. Bertha brought up bread and butter and tea—even Sophy's favorite seed cake—but her plate sat untouched on her lap. Eating seemed barbaric, somehow. Mrs. Upton shoved a slice of buttered bread past her square, yellow teeth. Crumbs of seed cake clung to Mr. Lynchem's fleshy lips, twisting Sophy's stomach. There was a tinny taste in her mouth; the visitor's words buzzed in her ears like the trapped fly. Fred's parents, Mr. and Mrs. Wilkes, lingered after the other guests departed. When Mrs. Wilkes, soft and familiar with her lace cap and graying curls, folded Sophy into her arms, she succumbed to choking sobs. Ashamed, she pulled away, swiping at her eyes, scowling at their concerned faces.

"I've spoken with Bertha and Mr. Lynchem. We've been through your mother's papers," Mr. Wilkes said, glancing uneasily at his wife. He thrust his large, spotted handkerchief at Sophy. She curled her hand around it, wadding it into a ball.

Why didn't I get to see them? Sophy suppressed a flare of anger.

"It appears your mother was not entirely without—connections," Mrs. Wilkes said. Sophy noticed the hesitation and wondered what it meant.

"Your mother chose a guardian for you, if it chanced she could no longer care for you. Mr. Lynchem has written to him."

"Who is my guardian?" Sophy asked, watching the color sweep into Mrs. Wilkes's cheeks. It was her husband who answered.

"Lord Fairchild. He lives in Suffolk."

"I have never heard of him before," Sophy said, swallowing.

There was an uneasy silence.

Of course you haven't, Sophy thought. *Easy for a Lord to pay to keep his bastard out of sight.* Her light muslin frock burned against her skin; her mother's pretty parlor was suddenly lurid and alien.

"He is the one who will look after me?" Sophy looked up from her tightly clasped hands, hating the quaver in her voice.

"That is what we believe, yes," Mr. Wilkes said. "Though it will be some days before Mr. Lynchem can expect a reply."

Glancing at her husband, Mrs. Wilkes added, "Don't fret Sophy. If anything should happen . . . if things go wrong, you have a home with me and Mr. Wilkes."

Sophy's throat swelled hotly. Blinking back tears, she mumbled her thanks. The Wilkes already had six children, sleeping in two small beds like pencils in a box. Mr. Wilkes, red-faced and gruff, brushed her gratitude aside.

"That's enough serious talk for you today. Why don't you go out to the garden? Let me and the missus speak to Bertha about packing up the house."

With automaton-like obedience, Sophy descended to the garden, heading straight for the shrubbery below the parlor window. Sometime during the torturous afternoon, someone had opened the leaded diamond-paned windows, but Bertha and the Wilkes's conversation was pitched too low to carry outside.

Late roses climbed the trellis leading to the kitchen garden, imparting a sweet and heavy scent to the air. Sophy licked dry lips. If Bertha was to pack up the house, it was certain she was leaving. Her eyes stung. Parting from mother's house cut sharper than she had expected, though in all her imagined futures she went away.

Who was Lord Fairchild? What was he like?

She hugged her knees to her chest, burrowing her face out of sight. Whoever he was, she was certainly his bastard. She tried to reject the truth, but could not. She felt unclean, different. Everything Mrs. Upton said was true.

Her throat was thick and hot. There was nothing she could do. They might say what they liked about her and her mother now. She had no defense. It was hard enough, she thought, biting down on her quivering lip, being so utterly alone. How was she to bear it, with the shame as well?

"Stupid," she told herself in a stern whisper. "You may as well get used to it."

TIMOTHY, THE THIRD FOOTMAN, WHOSE REAL NAME WAS JOHN, walked on silent feet over the thick library carpet, bearing a silver tray with three letters. With white-gloved hands, he placed the tray onto the gleaming surface of Lord Fairchild's desk, the noise as he set it down no louder than a heartbeat. Viscount Fairchild did not look up and Timothy withdrew as soundlessly as he had entered.

The library at Cordell Hall was Lord Fairchild's sanctuary. Tall windows looked out onto the east lawn. The heavy velvet curtains were drawn back, flooding the room with morning light and setting fire to the lone occupant's artfully combed copper hair. His hand moved steadily across the creamy sheet of paper in front of him. Dipping his pen in the inkstand, he continued writing, each stroke precise and methodical.

Twenty minutes later, Lord Fairchild set down his pen. He sealed and franked the letter, then picked up the correspondence waiting on the tray. Two of the letters were expected: one from his son Jasper, due to return from school for holidays, and one from his man of business in London. Reading Jasper's letter first and setting aside the second, he picked up the third, examining the direction. Though the sender's name was unfamiliar, the name of the village, Bottom End, arrested his attention. For five seconds he stared at the missive before turning it over and cracking the seal with unsteady fingers.

Scanning rapidly through paragraphs of obsequious flattery and apology, Fairchild found the heart of the matter buried in the middle of the second page. His breath caught; his hand faltered. Setting the letter onto the blotter, he stared unseeingly out the window.

Fanny was dead.

He had heard nothing of her for more than ten years, since the arrival of a polite note informing him that she had borne him a daughter and named the girl Sophy. Every quarter in the course of going over his accounts, Fairchild saw the entry inked in by his clerk recording the sum sent to Fanny Prescott of Bottom End. The sum had never varied in ten years; if Fanny had ever asked his steward for more, he knew nothing of it. He had promised Fanny, and his wife Georgiana, that he would not attempt to contact her.

Leaning back into the chair, he returned his attention to the letter, growing increasingly irritated with his correspondent's meandering sentences, dancing around the matter to hand—what did he wish to be done with Sophy?

It was a simple business. She could be brought here or sent to school. The writer—he flipped over the sheet to reread the name, a Mr. Horace Lynchem—had been bold enough to suggest a few. The presumption of the man was astonishing.

Bristling, Fairchild knew he wanted Sophy to be brought here, and not just to snub Mr. Lynchem. He wanted to see his child. Fanny, with her smooth brown hair and porcelain skin, would expect him to do his best for her daughter, as she had for his children.

Henrietta and Jasper had loved Fanny. Sweet and pretty, he had fallen for her too—a delirious escape during bitter, lonely days. Fanny had been delirious too for a time, but she had come back to earth first. It was guilt over the harm she was doing to his children that made her leave and confess to his wife. That and the baby.

Georgiana would not take well to him sending for Sophy, but Fairchild viewed that as an irritant rather than a deterrent. Let her chalk up a few grievances; their current détente served well enough she wouldn't declare open war. Rising from his chair, Lord Fairchild went in search of his wife.

THE RECTORY OF BOTTOM END WAS SOME DISTANCE FROM THE village, set in a small park. It was a comfortable house; two and a half stories of whitewashed stone. Identical dormers blinked on the slate roof like sleepy eyes. Mr. Lynchem, the rector, had held the living going on twenty years. In spite of the machinations of local widows and spinsters, he remained unmarried. His sister Euphemia kept house for him and she defended her hearth rights with vigor. She had a comfortable home with her brother, and did not intend to lose it.

When the post came, she noted the letter from Lord Fairchild, written on heavy paper and embossed with his seal. The paper was too thick for the writing to show through when she held it up against the sunny window, so Euphemia Lynchem set the letter aside and dashed off notes to her particular friends, Miss Myra Bowles and Miss Honoria Sikes, telling them the expected missive had arrived. She could count on them to spread the word.

Her staff—she economized unnecessarily, limiting herself to a cook and a maid—knew better than to touch the luncheon she would carry up to her brother. Euphemia had convinced him he had a delicate stomach, and that only she understood properly which morsels of food he could partake of and live. So it was her alone who laid out the poached chicken breast, the arrowroot biscuits and the dish of stewed apricots with a minuscule glass of canary wine. Placing Lord Fairchild's letter above the rest on the tray, she sailed down the hallway and carried it into her brother's book room.

Horace Lynchem acknowledged her with a grunt, hunched over the tiny, splayed wings of a dragonfly, a magnifying glass in one hand and a pin in the other. The point hovered over the abdomen of a particularly fine specimen of Oxygastra Curtisii as he prepared to pierce the tiny corpse.

"The Letter has come." Euphemia spoke loudly in his ear, startling him.

"What? Oh. That letter."

Euphemia pointed to where it rested beside his wineglass with a skeletal finger. Horace set down the magnifying glass on the blotter, frowning over the right wing of the dragonfly, now sadly mangled.

"I wish you wouldn't creep up on me," he said. "Now this one is completely ruined."

Euphemia concealed her smile. She had read Linneus's entire Systema Naturae, accompanied her brother on far too many tedious net-wielding expeditions, and labelled all his specimens in her elegant copperplate script. She hated insects. Horace had cases of the nasty things, pinned in precise rows, covering the walls of the room.

She hovered, waiting to watch him open The Letter, but Horace made a show of sangfroid and reached for his glass, as if receiving a letter from a peer was no extraordinary event. Defeated, she returned to the parlor.

When the door shut behind her, Horace set his glass down in such a hurry he nearly spilled his wine. Carefully, he pried the seal with his pen knife so it would stay intact, then opened the letter with eager haste. It was disappointingly short. Lord Fairchild asked him to have his daughter ready to travel on October first. He would send a coach for her and bring her to Cordell. His man of business would arrange for the sale of Fanny Prescott's house and furnishings. He asserted that he was Sophy's legal guardian and Mr. Lynchem could contact his lawyers, at the address given, if he had any concerns. The letter closed with perfunctory thanks.

Horace hooked a thumb into the pocket of his waistcoat and leaned back in his chair, sitting in silence for some moments.

"Euphemia!" he called. Her approach was silent as always, yet she answered his summons with suspicious haste.

"What do you need, Horace?"

"Ask John to bring Sophy Prescott to me."

Chewing a sliver of chicken, Horace reached for his next specimen.

SOPHY CAME TWO HOURS LATER WITH BERTHA A STEP BEHIND. Mr. Lynchem lowered his magnifying glass to look at her. Her hair had been damped down and tied back with a ribbon, but the drying strands were already regaining their unruly shape. Her cheeks were flushed and Bertha was puffing heavily.

"Thank-you for the message, sir," Bertha said, dipping into a curtsy. "Your John said the letter's come?"

"Indeed it has," Horace said, using his pulpit voice, at slightly lower volume. He had never liked Fanny Prescott. She was too pretty for a widow—smiled too much. Now he congratulated himself on his instincts.

"Lord Fairchild has acknowledged Sophy. He is sending for her. The house is to be sold. You will be required to make Sophy and the house ready," he told Bertha.

Turning to Sophy, he added, "Unbeknownst to you, child, you have lived on Lord Fairchild's charity and sufferance. You must prepare yourself to meet him, and to show him the gratitude, meekness, and obedience that is proper. Try him too much, and he may cast you off at any moment."

"Where does he live?" Sophy asked.

Horace blinked, annoyed to be interrupted just as he was finding his stride. "Suffolk. Lord's Fairchild's seat is Cordell Hall."

Bertha took Sophy's hand, giving it a squeeze. "And don't they say Suffolk's a pretty place? Not so rolling as Herefordshire, but very nice."

"That is immaterial," Horace said.

"Not to me," Sophy said.

"You will likely go from Cordell Hall to school," he warned. "And you had best take every advantage of the education that Lord Fairchild chooses to give you. Children like yourself must be prepared to earn their own bread. There is little place in society for your kind, black-blooded and born in sin."

He delivered his prepared sermon, but instead of reducing Sophy to tears as he had envisioned, she stared at him with stony, dry eyes, finally unsettling him. He stopped, faltering mid sentence like a wound-down clockwork.

"I shall make sure Sophy is ready, sir," Bertha said.

"See that you do," he said, trying to recover his dignity, but Sophy had already curtseyed and turned for the door.

CHAPTER 3
CORDELL HALL

Bertha fitted Sophy's things into her mother's battered old trunk. It was a small box, Sophy thought, to carry her whole life in. Together they lugged it downstairs and out to the front gate. Leaving Sophy in the garden to get her fidgets out, Bertha returned to the kitchen.

"The removers are coming!" Sophy called after her. "Who cares about crumbs?"

Bertha's mumbled response was indecipherable except for the words, 'properly clean.'

Sophy watched the ants scurrying across the flagstone path cutting through her mother's overgrown flowerbeds until her feet went numb from crouching. When Bertha brought out buns and tea, they ate together in silence under the climbing rose, now bare of blooms. Exhausted by her cleaning marathon, Bertha soon fell asleep and Sophy drifted through the garden, swinging a stick through the flower beds, decapitating drying poppy heads. Every few minutes, she went to peer through the gate and down the road. Bertha had predicted the coach would arrive this afternoon. Bored, Sophy finally sat down on her corded trunk, occupying herself by scraping a rut in the dirt with her shoe.

Leaving home frightened her, yet she was anxious to go. Grief and the preparations for departure had drained her like a blood-letting. She hadn't told a soul that she had thrown the chestnut that lodged in her mother's throat. Every so often, the sickening guilt lifted enough for Sophy to feel fear. She wasn't certain they could accuse her of murder, but she knew it was her fault her mother was dead.

"Oy! Sophy!"

Startled, Sophy turned to see Fred loping through the garden, entering through the gap in the hedge. The loose hem of his smocked shirt was gathered in one hand, the front of his shirt weighted down with apples.

"Hello, Fred."

He had the last remains of an apple in his free hand, nibbled down to its' bones. Tossing the core into the lane, he handed an apple to Sophy and sat down beside her on the trunk.

"So—you get to ride—in a—lord's carriage," he said, between mouthfuls.

"Yes," Sophy said, chewing slowly.

"Wonder what the horses will be like."

"Dunno." Her mother had hated it when she spoke like a farm girl. Sophy realized that wherever she was going, she ought to be more careful with her speech. Glancing guiltily at her dust-covered shoes and greying stockings, she straightened her back.

"How long will it take to get to Suffolk?" Fred asked.

"Mr. Lynchem said about three days."

Fred lifted his eyebrows, impressed.

"Will you thank your mother and father again for me?" Sophy asked.

"Sure. They heard you yesterday, though. And Mam's coming with a basket. Some pies you can eat on the way."

"Where is she?"

"Went to see Bertha. We'll miss you. I'll miss you." Fred wiped the back of his hand over his mouth. His tone was matter of fact, but Sophy was surprised Fred had admitted so much.

"I will miss you, Fred," she said, horrified when her voice turned high and squeaky at the end.

Fred leaned away from her, his eyes going wide.

"Yes, well, I might write you a letter. Every now and then."

Sophy didn't cry and Fred relaxed. Hurling another apple core into the road, he asked, "What do you think he'll be like?" He didn't need to specify who. Lord Fairchild starred in both their imaginations.

"He's probably all stiff in fancy clothes with a pointy nose and a disappearing chin," said Sophy, revealing her own inventions. Speculation had filled her thoughts in recent days.

"Like the villain in the traveling farce last year?"

Sophy scowled, realizing the resemblance. "Mr. Lynchem says I must be good and quiet. On the journey and after, too."

"Hmmph." Fred's frown told her he doubted she was capable of this feat.

"He gave me this to read on the journey," Sophy said, drawing a thin booklet from the drawstring bag beside her. She passed the flimsy sheets to Fred, who flipped through them.

"Matilda Ann," he read. "The tale of a wicked girl cursed with the sin of ingratitude who became a match seller." He erupted into laughter. "Think you'll end up a match girl?"

Occasionally, in Sophy's dire imaginings, she ended up a starving figure huddled in a ditch, prompting brief storms of weeping over her own fate. A match girl sounded much worse. Sophy had heard some talk of cities; rife with disease, they were filled with thieves and disreputables who preyed on the unwary and weak.

Seeing the fear in Sophy's face, Fred tried to reassure her by punching her in the arm. "Come on. Da says you'll be looked after proper. Lord Fairchild's sending his own carriage for you. Why would he go to such expense just to throw you out on your ear?"

Sophy swallowed. This circumstance had given her some confidence, but still . . .

"There you are," Bertha said, bustling down the walk with ferocious brightness. Mrs. Wilkes walked beside her. "Mrs. Wilkes has brung a hamper for you, love." Sophy stood and curtsied her thanks.

"What's this?" Mrs. Wilkes asked, plucking the booklet from Fred's hands. She turned it over and read the title, annoyance flashing across her face. "Take this instead," she said, handing Sophy a green cloth-covered book from the basket on her arm. "You'll like it better."

'Nursery Tales' was printed across the front in black letters.

"Thank-you, Ma'am," Sophy curtseyed again. She had seen this book at the shop in the village; it was a handsome present, and one which Fred watched her tuck into the basket with reluctance.

Blinking and turning red around the eyes, Bertha launched into a list of instructions: Sophy was not to speak to strange persons at wayside inns or pester the maid and coachman who were escorting her with questions. She must always wear her flannel petticoat and keep a clean handkerchief about her. "I've tucked two spare ones in the top of your basket, dear."

Four heads swiveled at the sound of wheels jolting down the rough road. Waiting with stopped breath, they saw a handsome, if dusty, carriage appear beneath the trees.

"They've come," Bertha breathed, her sigh of relief a strange contrast to her paling face. Fastening her eyes on Sophy and lifting her face in her hands, she instructed: "You write to me, Miss Sophy. Master Fred will read to me. I'll expect to hear from you regular." Voice a-tremble, she swept Sophy into a bone-cracking embrace.

"How I'll miss you, child," she whispered, low enough for Sophy's ears alone.

"Good-bye Berfa," returned Sophy, reverting to her baby's lisp and blinking furiously.

With unaccustomed brusqueness, Bertha set Sophy aside, questioning the coachman as he fastened Sophy's trunk to the back of the coach. Fred gave Sophy another punch to boost her confidence, and Sophy returned the gesture with a hug that made him color and shuffle his feet. Then the coachman handed Sophy into the carriage.

Sophy froze, surprised. Surely the elegant woman seated inside wasn't a maid.

The coach lurched forward and Sophy returned to immediate concerns, tugging down the window and leaning her head outside, blowing desperate kisses to Fred and Bertha, who were running behind the coach. Bertha's trot was heavy, her arms and bosom jiggling as she ran. The sight of her waving and running, cap askew, was too much and Sophy burst into tears.

"Goodbye!" she called, and ducked into the coach.

SILENTLY, THE HAUGHTY WOMAN HANDED SOPHY A handkerchief, her face marred with a frown of distaste. Sophy lapsed into cowed silence.

"Finished, miss?"

She was the maid then, despite her fine wool dress and her bonnet with a single purple plume. Her raised eyebrow and belated 'miss' told Sophy that though she was a servant, she was a superior one and not pleased with her current assignment.

"My name is Liza Pritchard," she said. "I'm to escort you to Cordell Hall. And you are Miss Prescott."

"My mother called me Sophy."

"I dare say she did," Liza smiled. "But I'm certain Lady Fairchild won't countenance that. You'll be Miss Prescott to the servants, and if the family calls you by your given name, I expect they'll prefer Sophia. It sounds better."

Flushing, Sophy turned her face aside, finding oblivion in the changing leaves of the trees as they swept past the window. The coach seemed luxurious to her, with its soft brown velvet squabs and glass windows that could slide open and shut. She had even glimpsed a crest on the door before being helped inside. She was not to know that this was the oldest of Lord Fairchild's traveling coaches.

When the passing scenery lost its charm, Sophy brought out Mrs. Wilkes's book. She shut it in disgust after the first tale. 'The Princess and the Pea' was not a real fairy story. It had no magic, only a nameless girl whose quality was evident in her easy bruises. Offended by the absurdity of the Queen's test, Sophy slammed the book shut and sank into memories of her mother's stories: corsairs and sorcerers and houses of gingerbread. Her mysterious father had figured in many of these, always a hero, taken from his family by duty or tragic death.

Sophy glared out the window, her throat tight. Her mother's stories were rubbish, all of them. Her father was a lecher, not a valiant, who had sent her mother away and never troubled to find her.

It was a bewildering journey, the anticipated three days lasting an age. Sophy asked no questions, merely watching the succession of villages, rivers, fields, and towns. Tom Coachman, despite his friendly smile, gave Liza a wide berth whenever they stopped, and so hardly exchanged a word with Sophy. The inns where they rested were noisy and frightening, and Sophy derived no comfort from Liza, sleeping noisily on the nearby trundle bed. Though she denied herself the refuge of remembering her mother's stories, each night Sophy fell into dreams of dark forests, lumbering bears, and twinkling fairy lights.

At last the land stretched out broad and flat. Sophy had counted seventeen windmills when Liza announced they were only two miles from Cordell Hall.

They stopped a short time later. "Is this it?" Sophy asked, scowling to hide her fear. She could only see one small house through the window. It didn't look anything like the hall she had imagined.

Liza's lip curled. "This is the lodge."

The keeper stepped outside, swinging aside a wide iron gate and waving them on their way. Driving down an avenue lined with giant trees, Sophy saw a lake and spreading lawns. The park, she thought. The carriage swung around sharply, and Sophy saw the house.

She had never seen such a large edifice. Two wings of warm, weathered brick receded on either side, each boasting a tower that stretched above the chimneys standing like soldiers along the steeply slanted roof. Though it was too late to hide her amazement, Sophy snapped her mouth shut.

The carriage stopped. Quaking, Sophy leaned back into the velvet cushions as the crunch of feet on gravel drew near. The door opened and a white-gloved hand materialized in front of her.

"Go on," Liza said.

Taking the hand, Sophy stumbled down the coach steps, which today seemed absurdly high above the ground. She had removed her bonnet in the carriage; now, she squinted in the bright sunlight. Glancing up from the gloved hand in her own, she saw the man's face was expressionless as a carving of a saint. He wore a pristine powdered wig and a long blue coat trimmed with gold. Could this be him?

Spinning smartly on his heel, he marched up the steps into the house.

"Why are you waiting?" Liza hissed. "Go!"

CHAPTER 4

MIND YOUR MANNERS

The hall inside was dim and bigger than the chapel back in Bottom End. Sophy's footsteps echoed on the shining tiles. Another man, dressed identically to the first, silently closed the door. They were alike as a pair of bookends. Clearly neither was Lord Fairchild. She followed the first up a wide stairway and along a gallery lined with looming paintings and towering doors. The man opened one and led Sophy into the room, halting four paces inside.

"Miss Prescott," he announced and withdrew.

Eyes fastened on the carpet, Sophy sagged into a curtsy, willing her legs to straighten again instead of crumpling under her as they seemed likely to do. She succeeded and rose. Fighting the urge to flee, she glanced up.

A man, long and thin, his shock of red hair tamed with moderate success, sat in a huge armchair, his fingers steepled before him. His shirt and cravat were brilliant white and starched as stiff as pasteboard. A lady sat across from him, holding an embroidery frame. She was fair, her silvery blond hair coiled round her head with a few ringlets falling down her neck, smooth as tapered candles. His wife, surmised Sophy, her stomach lurching. The lady set her embroidery aside, her gown rustling as she moved—the sound of a serpent gliding over dry leaves. Sophy glimpsed the stitchery forming a fantastical bird in jewel bright silks with cruel eyes. She couldn't look away.

A stifled laugh made her turn. Leaning against the wall stood a young man, perhaps sixteen or so, negligently dressed compared to his parents, but sharing his mother's silver blond coloring.

"Don't laugh at Miss Prescott, Jasper," chided Lady Fairchild.

"Forgive me mama," he replied. "It amuses me that she looks more like father than either of us."

Lady Fairchild pursed her lips as Lord Fairchild cast a quelling look at his son. There was another person—a girl—sitting in the far corner of the room, but Sophy had no time to study her, as her attention was immediately reclaimed by Lord Fairchild, who beckoned her forward.

"Come here."

Feet dragging in the heavy pile of the carpet, Sophy stepped closer. She did look like Lord Fairchild. She had his sharp nose, his dark pointed brows, his bright red hair. Taking her hand, he pulled her alongside the arm of his chair and lifted her chin with his free hand. His skin was too soft, Sophy decided, bridling at his touch. He smiled ruefully, turning her chin to the side and back again.

"Jasper's right. I'm sorry Georgiana."

Lady Fairchild sniffed. "It can't be helped. Certainly now, I agree she must stay. Impossible to pass her off as a distant relation." Lifting one finger, she beckoned her children.

"Jasper, Henrietta, come meet Miss Prescott."

They both stepped forward, bowing and curtsying in turn.

"*M. Lynch a écrit que tu parles français?*" Lady Fairchild inquired, arching her brows at Sophy.

"*Oui, madame.*"

The questions continued, in French, but Sophy held her ground. Yes, she knew her sums and her psalms, and had been taught to draw. She did not admit that she only memorized psalms because Bertha rewarded her with gingersnaps, or that her sketches had long been a source of amusement and despair to her mother.

"Henrietta's governess will teach Sophy," Lord Fairchild interrupted. "It's obvious her task is well under way."

Lady Fairchild fell silent with an acknowledging nod.

Sophy waited, feeling unspoken conversation pass between them, while Jasper watched his parents with a malicious grin. Though her gaze was friendly, Henrietta's open scrutiny brought a stain to Sophy's cheeks. Setting her teeth, she focused on the wall. Her mother had always told her staring was rude. At last Lady Fairchild commanded Jasper and Henrietta to show Sophy to the nursery.

"You will have it to yourself," Lady Fairchild said. "Jasper and Henrietta left it long ago." Sophy's breath loosened.

"Someone will bring you supper," Lady Fairchild finished. Sophy filed after Jasper and Henrietta in an orderly procession until they passed into the gallery. Jasper closed the door, then he and Henrietta flanked Sophy on either side. Shoulders twitching, she was conscious of their advantage in height, in years, in everything. She did not like climbing up the narrow stairway with them so close beside her, unable to trust them.

Halfway up the stairs, Henrietta caught Sophy's eye and smiled, stunning her with pink and blue and gold prettiness. It was a disarming smile. "We never knew we had a bastard sister," Henrietta said, eyes twinkling. "How exciting!"

As the door shut behind Sophy, William pushed to his feet and crossed the study to pour himself a brandy. Lady Fairchild watched him, but his hands were steady.

"Can I offer you anything, my dear?"

She declined with a shake of her head. When her husband was again seated, she picked up her embroidery. She wouldn't work on it here long—she found the chairs in this room uncomfortable— but she felt the need of a prop. Though William appeared calm, surely he was as surprised as she. The girl's resemblance to William was striking. It was an unexpected blow. Lady Fairchild had imagined her as a miniature Fanny, but only her diminutive size tied her to her mother.

The child would become her husband's ward, and while no person of breeding would think to say more—at least in her presence—Lady Fairchild did not like it. But she could not prevent William from keeping the girl here, since it was his whim to do so. Her best defense was to accept the situation with equanimity. She was not the only lady in her acquaintance called on to tolerate her husband's by-blows, and complaining about the child would only stir up more talk. There were some things, though, that she would not accept.

Rolling her needle between her fingers she looked up at William, who was watching her carefully over the rim of his glass. "You'll expect me to look after her, I suppose?" She failed to keep the bitterness out of her tone. "I must count myself grateful she's the only one."

William smiled tersely at his drink, denying her the satisfaction of confirming her last statement. "I don't expect you to concern yourself with Sophy, or do anything that displeases you. You haven't with my other children. I said we'd keep Henrietta's governess and get a new nursery maid."

Henrietta was fifteen; they had planned to dispense with the governess in two or three years.

"Miss Frensham may object," Lady Fairchild said, ignoring his complaint and piercing the silk in her frame with delicacy and precision. "I chose her for her impeccable morals."

"Not her hatchet face? It's no matter." Lord Fairchild brushed a non-existent speck from his sleeve. "For thirty pounds a year she can keep her objections to herself."

"Sophy seemed well brought up," she conceded. "And I detected no fault in her education."

"You did hire her mother to educate your children," William said laconically.

Lady Fairchild did not rise to the bait, placidly re-threading her needle with a skein of emerald silk. "I would not prevent you from doing your duty to your child," she said, making a neat stitch. "But I will not let you make her Henrietta's equal."

"Such was never my intention," he said.

"Thank you." As she relaxed, he spoke again.

"I do intend to settle an independence on her. If something were to happen to me, I must see she is provided for."

Lady Fairchild felt her hackles rise, but she didn't allow her needle to falter. She had years of practice at containing fury. William wouldn't take anything from Jasper. "Her independence is to come from Henrietta's portion, then?"

William rose again and walked to the window, apparently in deep study. Out of his sight, she let her mouth twist.

"Henrietta's portion is sufficiently large you will have a hard time fending off the fortune hunters. And she has your looks. She will not be lacking suitors," he said. His accusation was unspoken; he did not trust her with the girl.

"Very well," she said. A few thousands would not make a difference in Henrietta's prospects. Still, she would not give up Henrietta's money cheaply.

Watching her husband silhouetted against the window, she stitched with martial calm, letting her displeasure fill the room like smoke. Breaking the silence, he returned to her, bowing and bringing her hand to his lips.

"You are very good to me, Madam. I know this is an imposition. Thank you."

Lady Fairchild packed up her embroidery frame once he left.

She might have to take in the brat, but she had driven William from his library, letting him know he would pay for her compliance.

∞❦∞

NORMALLY LORD FAIRCHILD DID NOT TROUBLE HIMSELF TO walk softly, but he did now, climbing the nursery stairs. He was not accustomed to feeling nervous.

Sophy had hardly dared to look at him the whole interview. He knew nothing about her, but the arch of her neck and her frail shoulders, bravely squared, reminded him of Fanny and brought an ache to his throat. For one instant, he had been tempted to seize Sophy, as if only clutching her could assure him she was real. He had let the impulse pass without betraying himself; it would have frightened her and infuriated Georgiana.

Heart thumping, he paused outside the door. Jasper and Henrietta were still with her, the murmur of their voices seeping into the hall. Henrietta laughed. What did they make of her? Georgiana's icy distemper he had anticipated, but he had given no thought to how his other children would react. They sounded friendly enough.

Henrietta burbled on, punctuated by breezy asides from Jasper, who'd acted the bored sophisticate since he was eight. Sophy's own words were rare and scarcely audible. He would have to wait. He couldn't ask her about Fanny in front of Henrietta and Jasper.

Georgiana had staked her pickets in his library, so he went outside. A ride would take too long, so he paced between the parterres in the garden for three quarters of an hour, questions tumbling through his mind.

The second time he mounted the nursery stairs he found Sophy alone.

She was hunched in a straight back chair, her bread and milk untouched on the table beside her. The floor creaked under his foot and she spun around, a battered book in her hand.

"Miss Fairchild said I might look at the books," she said, setting it on the table.

"Who?" he asked. "Do you mean Henrietta?"

She nodded.

"Her name is Henrietta Rushford," he explained. "Fairchild isn't my name, you know, just my title. My name is William Rushford."

"Oh." Embarrassed, she turned her eyes away from him to the window.

"I'm sure Henrietta no longer wants the books," he said. "They are yours now." She said nothing. "You aren't hungry?" he asked, his eyes flicking to her untouched supper.

"No."

"You must be tired, after such a long journey."

"Not really," she said.

"May I sit down?" he asked, after an uncomfortable pause. He didn't know how to begin.

Crimson rushed into her cheeks and she gave a tight nod. There were two large chairs by the fire, but he wanted to look at her, hoping being near her would help him cross the distance he felt stretching between them. Unsuccessfully, he tried to fit himself into the other child-sized chair at her table. He turned the chair backward and sat astride it, folding his arms over the back.

"Do you . . . Is there anything you would like me to get for you?" he asked.

"No, thank you." There was no sign of her baggage. The maids must have put it all away.

"Why do you not send me to school?" she asked. Her hands, brown and freckled, twisted in her lap.

The question surprised him. "I want you here. Surely you will prefer Cordell." Seeing that she didn't, he faltered. "Here, you may learn to ride, and . ." What else did small girls do? "There are dolls for you to play with." He swept one hand wide, indicating the shelf where Henrietta's discarded toys lay.

The toes of her boots were scuffed. Though he looked at her with open curiosity, she studied him covertly, never meeting his eyes. "I have often wondered about you," he said. "How you and your mother were faring."

Sophy blinked and met his eyes. "She always told me my father was dead."

It hurt that she had known nothing about him. He wished Fanny had told her his name at least. "The truth must have come as a surprise."

She nodded, her half-undone hair ribbon swaying with her copper curls.

"You were well, living in that village?"

Another silent affirmative.

"Was your mother well?" he asked.

"Until she died, sir."

"How did it happen? Was she ill?" Why had Fanny not informed his man of business? He would have paid for doctors and treatments.

Sophy's throat contracted. "No, sir. It was an accident." He waited for her to continue. "She—she choked on something."

"I am sorry," he said, looking away. What a ghastly way to die.

The shadows on Sophy's face told him Fanny's death was still too raw a wound for probing. Looking away, his eyes caught on two paintings, propped against the wall above the wainscoting. He frowned. Henrietta had never drawn like that.

"Are those yours?" he asked. They were remarkable for a ten-year-old, but perhaps that was not surprising—

"They are mine, but I did not draw them," she said.

"Did Fa— are they your mother's?"

"Yes."

He smiled. "She was a wonderful artist. She made beautiful pictures, didn't she?"

Sophy looked at him, revealing a hint of a smile. "I have others, too. Bertha helped me put them into a book, so I could have them always. But I left these two out, so I could see them everyday."

"May I have them framed for you?" It was the right question. Sophy's tentative smile grew, transforming her solemn face.

"I should like that."

"I will have to send them away," he explained, "but it will not take long. And you will still have the book while you wait."

"Should you like to see it?" she said at last.

"Please."

With lighter steps than he had seen her use before, she crossed the room to retrieve a thick album from the drawer of the bedside table. She carried it back to him wrapped in her arms and spread it open before him, moving her untouched supper aside.

"My mother didn't have a lot of time for painting and sketching," she explained, turning the first pages. "But when she had a free afternoon with good light, there was nothing she liked more. She was the teacher at the village school, you know."

He hadn't.

"This is you," he said, pointing to a pencil drawing that was unmistakably Sophy, though some few years younger. "How old are you in this picture?"

"Eight, I think. Often she did likenesses of our friends."

"Did she do her own?" he asked, looking up quickly.

"No." Sophy turned the page.

Sometimes she said nothing, letting him look at the picture himself. Sometimes she would tell him something of the subject: whose cottage or garden it was or when the picture had been done. He liked watching her, her head bent, showing her mother's drawings with obvious pride.

"Wait," he said, stopping her as she made to flip quickly past one page. "I must see this one."

Pulling the book closer, he smoothed the page with his fingers, staring at the picture of a ruin of grey, tumbled stone, set in a garden. His garden.

"Your mother painted this?"

Sophy nodded, confused by his close questioning.

"When?" The precise detail of the folly and the garden stunned him, rendered almost more beautiful than it had ever looked in life. Sunshine gilded the edges of the stones; despite the ruin in the foreground, it was not a gloomy scene.

"Do you remember when she made this picture?" he asked again.

Sophy looked away, her hand twitching in her lap. "She made it the day she died."

He closed his eyes. She had remembered Cordell then, until the very last. Perhaps she'd recalled the place fondly, if the feel of the picture was any guide. He swallowed.

Sophy was staring at him. "It's incredibly like," he said.

"No." Sophy shook her head. "This is an imagined scene."

William smiled. This picture was a benediction, confirming that Cordell was the right place for Sophy, giving him the absolution and the answers he had scarcely dared to hope for. "It's real, Sophy," he said, standing. "Come, I'll show you. This is my garden."

"Yours?" Sophy froze, ignoring his outstretched hand. "I don't believe you. Why would she paint this place?" Her eyes were dark and full of disdain. He reeled, as if she had struck him with her hard little fist.

"You're tired," he said at last, mastering his galloping anger. "Eat your supper." He would excuse her today. She was merely a ten year old girl who had lost her mother. He should not expect her to immediately understand, or to like him. And yet it infuriated him that she didn't.

Bidding her good night, he left the room, telling himself she needed time. Halfway down the stairs, he heard the sound of tearing paper. He froze. Anger surging again, he rushed back up the stairs, throwing open her door. "Stop that!"

She jumped, the heavy paper falling from her hands.

"Wicked girl!" Long strides carried him to her; her eyes were wide, opaque. He reined in the urge to shake her. Fanny's drawing —his drawing—was already torn free from the book and rent down the middle. "I'll take these." Tight-lipped, he slid the torn painting between the other pages of the book. Fitting the book under his arm, he plucked the remaining two pictures from the wall.

"Those are mine!" Sophy cried, trying to snatch them away. He held her back, laying a hand on her shoulder. Immediately she stilled, but there was brimstone in her eyes.

"I will not let you destroy these," he said. "Someday you will regret damaging this. In the meantime, I will keep them safe. When I can trust you will not cut them into curling papers, or chuck them in the fire, I will return them. You will stay in this room tonight, and consider your apology."

With that, he stalked away, carrying the pictures to the gun room, since he hadn't retaken his library. When evening fell, he was still looking through the album, returning to thumb the torn edges of Fanny's last work again and again.

You gave your girl a wicked temper, Fan, he thought, reliving the scene with Sophy. Fanny too, had defied him at the end.

He thought he heard a faint chuckle in reply. *Your own temper, morelike,* she whispered. *Be good to our girl.*

He sighed. He would have the damaged picture mended. Someday, he would return the others, but this one was his.

CHAPTER 5
A BOY'S LIFE

S carcely more than a mile from Cordell Hall as birds fly, stood another Tudor house. Chippenstone had turrets, steep roofs, and towering chimneys like Cordell, but Chippenstone was also surrounded by a rectangular moat. A narrow bridge, skipping across the water in three arches, gave access to Chippenstone's geometrically perfect island.

Unlike Cordell's gently weathered brown, Chippenstone was built of cheerful red brick, with contrasting white stone around the windows. Few could look on the house and not smile, for it was exactly that warm color that reaches the toes, even through a heavy rain. In the summer sun, the warm facade conjured that delicious feeling of discovering chance-found strawberries or entering a room heavy with the aroma of fresh baked bread. Few homes could hold themselves next to Chippenstone and not retreat with a shamed blush. Palladian mansions looked starved; Norman buildings austere and uncomfortable; Stuart houses looked simply rude. But like those ancient goddesses competing for the prize to the fairest, Chippenstone was a problem for the homes in the neighborhood. It was an unlucky house.

Both Chippenstone and Cordell were built in the early

sixteenth century. Unlike the Rushfords, surely propagating to
infinity, Chippenstone's family lasted only a century and a half.
When the last one died, the home passed through a succession of
lawyers, every one of them unable to sire a dynasty and keep their
wealth more than a generation. The house was regularly plagued
by scandal; one wife was divorced after having criminal conversation with the estate steward; one daughter eloped with a tradesman; at least two of the owners lost the house because of
enormous gaming debts. After twenty years of tenants, the final
insult came when the mortgaged property was bought by a
merchant, a chandler's son from Liverpool who'd made a fortune
in the Canadian colonies. He had lived in the house for two years,
but was still quarantined by his neighbors. Lady Fairchild would
not admit to knowing his name.

That name, never spoken by the county families, was Bagshot.

LIKE HIS HOUSE, HENRY BAGSHOT WAS GENIAL AND RED-FACED,
his cheeks roughened by wind, sun and cold. As a young man,
he'd decided there was not enough scope for his talent in the
candle making business. He converted his humble inheritance
into tea and tools and other supplies. He could sell anything, and
he intended to sell these goods for a healthy profit across the
Atlantic. Before he left, he sold his ambitions to Sally, the
buxom innkeeper's daughter he'd been walking home from
Sunday meetings for six years. They married a week before he
sailed, and though they exercised their marital rights enough
within those days to carry them through two years apart, Sally
welcomed Henry back alone, no baby balanced on her hip.
Henry remained in England long enough to sell the furs he
brought back, buy a share in a ship and take on new cargo.
Twenty years they lived like this, and though they loved
frequently during Henry's visits, they were never given a child to

fill Sally's loneliness. Henry bought his first ship, then a second. He bought into a mill and then a steel foundry, still feeling like he had failed his wife until, like Abraham and Sarah, they had their miracle.

Henry was forty-four, Sally nearly forty when she listened, disbelieving, as her physician explained she was going to have a baby.

Henry sold out of most of his business ventures. He sold the giant house he'd built in Liverpool, and took his wife to London to the best doctors. Six of them were consulted in Sally Bagshot's care, but after two days of labour she lost her awe for them, and her patience. Sending them to bite their nails outside her door, she summoned an illiterate midwife. Despite the grim prognostications of the doctors, she safely delivered a son.

They named him Thomas, and Henry swore that his son would have everything. A sickly infant, little Tom was gowned in lace, with two nurses and his parents at his command, all watching anxiously, lest his foot dash against a stone. He contracted measles, scarlet fever, and pneumonia—twice— gouging deep lines of care across his father's face.

Henry decided his son would be a scholar, that he would lead a gentleman's life, suited to his frail constitution. But blood runs true.

Tom was not made for study, and laid waste to the string of governesses, tutors and pedagogues hired by his father at enormous expense. He had to pay a premium, first to lure them into his bourgeois household, and then to convince them to stay past the first week. Many could not be persuaded at any price.

Tom rode indifferently, saw little point in study after mastering his letters and numbers, and displayed an alarming propensity for commerce. At six, his father had to yank Tom by his collar off the street, where he was hawking sweet buns made by the cook. At eight he began manufacturing slingshots, selling them to other children in the park, usually girls.

"I'll give you money," Henry said, exasperatedly running his hands through the remaining strands of his grey hair.

"I want my own," Tom insisted.

One of the doctors recommended country air, so Henry bought Chippenstone, and Sally, who'd never lived outside a teeming city, set her mind to becoming the lady of the manor. The house was still a hive of carpenters, upholsterers, and plasterers, when Henry decided it was time to send Tom to school.

The current tutor was near to breaking, and Tom needed a gentleman's education. Moreover, he needed to meet the sons of gentleman and he wasn't going to meet any of them in Suffolk. They couldn't even hire locals as servants and had to import all their domestics from London.

Tom raged, sulked, and begged, but he was packed off to Rugby nonetheless, accompanied by the shattered remains of his tutor and a generous bribe for the headmaster.

The tutor left Tom in the hall; the headmaster pocketed the bribe and promptly dropped Tom into the snake pit that was the first form of boys.

These little serpents knew immediately that Tom was not of their kind and so they made his life hell, as only boys can. No one spoke to him, unless it was in mockery; the name they gave him was more commonly used for excrement. Under his clothes, Tom's spindle-shanked body was a lacework of bruises.

Tom's letters home made his mother weep, and though his father wanted to bring him home, he could not. What if he had given up the first time he encountered an ocean storm, sold goods at a loss, or lost a cargo? Tom must persevere. The time for indulgence was past.

In his second year at school, Tom gave up on Latin and learned to sneak away to the village instead, where he could sell his possessions for real food. Even if his schoolmates allowed him to keep his portions, the food at school was terrible. In six months Tom sold nearly everything—his books, his jackets, all but one pair of stockings—and ate better than any of the thieves who shoved him in the hallways and twisted his arms until he gave up his meals. Tom grew six inches and made friends with the village smith, the local boxing champion. That was a turning point. After Tom knocked an older boy unconscious, no one challenged him. Not alone, at any rate. Tom learned to trail close to crowds everywhere he went. His friend the smith taught him to bar his door by wedging a heavy stick between the door and the wall.

They caught him anyways, leaving him with a split lip and a black eye. That night, Tom ran away.

It was an impulsive, ill-planned flight. Three days later Tom was pulled out of the stagecoach he was riding by two solid looking Bow Street Runners, hired by Henry Bagshot to track down his son. They hauled him back to the village, where his father and mother were waiting at the local inn. Once he was sure of Tom's safety, Mr. Bagshot's panic gave way to wrath and he blasted Tom with spittle and invective for a good five minutes.

"You frighten your mother again like that and I'll skin you alive! You will not leave that school. You'll face them and win!"

Sally interrupted her husband by handing him a glass of water. Her husband's face was scalding red, and his doctor had warned him against such fits of temper.

"Must he go back?" she asked.

"Yes, dammit! I'll see my son a gentleman while I live—"

"I've told you what it's like—" said Tom, but he hadn't, not all, for the truth hurt his pride. "You still want me to go back?"

"I want you to have this. It's the only thing I can't give you. The one thing you must claim for yourself."

"I don't want it. You do," Tom said, and Henry, who'd calmly accepted a lifetime of insults and snubs, exploded.

"Yes, I bloody well do! My son will not be sneered at. My son will be welcomed at their clubs and their frippery parties and—"

"Fine. I'll go now." Betrayed and furious, Tom stormed out of the inn's parlor and flung himself outside into the stable yard. His arms were inflexible iron at his sides, but if he looked at his father for one more second, his rigid control would break.

Another word, and I'll knock your daylights out. Silently, he heaped insults on his father. If his classmates had been flinging them, he'd have broken their teeth.

Mr. and Mrs. Bagshot returned Tom to the headmaster, and though Tom suffered his mother's teary caresses, he wouldn't meet his father's eyes. Mr. Bagshot's warning, that he would not tolerate his boy being bullied, earned only contempt—from Tom and the other boys. It made Tom look weak, and he knew he wasn't.

AT FIFTEEN, TOM WAS STILL A LONER. THERE WERE BOYS WHO would have befriended him, for he could level an opponent with a single punch. But Tom let no one close, making no attempt to hide his disdain for them all: the headmaster, the dormitory wardens, the choir master, the shy, asthmatic boy everyone knew idolized him. Especially the handsome, vicious winner of the school fencing cup, already an Earl.

Knowing the frustrated masters would look the other way, Tom's classmates determined to take him down. It was the fencing champion, the young Lord Harvey, who hit on the idea and paid the mathematics teacher to keep Tom after class.

It was late, night's curtains drawing over the sky when Tom finished scrubbing the schoolroom desks and braced himself to cross the quadrangle alone. Dinner was long past, but up in his room, folded in a napkin, he had the remains of one of Mrs. Finch's pies. The mother of his blacksmith boxing teacher was an excellent cook.

Since six o' clock, Tom's stomach had assumed the form of a ravening beast; now he was only dimly aware of the clock chiming half-past seven as he climbed the stairs two at a time, thinking of his supper. He did not notice how quiet it was in the corridors. Breezing through his bedroom door, he only had time to halt, widen his eyes, and utter "Wha—" before they jumped him.

They had dressed themselves as savages, stripping to the waist, and painting their faces. Falling on Tom, they were savage indeed, throwing a pillowcase over his head and bundling him down the stairs and into the dark churchyard. Binding Tom to a tall grave marker, they fell back, allowing Lord Harvey to remove the bag from Tom's head with a flourish and a sneer.

"You belong on a midden heap Bagshot, not here," he said, and planted a punch squarely in Tom's gut. Striped with charcoal and chalk, the boys leered and hooted like demons as each one stepped forward to take a turn.

Still gasping from Harvey's punch, Tom willed his stomach muscles to turn to stone, as hard as the grave marker that was scraping the skin off his back. It was his only defense against the blows. Some of the fists were weak, but others robbed him of breath and made him retch. He counted twenty-two punches but didn't know when he started crying. Dying from shame, he scarcely heard their parting taunts as they doused him with a pail of water and left him.

He stopped crying once his teeth were chattering too hard. The meandering breeze was scarcely stirring the overhanging oak leaves and the ivy climbing over the graveyard walls, but it drove through Tom like a musket ball. He could hardly stand, but letting himself sag against the ropes binding his chest hurt worse. He could call for help, but who would hear?

Through breaks in the cloud, he could see the stars, so very far away. A black shape obliterated their gleam for a moment, and Tom flinched. Owl, or bat? He wasn't keen on either. Night noises pressed on him, and he glanced from side to side, afraid of what he might, or might not see.

Maybe a grim. Those great black beasts with slathering mouths were fond of graveyards. The creature would come on huge silent feet that left no mark, his misty breath a fog around his fangs.

Stop it!

Tom clamped back a whimper, seizing and discarding thoughts as they blew away like sheets of paper. His fraying bootlace, rice pudding with sultanas, the crack of Harvey's nose when he broke it—surely he would do that—the Latin declensions he'd been unable to completely ignore. Doubles to four thousand ninety six, the eight times table, the changing price of beaver pelts in England in the last three years. Something moved in the long grass, and thought fled, leaving his brain bare and open.

"Help!" he called, but there was no answer.

He tried again, yelling until his throat was hoarse. His fingers were stiff with cold. His wet clothes stuck to his skin, but was that from the water or his own sweat? His lips were swollen, and it hurt to breathe.

A cat prowled atop the graveyard wall. Just an ordinary cat looking for mice, Tom told himself, not a familiar. He stamped his feet and curled his hands into fists trying to keep warm. They were long, long hours, filled with fear and cold and despair. Tom imagined the dawn long before he saw it.

The sexton found him in the early morning, cut him free and supported him back to the school. Tom was not the first boy he had found left in the graveyard. The night porter put Tom to bed with a nip of brandy and a hot brick. Safe in his bed, Tom swore he was done with school. Once he'd evened the score with Harvey, that is.

CHAPTER 6
REVENGE

Tom was prepared to bide his time, waiting for the perfect revenge, but it fell into his lap two weeks later. Surely this was the work of divine providence, and not just Bella Finch.

One hesitated to mention Bella Finch in any relation to providence, unless it was her making—she had clearly been drawn on one of God's better days. But she was the younger sister of Finch, the Blacksmith, and though the men in a five mile radius might lust after her, she was given a wide berth. Finch was an attentive brother and a strict Methodist.

Tom was such a fixture at the smithy that Finch scarcely noticed his comings and goings; certainly he didn't know that Bella had allowed him to kiss her twice. For practice, she said. Tom knew full well that Bella intended to marry a certain local farmer with a fine house—it was only a matter of time before the farmer realized it himself and bowed to the inevitable—but he was no fool, and made the most of Bella's offer. Two afternoons he had spent with her. They talked, when their mouths weren't busy kissing. Tom might even have fallen in love with her, if she had let him, but Bella was a sensible girl. Tom liked her immensely.

JAIMA FIXSEN

Bella made good use of Tom, and often asked him to walk with her to the green when she knew her farmer would be sitting outside the tavern nursing a pint. Bella's farmer was not the only one who noticed. Lord Harvey noticed too.

As Tom reluctantly strolled back to prison (school could never be home), Harvey stepped out of the tavern and joined him, keeping pace but staying out of arm's reach.

"You've an eye for a sweet arse, Bagshot," he said.

"Do you mean Bella Finch?" Tom asked, missing a step.

"Yes." Harvey knew her name. All the Rugby boys did. "How is she?"

Not a twitch of an eyelid betrayed Tom's flaring temper. He said coolly, "Damn good."

"I knew it!" Harvey tipped his face up to the sky, exulting. "Stolen a march on all of us, you lucky dog."

Revolted equally by Harvey's crudeness and his friendliness, Tom kept his eyes on the road, listening to the gears whir in Harvey's head. Fearing intimate questions that he wouldn't be able to stand, Tom moved first, asking levelly, "Fancy a go yourself?"

Harvey laughed. "Who wouldn't?" When Tom said nothing, he added. "Of course I would! Is it possible, do you think?"

A keener fellow than Harvey would have taken note of Tom's crocodile smile. "Sure. I'll put in a good word for you. Give me a week. I'll let you know."

Harvey clapped Tom across the back, then hesitated, sensing something not quite right in Tom's face. "You're a decent fellow, Bagshot," he said lamely. "Think I made a mistake before. Misjudged you, you know."

"Don't," Tom said, waving away the apology like a trouble-some insect. "I assure you, there is no need."

All week, Harvey grew twitchier as he tried—and failed—to catch Tom alone. Finally on Thursday, Tom let himself be cornered in the study hall. Spying Tom from the doorway, Harvey

44

glanced nervously about the room before joining Tom at the table in the far corner.

"Well?" Harvey asked, licking his lips. Unable to resist, Tom looked up from his book, presenting Harvey with a mystified face.

"Bella Finch," Harvey prompted in an urgent whisper.

"Oh yes. Nearly forgot. She'll meet you tomorrow at midnight, in the choir loft."

"Not in the church—"

"That's where I did it," Tom said, challenging. "Where else can you go where you won't get caught? You've seen her brother, right?"

Harvey licked his lips again, blinked twice. "I see what you mean. All right then. But how do I get in?"

"I'll look after that." Tom's night in the graveyard had not scarred him so much that he had failed to notice where the sexton kept his keys. "I've done this before, remember? I'll unlock the church and leave the keys in the choir loft."

"All right," Harvey nodded. "Thanks, Bagshot."

Tom smiled, flashing teeth.

৩৩৩

TWO NIGHTS LATER, HARVEY SLUNK OUT OF THE DORMITORY alone, clutching a stolen lantern that was shuttered so it let out only a razor blade of light. The lapels of his coat were turned up to hide his white shirt, so only his pale face floated ghostlike across the quad. Distracted by the dark, his moist palms and dry lips, Harvey squelched into a pile of muck crossing the road to the churchyard.

Idiot! Now your shoes will stink! Closing his eyes, he swore fluently. He wiped his foot on the untrimmed grass against the wall surrounding the churchyard, scuffing his shoes against the stones, but hopefully removing any signs of his misstep.

The creak of the gate as he swung it wide was loud enough to summon the seraphim. Harvey hunched and looked over his shoulder.

Bagshot had to be the hardest, coarsest fellow alive if he was able to meet his doxies here. Suppressing a sigh of envy, Harvey crunched up the gravel walk to the church door, muttering under his breath that superstition was for fools. This injunction did not, however, make him immune to the gothic atmosphere. The grave-stones were mottled and diseased in the shaky light of his lantern, and rolling fog covered the ground. Feeling his own dread creeping up behind him, Harvey closed the distance to the church at a sprint and shoved against the door. It was heavy enough he had to shoulder it wide, flinching as it groaned like a waking spirit.

"Bella?" his frightened voice echoed in the church, a high falsetto. Clearing his throat, he tried again. "Bella?" There was no answer. He left the door open behind him. Cutting off his escape was more terrifying than the imaginary creatures that might be following him.

His footsteps seemed to shake the floor. It was a fight to keep his tread slow and measured with his heart whirring like hummingbird wings. Doing anything with Bella here was impossi-ble. He'd have to bring her somewhere else. Hang Bagshot and his iron nerve.

The stairs to the choir loft were narrow and steep. He heard a noise, like someone shifting their feet and raised his lantern so that he could see the door above him. It stood halfway open. Dropping his fear on the steps, he gathered the remaining antici-pation and anxiety into a knot in his stomach and pushed past the door.

"Hello?"

Something collided with his head, sending him sprawling. He picked himself up as his cry of surprise echoed through the church, buffeting him from all sides. His lantern was gone, flung into a far corner, the whip thin slice of light tilting crazily at the wall. He could not see, but he could feel the person approaching. Without thought, his feet found a defensive stance and he raised his fists.

A low blow stole his breath, collapsing him like a set of empty bellows and he fell again, hard on his tailbone. Understanding came as he rose. Bella wasn't here. Bagshot hadn't even spoken to her. He'd used her as bait to draw him here so he could pound him like a piece of meat.

"What do you want?" he asked, clinging to anger lest he betray fear. He and Bagshot were matched in height, but his strength was with the blade. He stood no chance with his fists, tripping in the dark over the rails and benches of the choir loft. Maybe he could pay Bagshot off.

"Just the satisfaction of using my fists," Bagshot grunted. Harvey dodged the first punch and the second, but the third caught him hard in the shoulder. He shuffled back between two benches. Bagshot wouldn't have as much room to move here.

"Settling the score? You got me this time, Bagshot. But what about the next? You can't—" Bagshot's fist cannoned into his face and Harvey spun like a drunken dancer. He raised a hand to his jaw, tasting warm blood from his split lip, but Bagshot was done waiting. With businesslike efficiency, he yanked Harvey's arms behind his back and bound them together with a leather strap, towing him out of the benches and throwing him up against the wall.

"My father's been to Canada you know," Bagshot said and dropped him. Harvey choked back a cry as his hip slammed into the floor. Leaning back against the wall, he watched Tom circle him. His lips were moving, but he couldn't hear the words over the blood pounding in his ears. Bagshot's cheerful face made the hairs on his arm stand on end.

Harvey swallowed, wiping the blood trickling down his chin

on the shoulder of his coat. Bagshot moved closer and Harvey whipped out a leg to kick him, but Bagshot was kneeling overtop of him in an instant, drawing a cord tight over his ankles.

"You like playing Mohocks, so I thought I'd share some of my father's stories with you. He's met many Indians." A heavy threat lay under Bagshot's conversational tone.

"You can't hurt me," Harvey sputtered, marshaling scattered thoughts in his ringing head. If anything happened to him, his father would—

Bagshot raised his hand. He was holding a knife.

"My father said he's never seen a neater piece of work than an Indian skinning and gutting a beast," Bagshot said over a high squeal that filled Harvey's ears. It was the sound of uncorked terror, and it was coming from his throat. He strangled the sound with an effort that left him panting. His eyes were riveted to the blade in Bagshot's hand. Surely he wouldn't. He must be mad.

"No doubt you've heard what they do to their enemies," Tom said and he took a step closer. Harvey froze, then his heart thundered back to life, his breath coming in shallow gasps as Bagshot stretched his fingers into his hair, yanking it so that his neck stretched, long and vulnerable.

"For God's sake. Don't. I'm sorry," Harvey gasped. Bagshot stopped, his knife halfway to Harvey's head, level with his eyes. "Please," Harvey begged.

"You're apology isn't worth anything to me." Bagshot shrugged. He slashed the knife through Harvey's hair. Harvey screamed, unaware that he felt nothing, only strands of his hair sifting over his face and shoulders. Bagshot grabbed another handful.

"God's mercy!" Bagshot was going to kill him. Sobs rattled out of his chest, and he thrashed, trying to tug free from Bagshot's hands. Bagshot forced his head back against the wall, pressing his lips together as he executed another swipe and released another handful of hair over Harvey's shoulders.

"I might listen to an apology for Bella," he said.

Incoherent, Harvey retched out words. He was sorry, he ought never to have presumed. Miss Finch was a virtuous lady, who ought never to be touched. He wouldn't speak of this; he wouldn't even look at her—

"Good. Cause I told her brother. You won't be handsome when I'm done, but you'll really lose your looks if he gets his hands on you. Might be best if you stay away from the village."

Harvey's shrill wails rang through the church. Even when Bagshot put away the knife, he only quieted to ratcheting sobs, fearing what was next. Bagshot was staring at him, exasperation pinning his lips together.

"Maybe I belong on the midden heap, Harvey, but you're the fly who eats it." Turning, he disappeared down the stairs. It took a half-hour for Harvey to realize he wasn't coming back.

GROWLING, MR. HENRY BAGSHOT CRUMPLED THE LETTER FROM the headmaster and stormed from his study. "Sally! He's run away again!"

She came running from her parlor, where she did worsted work when the maids weren't looking. She had never been good at fancy stitchery.

"What?"

"Yes. Run away again! And this time the headmaster says he's expelled! Some rubbish about leaving one of those starched and ironed boys tied up in the chapel and hacking off all his hair. They won't have him back, not after this."

Sally's face blanched. "Not our Tom. He would never do such a cruel thing."

"He ran Friday last. Who knows where he's got to in this time. Have to call out the runners again."

Sally clutched his sleeve. "Harry," —for that was what she called him—"Do you think he's all right?"

"Of course he is. We'll have him in no time."

But it took three weeks.

Three weeks of combing the countryside, asking at roadside inns, and checking shipyard manifests. Three weeks of Sally growing paler and paler, praying with every thought and word for her son to be restored, while Henry sickened with guilt and grief. At last they found him in London, working in a livery stable. Sure of a handsome reward, the lucky runner brought Tom back to Chippenstone, whistling in appreciation as they drove up to the house.

"Why'd you run from this then?" he demanded, but Tom, who had not spoken since his arrest, merely scowled.

After Rugby, he hated this house and all it represented. Give him honest folk and honest work.

When he owned this house, he would tear it down brick by brick, just to spite his father. In the meantime, he allowed himself to be escorted inside.

It was a remarkable day for the neighborhood, though no one knew of it, for both Cordell and Chippenstone were welcoming children home. As Sophy tripped up the nursery stairs, flanked by Henrietta and Jasper, Tom marched into the hall and into his sobbing mother's arms.

There was no help for it. Tom had to be birched, but Henry deliberately softened his arm. Tom didn't even squeak. That told Henry more than anything else. His son was not a boy anymore. He had no idea what to do with him. The boy he had threatened to scalp was an earl. Word got around; it was unlikely another school would take Tom after that. With an earl as his enemy, it would be hard for Tom to ever gain entrée with England's elite.

Henry glared, leaning over his desk. "You're well and truly finished, boy."

"Good."

"Just what do you plan to do now?"

"I was doing well enough for myself."

"Working at a livery!" Henry snorted.

"I enjoyed it. If you won't let me work with you, I'll find my own way."

"I meant you to have better than this."

"I don't want it. You can't make me."

His dream of his son being a gentleman was finished, impossible. Henry sighed. "You're right I can't. Sit down."

Surrendering to the inevitable, Henry gestured Tom to one of the armchairs by the fireplace. He sat without a grimace, causing Henry to reflect that he really had done a poor job with the birching.

"Well, Father?"

Henry rubbed his thumb over his side whiskers. "I won't have you worrying your mother again, hear?"

Tom had the grace to look ashamed. "I am sorry for that."

"You should be. Since you've left me no other choice, I'll give you a start. You can go with Fulham on the next ship. If you want to be in business, you'll have to learn. I'll expect you to work hard."

"Of course. I can earn my place."

Henry gave a loud humph. "You'd better. You'll leave before the month's out. In the meantime, you do what you can to make your mother happy." Sally would not like seeing her son take to sea. But what else was there to do?

Tom's lips parted, as if he couldn't believe his good fortune. Well, and if this was what the boy wanted, why shouldn't he have it?

Springing from his chair, Tom crossed the distance to his father, then hesitated, swinging his empty hands. His face was bright, flushed with pleasure. "I won't disappoint you father," he promised.

Henry smiled, and took his son's hand. "Of course not. You should tell your mother."

Long after Tom raced from the room Henry sat there. He had known for a long time that Tom would be good in the business. He'd also known that no matter how Tom succeeded in the world of commerce, he could not help but be disappointed. It was not the life he wanted for his only son.

CHAPTER 7
SEASONS

U p in Cordell's nursery, Sophy spent a sleepless night, agonizing over the loss of her mother's sketches and the consequences of angering Lord Fairchild. She could not afford to offend her only protector. In the morning, she trembled as the new nursemaid conducted her to the library. Though Lord Fairchild accepted her wooden apology, she seemed to have killed any interest he had in her. She glimpsed him only once in the following fortnight.

The nursery was lonely and dark at night; she often woke, cold and terrified, too afraid to leave her room and with no one to call. Awake or asleep, she dreaded being sent away from Cordell Hall.

Escaping in her free hours to the park, it didn't take Sophy long to find the ruin her mother had painted. How she longed for those pictures! Surely she would not be so troubled in that great empty nursery, if only she had them with her. After her angry outburst she was too afraid of Lord Fairchild to ask for the pictures back. The more time passed without speaking to him, the more timid she became. It hurt, knowing he had taken a share of her mother's love, but she locked pain and resentment away.

Lord Fairchild did not guess she was lonely, or he would have gone to her again. After her rebuff, he told himself he must wait until she was willing to know him. He watched carefully, but she never gave any sign. Always, she subdued herself in his presence, retreating as soon as possible. Only when he watched her unobserved did he see her come to life: running back to the house, red-cheeked, from the gardens; rollicking with Henrietta in an empty salon; flitting away from the kitchen with a ginger biscuit in her hand. He waited, increasingly impatient, but the sign never came.

Despite his own repeated counsel—she was young, she knew nothing of him, she was grieving—he was wounded by her cool dislike. She lived in his house, yet he felt almost as removed from his love-begotten child as he had the past ten years.

Sophy spent most of her time in the schoolroom with Henrietta and the adenoidal Miss Frensham. From the beginning, Henrietta had been eager to embrace her half-sister. Illicit novels were her lifeblood. She viewed Sophy as a tragic heroine, becoming quite disappointed when she learned Sophy had not been rescued from the workhouse. But she was an eager listener and Sophy's stories turned out to be better than the one she had imagined. She liked few things better than hearing Sophy's caricatures of Mr. Lynchem and the worthy ladies of Bottom End, or her retellings of Fanny Prescott's fairy tales. Sunny natured, there were truthfully very few people Henrietta disliked; even dour Miss Frensham was not wholly despised.

It didn't take long before the girls began swapping schoolwork. Henrietta might have made a mathematical genius, had her mother allowed it, but she had almost no facility with French. Sophy spoke with a delightful accent, but needed help marshaling her thoughts when confronted with a row of numbers.

Cordell was an unhappy house, Sophy realized, with Henrietta its one bright flame. Lord Fairchild indulged her, fond of his beautiful, high-spirited daughter. Lady Fairchild was proud of her and ambitious for her, already mapping out her marriage prospects and her brilliant social life. Even Jasper's teasing was done with obvious affection. Henrietta was the pride of the all the servants, more so than Jasper, who could be churlish under his smooth veneer. Like everyone else, Sophy could not help loving her.

Henrietta's company was some solace, but still, Sophy was often alone.

Vast and sprawling, the park at Cordell was moist with rotting leaves in the fall, rimmed with frost and blighted by wind in the winter. A hardy soul, Sophy ventured out in all weather, until the day that Jasper spied her sliding across the frozen lake. Hauled back to the house, she was lectured by Miss Frensham, by Dessie, the nursery maid, and most awfully, by her father, whom she still called Lord Fairchild. He sentenced her to a fortnight indoors, so Sophy took to exploring the house. Venturing undetected into rooms, eventually she mapped it all, from the fastness of Lord Fairchild's library to the steaming laundry. She tiptoed through the airy prettiness of Lady Fairchild's suite, wandered the state-rooms and finally ingratiated her way into the cellars, the exclusive domain of Jenkins, the butler.

"She's an endearing mite," Dessie admitted at table in the kitchen, "Even with that naughty streak. Lord, it's impossible to keep her in the nursery." Just that day, Dessie had found Sophy in the gunroom and the dumb waiter.

Liza sniffed, exchanging looks with Millie Dawson, Lady Fairchild's maid. The two were united in their disapproval of Sophy's presence in their Lady's house, but otherwise the servants liked her.

When Easter came, Lady Fairchild punished her husband by inviting her family for the holiday. Sophy spent her days hiding from the guests. Once she was summoned to the library to speak to her guardian; it was a difficult interview with long silences, but she hoped she had convinced him that she was doing her best as a scholar and endeavoring not to make trouble. He was still a stranger.

At first, Jasper saw little of his half-sister, being away much of the year at school. Uninterested in young children, he had intended to ignore Sophy, but discarded this notion over the summer in favor of making a pet of her to annoy his mama. He spent most of his time at Cordell tramping through the fens with his dog and a fowling piece and one day he saw Sophy drifting away from the house as he made his own way through the gardens.

"You may as well carry my bag," he said, tossing it to her. "If you're going to spend the day outside. Come on."

She was a game little thing, he learned, solid as a soldier, gladly following him under hot sun or chilling mizzle, begging for stories of his adventures at school. She was, as he suspected, a regular hoyden and knew how to climb trees and make a whistle from a blade of grass. He laughed, seeing how pleased she was when he showed her the best places to find tadpoles, though he was past that kind of thing himself. Seeing her sitting like a sack as one of the grooms led her around on Henrietta's old pony, he decided he ought to take an interest in her training, if only for the sake of the horse. After a particularly hard fall, he discovered Sophy's collection of curses. Smirking, he gifted her a few jewels of his own, recognizing in the flash of her eyes a like-minded soul.

It pleased Jasper to escape with Sophy and watch her thin face vivify in his company. Naturally, she was a trial at times, being eight years his junior, but he did not hesitate to dismiss her when he tired of her company. He found he seldom did. They passed much of their time together in companionable silence or with Jasper giving orders. Rarely, very rarely, they spoke about Fanny Prescott, whom Jasper had not forgotten.

Sophy had tried to bury both guilt and grief, but sometimes she had to speak of her mother, though she was never certain if even the best memories would bring tears or laughter. Jasper listened avidly, imparting now and then a memory of his own. Sophy understood that he had been fond of her mother, and was comforted.

The year Jasper finished his studies at Cambridge, Lord and Lady Fairchild took Henrietta to London for the Season, launching her with all the pomp and circumstance of a ship of the line. She was eighteen and a brilliant success, receiving a flattering number of offers. From the beaus vetted by her mama, Henrietta chose Lord Percy Arundel, surprising many. Two dashing eligibles had made Lady Fairchild's list, and still Henrietta chose Arundel. True, he was wealthy and an earl, but he was balding and fifteen years her senior. He had bookish habits and a tendency to talk over peoples' heads, in no way resembling the heroes of the novels Henrietta had devoured for so many years. Lady Fairchild was puzzled by this choice, but Henrietta seemed pleased with the match and snagging Arundel was a coup of which any mother could be proud.

Sophy, who received regular letters from Henrietta, had a better understanding of her reasons and was happy for her sister, though grieved to lose her companionship.

"He adores me," Henrietta wrote. "He will not wander, and he will love me when my beauty is gone. Mother thinks he is a staid fellow. He is, but that doesn't stop me loving him. Just don't tell anyone."

Henrietta married in the fall and Cordell was a quieter place without her. Jasper seldom visited, though he was often at Newmarket, a scant fifteen miles away. In command of his own money now, he tended to avoid his parents, running with a younger, faster set of sporting gentlemen.

Her work completed with Henrietta, Lady Fairchild tried to turn her efforts to her son, but was speedily rebuffed. Her husband refused to lend his aid, and the truce that had held between them during Henrietta's season ended. Lady Fairchild resumed hostilities with a broadside of dinners and parties, and Lord Fairchild retreated to his stables.

· · ·

OVER TIME, LADY FAIRCHILD'S THOUGHTS TURNED TO SOPHY. It surprised her that Sophy seldom rode with William, since under Jasper's tutelage she had become a daring rider. The girl would probably have moved into the stables, if they allowed it, so strong was her fascination with William's bloodstock. Yet she rode with her father only by accident, if they happened to choose the same time and direction. Once, Lady Fairchild had feared Sophy would eclipse her own children in their father's eyes. A misplaced worry, it had turned out.

She was a surprisingly agreeable thing, always docile and polite. Neither Jasper nor Henrietta took pains to please her like Sophy did. Bored, and a little lonely, Lady Fairchild stopped ignoring the girl and began summoning her to the drawing room. Always she made some excuse to herself at first: Miss Frensham had a cold and was unable to pour the tea, or she wanted Sophy present to outshine Mrs. Matcham's two boring daughters. Lady Fairchild found comfort in Sophy's company, for since Henrietta's marriage, her life seemed to have lost much of its purpose. So it was natural, almost unnoticeable, when she began taking Sophy about with her and coaching her in the social arts of which she was an acknowledged master.

They spent many companionable hours together, shopping in the village and reading fashion magazines. Sophy's looks could not be compared to Henrietta's, but her taste was excellent. Within a year, Sophy accompanied Lady Fairchild most everywhere, assisted with her correspondence and wrote out the menus for her entertainments. Lady Fairchild began to depend on Sophy, to be just a little fond of her. In reflective moments, Lady Fairchild concluded there was a certain justice to it, since her own children preferred their father. She could not deny it was just a little satisfying, that she had succeeded where he could not. He tried to hide it, but she knew he envied her rapport with Sophy.

She never varied her imperious manners, but she valued Sophy more than she admitted.

Sophy was content. It was pleasant, being in Lady Fairchild's good graces, and her latent fears of being thrown out receded until she almost forgot them. Though she missed Henrietta and Jasper, she had Lady Fairchild's company, the horses and Cordell. She loved the wide expanse of the Suffolk countryside. Riding was her joy; racing her secret enthusiasm. Barred from the meetings in Newmarket, she extracted detailed accounts from John, the head groom, and was as proud as he each time Cordell fielded a winner. Her days were full, starting with early morning rides and ending with neighborhood parties; her thoughts never travelled beyond the next social engagement or the next race meeting. Her seventeenth birthday came and went without anyone seeming to notice. Lady Fairchild never spoke of the past, so it was easy to distance herself from her own memories. Sophy did not pause to consider the future.

CHAPTER 8
LADY FAIRCHILD DECIDES

"Thank you, Mrs. Larkin. I shall call again next week to see how you are getting on."

Mrs. Larkin, now the mother of six, curtseyed as Lady Fairchild gathered her sables and swept out of the cottage.

Tom Coachman helped her into the carriage. Females of Lady Fairchild's generation did not drive their own vehicles and nothing could persuade her to learn, though she had ordered Jasper to teach Henrietta and then Sophy, once it became fashionable for young ladies to drive a smart vehicle with one or two horses.

"Sophy?" she called. *What was keeping her?*

"Coming, ma'am." Sophy appeared at the carriage door, a large basket hung over her arm.

"What's that?" Lady Fairchild asked.

Sophy's face split in a wide grin. "One of Dash's puppies. Peter Larkin gave her to me, but I will let Jasper have her. I have wanted to thank him for giving me such a handsome Christmas present, and I think he will die of envy if I do not." Even Lady Fairchild knew that the Larkin dogs were famous.

"Very kind of Mr. Larkin, I'm sure." Lady Fairchild said,

looking dubiously at the basket and stretching her feet to the hot brick in front of her. It was late afternoon, but the slanting winter sunlight was too weak to melt the frost from the trees. Taking a small notebook from her reticule, she drew a check mark beside the last name on her list with a silver pencil. "He kept you outside long enough."

"That was my fault, ma'am," Sophy said. "It was so hard to choose just one."

"Drive on," Lady Fairchild instructed, rapping on the window of the carriage. Tom Coachman gave the horses leave to start.

Lady Fairchild was always diligent in visiting her husband's tenants. She brought gifts of linen and tiny gowns after a birth, distributed hampers of food and shirts when there was illness or misfortune, and had personally vaccinated all the servants and laborers belonging to Cordell Hall. There were few roles she found as satisfying as that of Lady Bounty. Normally, she was gratified by the simple gifts she occasionally received in return: rose cuttings for her garden, a bottle of liniment she thrust onto her housekeeper, a clutch of chicks from one of the farmers' prizewinning hens. This time she frowned at the basket, tapping her pencil against the list.

"If you do not like her, I will keep her in the stables," Sophy said, though it was plain the idea distressed her.

Lady Fairchild waved a hand. "My dear, I'm sure it's no matter if you keep her in your rooms. Heaven knows one more dog will make no difference."

William knew she hated his dogs in the house, but the dogs came inside nevertheless. It was not the puppy that displeased her. No, this dog was just the latest instance of a growing problem. When she and Sophy conducted their errands of mercy or drove into Bury St. Edmonds to visit the shops, farmers' sons increasingly found excuses to speak to Sophy. The shop boys were too attentive, following her with their eyes. Worse, Sophy was friendly in return, smiling as readily to Peter Larkin's bashful greeting as she did to Jasper's teasing.

Until now, Lady Fairchild had always been glad Sophy never tried to increase her privileges or insinuate herself higher. She had liked her for being content with her place. It had never troubled her before when Sophy failed to discourage the familiarities of the local people, but Lady Fairchild saw where it was leading now. Letting Sophy marry a farmer or a tradesman would be intolerable. She could not invite those men to her home, or visit Sophy in theirs. Day by day, she was realizing that she did not want Sophy to pass out of her life after reaching adulthood.

It was strange, Lady Fairchild thought, watching Sophy lift the lid of the basket and slip her hand inside to fondle the bundle of silky fur. She had never expected to like her.

Though not a beauty, Sophy was undeniably pretty. It surprised her that William's features had turned out so well on a female, but they had indeed. Sophy's face was arresting, her dark, mobile brows and pale skin topped by the bright tangle of her hair. Of course the local boys noticed. Sophy's self-deprecating manners only encouraged their presumption. These farmers' sons would never have dared to throw a second glance Henrietta's way.

It was a problem, but it didn't have to be. Finding an acceptable husband for Sophy would be difficult, but was by no means impossible. Examining the idea, Lady Fairchild's pulse quickened. Sophy was illegitimate, but acknowledged, and with a good dowry. She had all the necessary accomplishments and an eye for color and design. If she brought Sophy out, Sophy would do very well. Leaning her head back into the velvet upholstery, Lady Fairchild let a dreamy half-smile creep across her face. There was nothing that gave spice to the London Season like arranging a marriage.

It would be truly magnanimous of her.

Eyes narrowed, she watched Sophy, who was intent on her puppy. With her hair cut, some simple pearls, and a delicate figured muslin, nothing could look more appealing. She would show best at outdoor events, Lady Fairchild decided—rides in the park, Venetian breakfasts—they would have to pay special attention to choosing habits and walking dresses. Of course she could not bring Sophy everywhere. There would be no court presentation, no vouchers for the assemblies at Almacks, but otherwise she would have Sophy's company. Her one dissatisfaction with Henrietta's marriage to Arundel was that they lived so far away. She might have better luck there with Sophy.

"You look vastly pretty today, Sophy, but I think it's high time we got you some new gowns," she said.

"Thank-you, ma'am. That is most kind." A pink flush stole into her cheeks. "But I won't need anything until you and Lord Fairchild return from London."

Lady Fairchild didn't contradict her. No need to explain just yet. She would speak to William first.

"DON'T LET THAT OVERGROWN MOUSE CHEW ON YOUR DRESS," Dessie scolded, fastening Sophy up the back. "That flounce was three shillings a yard!" Letting out a cry of vexation, Dessie pounced on the puppy and stuffed her into the basket, cursing Peter Larkin under her breath.

"Sorry! She can't help it," Sophy said, crouching down to examine her hem. "It's just a small tear."

Dessie sniffed.

"I can mend it myself, you know," Sophy said. "No one will see it, but I can change if you think I should."

"This is your best dress and you are supposed to take special pains this evening," Dessie said, repeating Lady Fairchild's instructions for perhaps the fifth time.

"Who's coming?" Sophy asked. "She's never made such a fuss for any of the neighbors. And we have no house guests."

"You'll see," Dessie said, holding the secret in with a prim smile. "It's an occasion, and you ought to look your best."

Sophy rolled her eyes, submitting to Dessie's attack on her windblown hair, wondering who Lady Fairchild was entertaining tonight. It had to be someone important. Hastened by Dessie and her own growing curiosity, Sophy descended to the drawing room on light, rapid feet, took one step inside, and stopped. The room was empty, save for Lord and Lady Fairchild.

No impromptu party? She looked around. No guests lurked in the corners.

"Good evening, Lord Fairchild, Lady Fairchild," she said, curtseying to each. Then she followed behind as her father took up Lady Fairchild's hand and led her into the dining room.

The table had only three places, set in the usual gleaming china and sparkling plate. Yet it could be no ordinary meal, for Lady Fairchild was wearing her new rose satin. It was unlike her to bring out a new gown if they were merely dining with the family. Timothy, the footman, held out her chair and Sophy took her seat, eyeing Lord and Lady Fairchild carefully as she began eating her soup.

Lord Fairchild looked as he usually did at dinner: freshly shaved, in breeches, silk stockings, pumps and a dark coat. It was Tuesday, so he wore blue, a quirk Lady Fairchild could never persuade him to give up. His face was lined and he looked a little tired, but that was nothing extraordinary. He made conversation, his eyebrows dipping, lifting, and drawing together as he spoke. Apparently he had spent his afternoon going over the form books.

"And you Sophy?" he asked, between bites of turbot. "How was your afternoon?"

"Pleasant. I finished the work Miss Frensham set me and spent the rest of my time riding."

"Mmm?" He was interested in the ride, not the lessons.

"I took out Nemesis, the new Arabian. She was fresh. John says that bodes well for her race."

"Good."

"You said you finished all your set lessons?" Lady Fairchild asked, as Timothy brought out the second course.

Sophy nodded. "She'll give me more when she returns." Miss Frensham was gone for a three week holiday with her family.

Lord Fairchild shook his head. "She's not coming back." He wiped his mouth with his napkin. "Taking a new post in Surrey, with the Beauchamps. You've had lessons enough." Feeling the blood drain from her face, Sophy worked around a bite of pheasant, her mouth dry. Tonight was an Occasion, Dessie had said.

Not this.

Some fears Sophy had never been able to eradicate. She'd lived carefully for seven years, afraid of being sent away from Cordell Hall. Her stomach plunged at the thought.

Lady Fairchild frowned at her husband, displeased he had chosen to discuss family matters with a servant in the room. Pointedly, she asked him what he had thought of Sunday's sermon.

"I'm sorry my dear," he said. "I wasn't attending."

"Well, I am not certain I approve of the vicar choosing his text from Revelations," she said. "I dislike apocalyptic fervor."

Swallowing her dry mouthful, Sophy cut her meat into tiny pieces and managed to eat one spear of asparagus. She waited, her hands gathered in her lap, while Timothy removed the tablecloth and brought out dessert. Ignoring her favorite cake—was it a sign? —she took an orange from the bowl and dissected it with her silver fruit knife. She could not look up.

"You're seventeen now," Lord Fairchild said at last, setting down a half empty glass of burgundy. "It's time we spoke about your future."

Not yet, Sophy thought, desperately concealing her disquiet. But there were governesses her age, she knew.

"Georgiana has spoken to me. She has an excellent plan."

Lady Fairchild interrupted. "Let me tell her, William." She was excited, giving off fizz like a glass of champagne. "Sophy, dear. We are bringing you with us to London."

Sophy blinked. "Why?"

"For the Season, of course."

Sophy frowned, still not following. Lady Fairchild always looked forward to the Season, but—

"Seventeen *is* a little young," Lady Fairchild said, "but with your handicaps it might take two Seasons to come up with a suitable match. We may as well make the best use of your youth and beauty we can."

Hope and relief flared in her, hot and bright as a struck match. Always, she shied away from thinking of her future; no wonder, with Miss Frensham's dreary life observable every lesson, every day. Hadn't old Mr. Lynchem warned her this was how it would be? Her mother had seemed happy as a teacher, but Sophy did not trust her memory. She couldn't have been really happy, spurned by her lover, suspected by the villagers, hiding a grieving heart.

Well, she would escape this future at least. Now, with the hope of marrying herself, she might enjoy reading the novels Henrietta was always sharing with her. She had three of them now, pasted into false covers (for Henrietta knew well what Lady Fairchild permitted Sophy to read) hiding under the clean hand-kerchiefs in her bureau drawer. Sophy hadn't opened any of them. With her history and prospects, she had always found romances painful, teasing her with something she did not hope to have. Henrietta had never understood. Surely her mother had loved Lord Fairchild, and look where that had led?

This wasn't the same. Lord and Lady Fairchild were helping her to a husband. Rather forlornly, Sophy reflected that it was not necessary to love one of those. But it was possible. Henrietta was unashamedly happy. Sophy brightened. How wonderful it would be, if she could have the same.

"I am to marry?" she said, finding her voice at last.

"Of course." Lord Fairchild set down his fork. "What else would you do?"

Work. Wither into spinsterhood. Teach Henrietta's children, or Jasper's, when he had them.

She was the only one at Cordell—the only one in the neighborhood—without a clear place and a clear path. When Sophy let herself want anything, it was only to remain at Cordell. If she was inoffensive and not too conspicuous she might be able to stay, blending into the background like a dappled fawn, scarcely noticed. Eventually the house would pass from Lord Fairchild to Jasper. He would keep her, she knew.

Lately, she had begun contemplating other paths. Peter Larkin did not quicken her pulse, but she liked his smile and his steady hands. If she—but she could not think it without blushing. He would want a bride with something besides youth and a modicum of looks. She had none of the skills a farmer's wife would need, and no money either.

"Don't worry, Sophy," Lady Fairchild said. "You shall manage perfectly well. Your father has given you an independence—"

"I have money? How much?" Sophy interrupted.

"You have enough to attract respectable men," Lord Fairchild said repressively.

Lady Fairchild exchanged a glance with her husband. "Respectability is key," she said. "We should like you to remain within our sphere. Imagine, if you will, how disagreeable it would be for Fairchild if you were to marry one of the locals—Sam Goodwin or Peter Larkin. Such awkwardness! How could he collect rent from his daughter's husband? Certainly they would use you to impose upon us."

Not Peter Larkin then. "Is it enough money that I could live on my own?" She had lived in plain circumstances before. A cottage was all she needed.

"What an idea!" Lady Fairchild said. "You are far too young to be thinking of any such thing. I do not approve of spinster households. And it is entirely unnecessary, for as I said, you cannot fail to attract someone worthy."

"It is important for me to see you are well cared for," Lord Fairchild said, straightening his knife alongside his plate. "And it is very good of Lady Fairchild to sponsor you." He looked up into Sophy's eyes. "Rest assured, I shall look carefully at all the men who apply to me. We will help you make a wise choice."

No one knew what Society permitted better than Lady Fairchild, but Sophy was skeptical. What sort of man of their rank would be willing to marry a bastard? Yes, the neighbors accepted her as Lady Fairchild's companion, but she did not think they would tolerate her when they knew she was dangling after one of their sons. When the Matcham girls learned she was entering the lists, they would have her blood. Or what little they could get of it with an embroidery needle. Sophy swallowed, forcing a tremulous smile to her lips.

What sort of man indeed? And what sort of marriage? Sam Goodwin had loved his young wife, until losing her a year ago to influenza. His heart might be given and gone, but he was a gentle man, who would be good to whatever girl he married. If she was to marry into her father's order—

Sophy glanced between Lord and Lady Fairchild and shivered. No one made marriage look more uncongenial than they.

"One would think you don't want to marry, the way you carry on," Lady Fairchild said. She looked offended.

"No, no. I'm merely surprised." Sophy said. "I—thank-you," she added, bowing her head to escape her father's pointed look.

"Think of London," Lady Fairchild said. "You shall have such a wonderful time!"

She was thinking of London. It was making her ill. London was not Suffolk. There, even Lady Fairchild could not protect her from the contempt of the Polite World. Some would never accept her. Some would scorn her. Mock her. Despise her.

She raised her eyes from her plate.

"This is a happy day, Sophy," Lord Fairchild said, smiling at her from down the table. "Only to be surpassed by your wedding, I hope." He raised his glass. "To your future, Sophy! And your happiness."

Would there be happiness in this future? She feared not. But her tension ebbed as she drained her glass. *Don't be a ninny. They want you to be well.*

Setting down her glass, she tried to catch some of their excitement. Her father was on his feet, already refilling her glass. "Have another, both of you," he said, overriding Lady Fairchild's weak protest. "This burgundy is for celebrating." Returning to his place at the head of the table, he remained standing, grinning broadly as he raised his glass. "The King," he said. "And confusion to Bonaparte!"

CHAPTER 9
LEAVE TAKING

Sophy spent the weeks leading to her departure for London alternately fearing that she would be shunned or that Lady Fairchild would succeed. Everyone was pleased for her, from the lowliest stable boy to Jenkins the butler. She accepted their well wishes with the best grace she could muster, but couldn't hide her feelings from Dessie.

"I wish you could come with me," she said.

Dessie snorted, tugging harder at Sophy's night plait, knotting the end with a piece of string. She had a young man in the village and was being promoted to housemaid. "Worriting will only spoil your complexion. You'll need a proper maid in London."

Nine days before Sophy and Lady Fairchild were scheduled to journey to London, she had a reprieve. Jasper wrote, offering to drive her down to London on his way back from Newmarket, giving her a few extra days. Sophy begged to delay her departure and Lady Fairchild agreed. As she waved Lady Fairchild goodbye, Sophy's spirits rose. She had five days to herself, maybe six. She wouldn't waste a single one.

She would play spillikins with Dessie and eat ginger biscuits. She would finish walking all the paths in the garden, ride through the marshes and sketch the house and the surrounding country. Her artistic talents were non-existent, but she would try to make a passable representation of the country for which she had grown such a painful love. She had always loved springtime at Cordell, when the family went to London and she had the run of the house.

Her first day alone dawned grey and wet. Sophy spent the morning staring out the window and writing a list of everything she wanted to do before leaving Cordell. In the afternoon, conscious of each passing hour, she ventured out of doors, cloaked and carrying a large umbrella. She returned an hour later, damp and defeated. Sketching was impossible while juggling an umbrella and she did not dislike any of the footmen enough to ask them to hold it for her while she drew.

The rain fell unabated the second day, so Sophy threw the list into the fire, and spent the day with John in his snug room off the stables, listening to him recount horse lineages and famous races.

The third morning was misty and damp. Good enough, she decided. Throwing on an old riding habit, she gulped a quick breakfast, scarcely pausing to chew. A letter from Jasper rested beside her plate. Eager to be on her way, she stuffed it into the pocket of her heavy skirt for later.

Only Jem, the youngest groom, was in the stables. Sophy seized her chance and bullied him into saddling Ajax. She had worshipped Lord Fairchild's magnificent roan hunter for a year, but been forbidden to ride him. Fate had blessed her with a chance at last. Sophy kept a sedate pace until she was out of sight of the house, then she booted him to a canter, sending clods of black dirt flying behind her. Overhead, the sky was stone grey, and as cold. Flying over the ground, the chill rasped her lungs, stinging her cheeks and stiffening her fingers through her gloves. The damp twisted her flyaway strands of hair into corkscrews.

She loved this, the heavy smell of earth and rotting bracken, the fens so green and alive. She didn't check when she came to the end of Fairchild land, though she was not allowed to ride beyond without a groom. None of the servants would know. Even if she was discovered, there was no one to whom they could complain. Smiling, she turned down the lane to the village. She made some farewells, thanking Peter Larkin again for the puppy, and bidding goodbye to Stokes, the farrier. Old Mrs. Stokes offered her tea and biscuits, silencing her growling stomach. As she left, Mrs. Stokes urged her to return home, but Sophy wasn't finished yet.

The servants couldn't complain if she was back late. She wasn't hungry, and she was free. She did not know when she would see these sights again: white windmills, the flat expanse of surrounding farms, flocks of sheep cropping the new spring growth. She'd never been this far on her own and was surely trespassing. It scarcely mattered. No one would see her. The chill had chased most people inside.

Her hand brushed her coat, crinkling Jasper's letter inside her pocket. She dismounted in a spinney of birch trees to read it. The missive was brief, full of his usual nonsense. It made her smile.

A fat raindrop splashed onto her hand and Sophy glanced through the budding branches at the sky. It was darker, and not just because night was fast approaching.

"Damn." It took a moment to find a large enough stone so she could mount Ajax. By the time she rode out of the spinney, the rain was falling fast. The plume on her hat, limp as the tail of a dead mouse, drooped over her eyes. Wincing over Dessie's displeasure, she yanked it free and let it fall. Her habit was plastered to her back. Water ran down her neck and her nose. Clenching her chattering teeth, she left the road to cut across the fields, urging Ajax faster. She needed to get home. John would be furious with her for keeping Ajax out in this weather.

There was a stream ahead, bordered by thick trees. Sophy ducked her head as she rode unchecked beneath the branches. Ajax gathered on his haunches, preparing to spring across and lurched beneath her, throwing her to the side. Before she could cry out, she flew from the saddle.

As the ground rushed to meet her, her left hand caught in the reins, yanking her arm, sending her into an awkward spin. She felt a tearing in her shoulder as she slammed into the ground and a moment of sheer terror before her hand pulled free from the reins. Waiting to be crushed by Ajax's hooves, it was some moments before she realized she had been thrown clear.

Lungs heaving, she rolled onto her back, gasping but making no sound. Frantically she gulped air, unable to exhale. At last she managed it, a high-pitched whistle of pain.

Wet leaves stuck to her cheek. She scraped them off with her right hand and tried to sit up. The movement sent a stabbing pain through her left shoulder. She let out a strangled cry. Gingerly, she tried to move her left arm.

It was useless. She couldn't move it, not without the edges of her vision swirling darkly. Flat on her back, she stared dizzily at the sky, drawing shallow breaths, her heart beating presto.

You can't stay here. No one will find you, and you're cold. And what about Ajax?

Turning her head, she spied him standing not far off. "Beast," she managed to gasp. He lowered his head, as if he was ashamed.

They had to get help, quickly. Something was terribly wrong with her arm.

Don't think about it. Just get up.

Reaching her right arm across her middle, she clamped her left arm against her side, and rolled to the right with a groan. Biting hard on her bottom lip, she lurched upward. Good. She was sitting now. Getting to her feet was easier. Her shoulder throbbed, but holding it against her side seemed to help. Unfortunately, she had to let go, to reach for Ajax's dangling reins.

The pain was staggering, but she caught the reins with a clumsy swing. Looping the leather around her right wrist, she clutched her left arm again.

"Come on," she said, unsure if she was addressing the horse or herself.

A slick layer of wet leaves covered the ground. No wonder Ajax had lost his footing. She'd be lucky if she didn't fall herself, the way she was trembling. Eyes on the ground, she picked her way out of the trees, leading an unusually docile Ajax.

There was little light left. She wouldn't be able to walk far. Getting herself into the saddle was impossible. Pressing her lips into a thin line, breathing noisily through her nose, she started walking, hoping it would not be long before she found the road.

CHAPTER 10
STRANGERS

I t was a foul day for riding, Tom thought, but that was England for you. It had rained all the way from Bury St. Edmonds, and he was wet to the skin by the time he glimpsed Chippenstone's lights.

His mother, of course, was waiting for him. As he dismounted, a groom ran out to lead his horse away. He hadn't taken two steps before the butler stood beside him, holding out an umbrella. Tom didn't recognize him, but he was used to new faces. Servants didn't usually stay at Chippenstone for long. Stepping inside, he very properly handed his hat, whip and gloves to the waiting lackey. His mother rushed towards him from the drawing room, her crisp purple silk rustling, the ludicrous tower of curls atop her head bouncing madly.

"Martin's preparing a bath," she said, helping him from his coat, pushing aside the hovering butler. She kissed him soundly on both cheeks. "I needn't ask about your journey. You look like a drowned cat."

"And you look your angel self, mother. Stand off, so I don't get wet all over you." He thrust his sodden greatcoat at the butler.

"May as well make just one puddle," he said, fumbling at the buttons of his coat with numb fingers.

"James, bring a dressing gown for Mr. Bagshot," the butler commanded.

It was, Tom knew, unusual for gentleman to strip down in the front hall. It didn't bother him to fret his servants; after all, they knew what kind of people they worked for. And if it pleased them to find more congenial employment elsewhere, that didn't bother him either. It was his mother who suffered agonies of humiliation when the servants explained to her how things should be done, or gave up and left. He wished she would let up, but had lost hope long ago.

"Thank you, James," Tom said, exchanging his waistcoat for a brocaded silk dressing gown. Lord, it felt good to pull on something warm and dry. Pity he had to keep on his wet shirt and trousers. He didn't mind upsetting the servants, but his mother would be mortified if he removed shirt and breeches down here.

"I'm for the bath," he said. "I'll be down in two ticks."

"I'm glad you're home," she said.

He winced. Chippenstone would never be home. Two years since his father's death, and his mother still hadn't given up this pile of brick, the evidence of her husband's last, failed dream. She was lonely here, but nothing Tom said could persuade her to leave. Visiting her was no hardship; he would ride twice as far, in any weather. But when she joined his father, he knew he would sell this place.

"I missed you, mum," he said and chucked her under the chin, before bounding up the stairs three at a time. Behind him, he heard the butler tell James to take his wet clothes away. Then he heard a knock. He stopped. His mother never had visitors. And who would call in this weather, at this time of night?

Turning round, he saw a dark wraith framed in the open doorway. Without thinking, he descended the stairs and crossed the hall. The creature was clutching one arm and shivering uncontrollably—no wonder, for water streamed from her skirts onto the floor. Her face was white as wax, her lips a ghastly purple. Muddy war paint smudged her cheeks and leaves stuck to her skirts.

"Forgive me for b-b-begging your assistance," she said through chattering teeth.

"You're hurt." Tom frowned, moving closer.

"Yes." She gulped. "But my horse . . ." She glanced worriedly behind her, out the open door. "He needs tending."

Looking past her, Tom saw a huge animal standing on the gravel drive.

"He's chilled," the girl explained, her voice close to breaking. "If he gets sick in the lungs, he'll never race again."

"See to her horse," Tom ordered, to no one in particular. "You must come inside." She wasn't thinking straight, he thought. Probably had the wits knocked out of her.

He offered his arm, but she hesitated, biting her lip. "The pain is too great to let go of my arm. If you will lead me—"

She attempted a step forward, her face contorting with pain.

"Wait," Tom said, wrapping an arm around her waist to steady her. Cold water seeped through the sleeves of his dressing gown. She must be half-frozen. "I'll carry you."

Probably he should wait for her permission, but that seemed foolish in the circumstances. She looked ready to fall to the floor. Scooping her up, he saw her wince though he had tried not to jar her shoulder. Every step he took, her teeth cut deeper into her lip. How in Hades had she managed to walk to the house?

His mother reappeared, burdened with a stack of towels. "We must get you warm," she said, bustling ahead of them into the drawing room.

"I'm going to set you down here," he said, indicating a large sofa by the fire with a jerk of his chin. "Ready?"

She nodded. He tried to lower her smoothly, but she was no featherweight, despite being so slight. Laying back, she let out a sigh. "I'm ruining the silk of your sofa."

He supposed she was. No matter. "What happened?" he asked, as his mother tended to her with the towels.

"I was riding across the fields, trying to hurry home."

"Oh?" his mother looked up, but the girl didn't elaborate.

"Ajax lost his footing jumping over a stream and I fell." Her lips shook.

"Let me see the arm," Tom said, moving closer. "You can't move it at all?"

She shook her head, shrinking away from him. "It doesn't work. When I try the pain in my shoulder is unbearable." Her reedy voice betrayed suppressed panic. Frowning, he studied her. The arm was straight and didn't appear swollen. "Did you land on it?"

She shook her head. "My hand tangled in the reins."

"Pulled your arm?"

She nodded, squeezing her eyes shut.

He considered only a moment. "I can help," he said.

"Are you a doctor?" Her gaze was desperate, but suspicious.

"No." He smiled. "I'm a sailor. I think you've pulled your arm out of your shoulder. I have a surgeon friend, who I've seen fix injuries like this a time or two. You won't feel a thing." That's what Jack told his patients anyways. He hoped it was true.

She tensed, drawing away from him.

"I'm just going to hold your hand and your elbow," he said, reaching forward. "Don't be afraid. This won't hurt you."

Moving slowly and maintaining a soothing patter of words, he cupped her elbow with one hand and clasped her wrist with the other. Her hands were like ice, the skin under her nails matching her purple lips.

"Wretched weather you choose to ride in," he said.

"You've been outside too," she said through gritted teeth. "Your hair is all wet." He saw her eyes flick to his dressing gown, but she didn't mention it.

"That's how I know it's so awful. I thought I was cold. How long were you out there?"

She didn't reply, just sucked in a breath as he lifted away her uninjured hand. Inch by inch, he bent the elbow of her injured arm until it was square, then turned her forearm, bringing her hand down to the seat of the sofa. When her hand was almost to the cushion, he felt her shoulder catch. She gasped, her eyes popping open.

"Leave it," she commanded. "I want to see a doctor."

"Breathe out," he said. "You'll be all right." It was nearly done. Jack said dislocations were best treated quickly, before the muscles could spasm. He nudged her upper arm forward, feeling it slide into place. He released her and sat back on his heels. "Try to move it now."

She lifted her arm tentatively, closing her eyes and letting out a wavering sigh. "Thank God." Relief crumbled her fragile control and her shaking returned. Staring past him with huge, catlike eyes, she let out a half-smothered sob.

"Can you lift your arm all the way up?" She seemed past hearing, so he took her arm and circled it around. The joint moved freely, and he felt his anxiety ebb away.

"We must get you warm," he said.

"You go make sure the surgeon's been sent for," his mother said. When he didn't move, she took his arm and steered him to the door. "I've got to get her out of those wet things. It's all right to move her arm?"

He blinked. "I don't see why not, though I imagine she's pretty sore."

His mother frowned. "If it's too difficult, we can cut them off. See if Sarah's bringing laudanum, like I asked. And don't forget to put on dry clothes yourself. I don't need you catching cold on top of everything."

"Rheum, more like," he said, winking as he closed the door. "I'm likely to cause you the most amount of trouble."

In the drafty hallway, away from the fire, cold pierced him again. He'd forgotten how chilled he was. Nights like this, no one should be out, certainly not lone girls. Jack had told him how terrifying a dislocated shoulder was and both times he'd seen him treat one, the patients had panicked.

He wouldn't soon forget her woebegone, desperate figure standing in his doorway and shrinking in pain on his sofa. He wondered how she had come to be riding in such weather, alone. Her speech, her horse and her clothing indicated she was too well bred to be allowed out without an escort.

Remembering his bath, and that the water would soon cool, he loped up the stairs. She would explain soon enough.

Swathed in a new dressing gown and with a warm drink in his hand, Tom sat in the plain nook of a room he had claimed for himself. The master suite here was too big and ornate for him. He kept his chair pulled close to the fire and his feet propped on the fender. If there hadn't been such strange happenings, he was quite sure he would be asleep by now. Lord knew he ought to be tired.

A soft knock sounded at the door. "Still awake?" his mother asked.

"As you see." He signed for her to join him in the opposite chair. "How is she?"

"Asleep," was all she said.

Close to the light of the fire, he saw that his mother carried the girl's clothes. Briskly, she shook them out and hung them over the screen to dry. Even after decades of wealth, his mother hadn't forgotten how to do menial work. Her fingers were thick and efficient, with sagging skin around the knuckles and liver spots showing through her lace mittens.

"You could have let Sarah take those away," he said.

She sniffed. "I'm trying to find out who she is."

"She couldn't tell you?"

"By the time we got her into bed, she couldn't put three words together, not so they made any sense. Didn't want to take the laudanum, either. Shouldn't wonder if she's brewing a fever, the way she raved. I thought I'd have to hold her nose, but she took it in the end, poor girl."

"So you have no idea where she is from?"

She hesitated before giving an answer. "No. I don't like the idea of her family not knowing where she is. They must be frantic."

"You forget that I know you of old, Mother." Tom said. "You suspect something, don't you?" She was wearing the same look as when she'd discovered the coal merchant inflating his accounts.

"She has red hair," his mother said.

"She does?" Tom hadn't noticed anything beyond that it was wet. "I don't see how that helps."

His mother pressed her lips together, but her pink cheeks betrayed her excitement. "Lord Fairchild has red hair. I've seen him from a distance, in Bury St. Edmonds. Red hair is unusual here." Her words picked up speed. "I think she's his daughter. She said she was riding home, and Lord Fairchild's house isn't that far."

"Seems slender evidence to me," Tom said. "He might not have any daughters."

"I pick up bits here and there," she said. "I'm fairly sure there's at least one."

He firmed his mouth against the chafing of old wounds, still angry that she had lived here nine years—nine years!—and couldn't say for certain. This was not the way things should be. He drew a long breath and stared into the flames.

"Ah," his mother said, drawing a sodden scrap of paper from a jacket pocket. "This might tell us something."

Carefully, she unfolded the paper, fragile as tissue from the damp, and laid it out on the table. The ink had bled in many places, but some of the writing remained.

"She might dislike you reading her letters," Tom commented, reaching for his brandy.

"What else are we to do, pray?"

He shrugged. "She is out of harm's way. Her family will rest easier, knowing she is safe, but it makes no real difference if they find out now, or tomorrow, or the next day." He would not turn away anyone in need. But taking extra pains for one of them . . . that was another matter.

"Tell me again, when you have children of your own," she said, dismissing him with a sniff.

He watched her scan the paper, her lips moving as she read, and he felt guilty that she was so alone. If she had been able to have other children, his father might not have been so bent on elevating him against his will. He could have avoided Rugby altogether, and his mother would have more than his occasional visits to keep her company.

His mother gave an excited squeak, lifting her hand to her cheek.

"Well?" Tom asked.

"I'm right," she announced. "Look here."

Reluctantly, Tom left his chair and moved to stand beside her.

"He signs his letter 'Jasper', which I'm told is the name of Fairchild's heir, the Honorable Jasper Rushford."

She pronounced the name as if it was sacred, like Shakespeare, or Nelson.

"Look here," she pointed. "There's something about their father, and taking her to London." She looked up at him, her eyes wide with shock. "Tom, we've got Lord and Lady Fairchild's daughter here!"

Wonderful.

His mother leaned back in her chair, fluttering her hands over her chest, as Tom returned to his, full of misgivings. Her unfocused gaze bespoke her agitation and rapid internal calculations.

Tom was annoyed. Fairchild's daughter had no business showing up on his doorstep and knocking his mother out of orbit. He would have to get rid of her as soon as decently possible. As long as she was here, his mother would scheme. He had no interest in cultivating a relationship with any of his toplofty neighbors, and he was reasonably sure they would not welcome acquaintance with him either.

It didn't help that the girl was young. His mother wouldn't be able to stop herself from matchmaking. Seeing him wed was becoming a mania with her. He wished she would understand that people like the Fairchilds would never permit their daughter to marry a Cit like him. Once, his father had tried brokering a marriage for him, but Tom had flown into such a temper he had never done it again. He regretted lashing out at his father for that, but it enraged him, being sneered at by financially embarrassed gentry who were reduced to selling their daughters. Brought him back to his schoolboy years at Rugby all over again.

The fact that the daughter in question had treated him like he carried a bad smell had not helped matters.

His mother was drumming her fingertips on the table beside her. A bad sign.

"We've done what we can for her tonight," Tom said. "You needn't go to any special trouble."

"You can't be serious. Miss Rushford is used to—she cannot be expected to—" His mother stopped sputtering and drew herself up with a long breath. "You'll see, Tom. I can entertain her as well as any one else. She will not find fault with any of my arrangements. She shall have everything she can possibly require."

"I'm sure she shall," Tom said. Tempted to remind her that beggars couldn't be choosers, he nevertheless held his tongue. This was going to be worse than he feared.

CHAPTER 11
TEMPTATION

S ophy opened her gummy eyes and frowned, confused by the unfamiliar draperies above her. She was in a bed the size of a barouche, buried in a white froth of pillows. Pushing her hands into the mattress, she tried to sit, but was stopped by pain lancing deep in her shoulder. Recollecting with a groan, she sank back into the pillows and stared up at the yellow silk bed hangings. Her shoulder ached something fierce.

She couldn't lay here forever. She owed some explanation to her hosts. They probably had all kinds of questions. Who she was, for one. And she should send a message to Cordell as soon as possible. Dessie would be frantic by now. Setting her chin, she swung her feet over the side of the bed and pushed herself upright with her good arm. The bed was huge. Perched on the side, her toes dangled well above the floor. The surrounding walls were decorated with painted panels of rose gardens, cherubs and a fatuous looking shepherdess ignoring her flock to flirt with an adoring swain. *It's the Pompadour's boudoir, transported to Suffolk*, she thought, unable to suppress a smirk.

It was an astonishing room, but over warm. The nightdress she wore clung to her back. Her teeth felt fuzzy and her mouth tasted sour. Licking dry lips, Sophy slid to the floor, stumbling on her ruffled hem. Snatching a glass of water from the table by the window, she gulped greedily.

"Good morning, Miss."

Whirling round, Sophy saw that a housemaid had entered the room. Damn, this house had silent hinges! Setting the glass down with a thunk, Sophy buried her hands in the voluminous folds of the nightdress. "Good morning," she croaked.

"Mrs. Bagshot was wanting to know what you wish for your breakfast."

Oh. "Is Mrs. Bagshot the cook?" Sophy asked.

The maid's face contorted into a gargoyle grimace. "No, miss." The maid wasn't angry, Sophy realized. She was trying not to laugh. Why?

"Mrs. Bagshot is the Missus," the maid informed her, recovering her arch manner. "If you are well enough, she'd like to see you."

Sophy cursed under her breath. Small chance this hench-woman would keep her gaffe secret. Already she'd offended her hostess.

"Of course," Sophy looked around. "Where are my clothes?"

"Mrs. Bagshot doesn't want you to make yourself uncomfortable. If you permit, she'll attend you here."

Mystified, Sophy nodded and climbed back into bed. This was famous solicitude for an unwanted guest, but she felt unequal to extracting an explanation from the maid.

"Your breakfast?" the maid asked.

"Oh. May I have chocolate and toast and a soft-cooked egg?"

"Of course, miss." The maid curtsied and left.

The door had scarcely shut behind her when it opened again, admitting the plump, grey haired lady she hazily recalled from the evening before. Her dress of shiny maroon silk strained over her bosom. A crepe in the same color would have looked much nicer, Sophy thought.

Sophy opened her mouth to express her thanks, but the lady sank into a deep curtsey before even glancing at her. Robbed of speech, Sophy could only stare, her mouth half open.

"We've been so worried for you. But you can be easy, for the surgeon's come at last. He'll take a look at you. Indeed, you're looking much better today. How do you feel?"

"Better, thank-you. Are you—Mrs. Bagshot?"

"I am indeed," Mrs. Bagshot said, sinking into another curtsey. "And I've been racking my brain trying to discover who you must be, thinking of your poor family, who must be out of their minds with worry." She gave Sophy a confiding smile. "But I have a guess. You must be Lord Fairchild's daughter." Sophy swallowed. Her cursed hair!

"You are correct, Mrs. Bagshot." She didn't know what else to say. People were never so direct. Nor could she recall ever hearing the name Bagshot before. Who were these people? Surely she wasn't that far from home.

"We will send word to your family first thing," Mrs. Bagshot promised. "And Sarah here—" seeing that the space beside her was empty, Mrs. Bagshot called again, louder, and the maid hurried back into the room, "—will be pleased to wait on you. Sarah, this is Lady Sophy Rushford."

Sophy coughed, hiding her shock. Mrs. Bagshot thought she was—that she was real, like Henrietta, and had then seen fit to present her to a maid. She didn't know whether to swallow her tongue or throw back her head and laugh. Introduce her to the maid, indeed! It was plain that Mrs. Bagshot was beyond her depth. A dark suspicion took hold of her.

"Is this Chippenstone?" she asked, interrupting Mrs. Bagshot's lengthy instructions to Sarah.

"It is indeed, Lady Sophy." Mrs. Bagshot beamed. Sophy choked back her laughter with another violent cough, wincing when her shoulder protested.

"More laudanum, my Lady?" Mrs. Bagshot asked, advancing solicitously.

"No, thank you," Sophy managed. Chippenstone was the only house of consequence in the neighborhood where Lady Fairchild did not go. It had been bought years ago, by some wealthy tradesman.

Of course none of the Rushfords came here, Sophy thought, seeing the room with new eyes. Mrs. Bagshot was exactly the sort of ridiculous person Lady Fairchild most detested.

As she watched Mrs. Bagshot's awkward bumbling, something took hold of Sophy: some imp of mischief or some half-formed wish. Without thinking, she donned her best Lady Fairchild manner and announced, "You are addressing me incorrectly, Mrs. Bagshot. My father is a viscount, not an earl, so I am a Miss, not a Lady. It would please me if you called me Sophy. It is what they call me at home."

This was perfectly true. It was not her fault if Mrs. Bagshot believed more than that.

It took two minutes for Mrs. Bagshot to curtsey herself out of the room and for Sophy to lose her nerve. As soon as the door closed, she collapsed like an accordion and sank onto the bed. She was trembling. What had she done?

She would be caught for sure. Lady Fairchild would skin her alive. She couldn't guess what her father would do, but she was afraid. Playing at being Miss Rushford was like setting fire to her own boat. She should confess the truth at once.

While she was rehearsing scenarios, the surgeon came. He pronounced that Sophy's arm was where it ought to be, and that she must rest the arm in a sling. The pain would diminish in the coming days. Sophy declined another draught of laudanum. Sarah returned as the surgeon left, bringing Sophy breakfast and a pink morning dress, which had been hastily taken in and shortened.

"Missus didn't want you struggling into your habit today, since you insist on dressing," she explained. Though the gown fit loosely and Sarah was a careful attendant, donning it was a teeth-clenching, eye-squeezing process. Sarah gasped at the ink black bruises marring her right hip and shoulder.

"Are you certain you should dress, Miss?"

"They look worse than they feel." Thank goodness they wouldn't show. Her hands and face were unmarked. When Sarah withdrew, Sophy sank into a chair, white faced and tight-lipped.

She ate her breakfast one-handed, sitting by the window. A sprig of apple blossoms stood on her tray, and a slivered pineapple fanned across her gilt edged plate. She drank her chocolate, considering again how different things would be if her name was Rushford. How pleasant it would be to automatically be treated with such deference, to always be confident of your place. Her life would be vastly altered, if Lady Fairchild was really her mother.

Traitor, she thought, recalling her mother's smile with sudden clarity. Fanny Prescott had owned a wide mouth with teeth that overlapped at the corners. Sophy could no longer construct her face completely, except as she had died, grey and gasping. Shutting her eyes, Sophy swallowed her mouthful with difficulty, shoving away guilt.

She hadn't meant it to happen, and surely she had been punished enough.

A lifetime of Sunday Sermons argued against her, telling her only eternal fires could atone. Sophy frowned, savagely chewing a bite of pineapple. Priestly blithering about heavenly rest and just rewards did not comfort her. Experience had taught her that justice was a word without application in life. Losing her mother was shattering enough. Need she suffer the stain of illegitimacy as well? She had done no wrong there; that had been her mother's mistake.

The chocolate in her cup had gone cold and bitter. It was no use, she knew, brooding about the same old things. Not when she had landed herself in such a scrape. Her energies were better spent finding a way out.

Leaving on the sly would solve things nicely, she thought, setting down her spoon. Then she remembered someone would have to saddle Ajax and help her to mount. She doubted she was equal to the ride home, even if she was successful in talking her way around one of the Bagshots' grooms. And surely the Bagshots would come to Cordell, looking for her. She could just imagine Mrs. Bagshot greeting her as Miss Rushford in front of Mrs. Lawson, the housekeeper. It was only one short step from them to Lord Fairchild.

Come clean, she told herself.

And yet, the more she thought of it, the harder it seemed. Confessing didn't actually offer a clear way out. For one thing, the truth would be very unkind. Mrs. Bagshot would know she had been making fun of her. Which was awful, seeing as Mrs. Bagshot had been entirely amiable: altering her clothes for Sophy to wear, giving her the best rooms, bringing the surgeon, not to mention taking her in from the cold and helping the young man to set her arm. He must be her son, Sophy decided.

They would both be very angry with her, and would probably spread the tale to everyone in the neighborhood. Which left her one choice. Keep on as Sophy Rushford, conceal the truth, and never see them again.

With luck, she might be able to manage it.

Rising, Sophy smoothed the wrinkles from the borrowed pink dress and made her way to morning room.

Mrs. Bagshot and her son were waiting for her. Both rose as she entered, but Mrs. Bagshot sprang forward, taking Sophy's good arm and leading her to a divan in blue damask, prepared with pillows and a silk shawl.

"We must take every precaution after yesterday's misadventure," she said, wrapping the shawl around Sophy's shoulders.

"You are excessively kind, Mrs. Bagshot," Sophy said, flushing as she remembered her own churlishness and that further deception was necessary. "I must thank you for your hospitality. And for your assistance, sir, in putting back my arm."

"I was happy to be of use," the son said, retaking his seat.

Sophy plucked at the fringe of the shawl. "I shan't continue to impose on you," she assured them. "If I can borrow a servant to carry a message to Cordell Hall, they can send a carriage to collect me this afternoon."

Mrs. Bagshot vigorously shook her head. "Oh no, my dear! Even if the surgeon would allow it, it would be unwise to tax yourself so soon. You are very welcome here, and besides, there's no one there to look after you!"

Mrs. Bagshot met Sophy's surprised glance and dissembled, nervously fluttering her fingers as she explained. "I stumbled across a letter in the pocket of your clothes last evening, after you were asleep, you see. Is it true, that your brother Jasper plans to collect you in a matter of days?"

"He is to take me to London, ma'am, perhaps as early as tomorrow. My parents are there already," Sophy said.

"And there are none but a few servants at your house?"

Sophy nodded, supposing it wouldn't do to explain that she was well accustomed to spending this part of the year alone, save for Dessie and the other servants left behind. "Truly, I—"

Mrs. Bagshot protested. "After such an injury, and getting so chilled! You still look very pale, and the surgeon says your arm must not be jostled. All the upheaval of traveling home, only to leave again? Tom, tell her she mustn't!"

Could she fool them for two days? Sophy calculated rapidly. It didn't look like she had a choice. Even if she insisted on leaving, she didn't think she could convince them to ignore the surgeon's orders. Staying here presented all kinds of difficulties: her horse, her lack of clothes, Jasper . . .

"I'm sorry for looking at your letter," Mrs. Bagshot said, handing over the paper in question. It was dry now, but Sophy could see the ink had run in several places. "I took the merest glimpse only, hoping to learn who you might be. Happily, that was not hard to discover."

Sophy licked her lips, trying to recall if Jasper had written anything that would reveal the truth. "Have you sent word to Cordell?" she asked. If Mrs. Bagshot's servants had already gone to Cordell with the news that a Miss Rushford was lying injured at Chippenstone, she was sunk.

"I'm sending a man over this very minute," Mrs. Bagshot beamed.

"Can he wait?" Sophy asked quickly. "I should like to inform them myself. If your servant could carry my letter—"

"Of course." Mrs. Bagshot rang the bell.

"And could my horse be returned as well? John, my father's head groom, will be anxious to look him over." A gross under-statement. John would inspect Ajax from ears to fetlocks, and if he had suffered as much as a bruise or a strained tendon, he would ban her from the stables. Staying at Chippenstone had some advantages, she decided, so long as she was not discovered. Dessie could send over her boxes and Jasper could collect her here as easily as Cordell.

The son cleared his throat. "I looked over your horse myself, Miss Rushford—"

"Please, do call me Sophy. I am not out of the schoolroom yet," Sophy interrupted. Less chance of slip ups, if they used her given name.

He inclined his head. "As I was saying, I looked over your horse this morning. He's taken no hurt. I wish we could say the same for you. It's lucky you didn't break your neck. That horse is much too large for you."

Inclined to argue, Sophy reminded herself that he had been obliged to rescue her. "John will give me quite a scold, I promise you."

He snorted. "Yes, but will you listen?"

She pretended to consider the matter. "Well, I might." Before he could roll his eyes, she fixed him with her most engaging smile. "This whole business has been rather embarrassing. You won't tell anyone, will you?"

"Of course not." Mrs. Bagshot said, reaching over to pat her hand. "You may depend on Tom and me."

Sophy did not fear Mrs. Bagshot, who adapted instantly to her whim. It was the son, Tom, who she seemed unable to charm. She bit her lip. "I shouldn't have taken Ajax out. It was dreadfully foolish, but he's such a beautiful horse. And I wanted to ride round the country here once more, in case I don't return to Cordell."

"Oh?" Mrs. Bagshot gave her a blank stare.

"This season is to be my debut," Sophy explained, forcing an attempt at the dazzling smile Lady Fairchild had taught her. It was as effective as a damp firecracker.

"How exciting, to be sure," Mrs. Bagshot said.

"Qualms, Sophy? If you can take on a horse like Ajax, I'm sure your courage is up to the Marriage Mart." Tom said dryly.

Sophy's lips twisted. "I was thrown, Mr. Bagshot. You are not very reassuring."

He quirked an eyebrow at her. "But now you've learned not to choose a horse that can overmaster you."

Heat swept over her cheeks. She arched her eyebrows. "I am not generally considered an incompetent horsewoman, sir."

"Dear me, no," he laughed.

Lady Fairchild would say this conversation was in poor taste, but Sophy rather liked him this way, throwing her quips and slumping in his chair. Certainly it was an improvement on the stiff formality he had worn when she first entered the room. He had been like this last night, she remembered, making her easy as he set her shoulder. He looked almost dashing, which was a thought Lady Fairchild would not allow, if she could have known it. Sophy pinched her lips together, remembering that yesterday he had carried her up the stairs. And not, she thought, while wearing his coat.

Yes, he had been without coat and waistcoat, in his dressing gown of all things. It had billowed behind him when he had come running down the stairs.

He let out a sigh and heaved himself out of his armchair. "Pleasant as this is, I have business to attend to, and you have a letter to write." Nodding to Sophy, he crossed the room and kissed his mother.

She retained his hand. "You'll join us for dinner?"

This time, his smile was a polite grimace. "Of course."

He left. Mrs. Bagshot, about to fetch a lap desk herself, remembered in time to send a servant instead.

Sophy knew she should be quick about her letters; the Bagshots' servant was waiting, and everyone at Cordell would be searching for her. If she took too long, her letter would come after they sent word to her father that she was missing. Brushing her chin with the end of her quill, she wondered if the truth would slip out from Cordell's servants. No, she decided instantly. The man from Chippenstone was just delivering her horse and her letter. Cordell's servants would not talk to him. They would snub him as surely as Lady Fairchild would snub his mistress.

She scrawled out a letter to Mrs. Lawson, the housekeeper at Cordell, including a postscript apology to John. She enclosed a letter to be forwarded to Jasper, asking him to collect her from Chippenstone instead. Just in case, she put in a third letter for her father. She couldn't ignore the possibility that Mrs. Lawson had already sent him word by messenger. If she was to carry off her deception, she needed to keep Lord Fairchild and, more likely, his servants, away from Chippenstone.

CHAPTER 12
DUTY AND DESIGN

Tom planned to see Miss Rushford as little as possible, but dinner was unavoidable. His mother expected him to dine with her and he tried to be a dutiful son.

He arrived in the dining room, intentionally late. Miss Rushford and his mother were already seated. "How is your shoulder, Miss Sophy?" he asked, as one of the footmen in eye-blinding green livery pulled out his chair.

"Better, thank-you." Tonight she was demure, unrecognizable as the wild apparition on his doorstep yesterday. He suspected this observation might offend her. Concealing a smile, he looked down the table as the pair of footmen swept away the covers. He nearly groaned aloud.

His mother had ordered an absurdly lavish meal. Frowning at his turtle soup, he wondered how long eating would take. He hadn't lied about his pressing business: one of his ships with a load of timber was two weeks late, and he'd found a potential buyer for furs, if he could guarantee delivery of specific quantities. He ate his soup silently, his body mummifying while his mind leapt elsewhere.

The second course was worse. There was asparagus in cream

sauce, ham, roasted goose and poached fish with leeks, washed down with champagne. It was a colossal waste, when only three people were eating. He had lived on weevil infested rations in His Majesty's navy and it bothered him that good and brave men ate so poorly, when his table was groaning under masses of china and plate and the carcasses of he knew not how many beasts. The servants would eat well tonight, but there was no way even they could eat this much food before it spoiled.

His mother looked at him, imploring him to speak. They ought to be having conversation, he knew. Well, what did she expect him to say?

"Did you have a pleasant afternoon, mother?"

"Yes. Miss Sophy slept and I looked over some magazines."

"How nice." He grinned and the conversation died.

Miss Rushford leaned back into her chair as a footman cut up her meat. It did not please her, having to be tended like a child.

"And how was your afternoon, Mr. Bagshot?" she asked.

"Profitable." He wasn't going to pretend to be something he wasn't. "Unfortunately, I wasn't able to conclude all the matters demanding attention, but I made a good start."

"That must be satisfying," she replied, unperturbed. "The sauce on this sole is excellent, Mrs. Bagshot. I must commend your cook."

But by the time the third course was brought in, she was drooping in her chair, shadows etched under her eyes.

"Are you in pain? Would you like to retire now?" his mother asked. "We mustn't fatigue you."

She rallied, though her answering smile was wan. "It's not seven o' clock yet. I ought to at least make it till nine."

"I'm an early sleeper, myself," his mother confessed. "Come, let's return to the drawing room. We'll take tea, and we can fetch you a book."

Sophy agreed, and Tom stood, preparing to bow and watch them leave.

"Give Sophy your arm, dear," his mother said, ruining that plan. He walked her to the drawing room, seated her on the divan and fetched her shawl, but his mother wasn't done yet.

"Will you read to us, Tom?" she asked. "I think that would be nicest. I'm a little tired, myself." He couldn't refuse. He nearly always passed his evenings at Chippenstone reading aloud until his mother fell asleep. She had always read with difficulty, having only a scanty education.

"Of course," he said, crossing the room to retrieve her book.

"Oh no," she stopped him, turning pink. "Why don't you fetch something new from the library? Marmion, perhaps."

Sophy missed nothing. "What is it you've been reading?" she asked, and Tom saw his mother writhe under all her lace.

"Just some novel," she explained.

"Which one?" Sophy asked.

Tom lifted up the book, ignoring his mother's unspoken protests. "It's called *The Wicked Duke*."

"You wouldn't like it," his mother said.

"I don't see why I shouldn't," Sophy said. "And I cannot take you away from your own book, ma'am. There is nothing more exasperating."

Tom deposited himself in a chair, while his mother tried to assume a calm face.

"Please begin," Sophy said, waving a limpid hand. Lord, her airs were infuriating. And yet, he had seen his servants respond to her with palpable relief, looking sideways from her to his mother as if to say, *See? This is how it should be done.*

Tom opened the cardboard cover, clearing his throat and removing the ribbon that marked his mother's place. *"Cassandra awoke in a cave, dark and damp. She couldn't move, and her hands and feet were bound to a heavy chair, upholstered in velvet. There was a fluttering noise behind her. Bats, she decided."*

"Really, Miss Sophy . . ." His mother was paralyzed, her mortification growing with every word. Tom cursed himself for giving her such an ill turn, for humiliating her in front of Miss Rushford. Making him do the pretty did not make it right for him to act like a bear.

"Please stop, Mr. Bagshot," Sophy said crisply. Tom glanced at her, surprised she would call halt, though his mother's distress was plain. "I would enjoy this story much more if you read with feeling. You make it sound like Cassandra is trimming a hat." She gave his mother a warm smile. "I don't think your son has any sensibility ma'am. He had best give the book to me." She stretched out an imperious hand.

"You like this kind of story?" his mother asked faintly.

"Absolutely," she said, and his mother relaxed in her chair.

Stunned and not a little grateful, Tom handed Sophy the volume and returned to his chair. She could not possibly—and yet there was a gleam of genuine enjoyment in her eyes, a spark he hadn't seen before.

"Marvelous," Sophy said, scanning the lurid page. Then she began.

"From the velvet blackness came the sound of footsteps, booted heels crunching the gravel like a giant grinding bones. In vain, Cassandra tugged at her bonds. Helpless, she stared in horrified fascination after the sound, listening to the sinister footsteps drawing nearer and nearer.

Her plea for help died in her throat as Roberto stepped into the guttering candlelight.

"Have mercy!" she gasped.

A cruel smile crossed his face. His eyes glistened like polished stones, barely visible under the wide brim of his hat.

"So! You are caught at last!" Sophy jumped to her feet, throwing herself into her role, tottering as she nearly stumbled over the hearth rug.

"Careful," Tom said, starting forward in his chair. With her injured arm bound in the sling, she would have trouble catching her balance.

"I'm fine," she said. "At last my Italian lessons will be useful."

Adopting a gruesome accent, perfect for the villainous Roberto, she resumed reading, pacing across the drawing room, making wide theatrical gestures with her good arm. She was a rather astonishing actress, and his mother settled in to enjoy the performance.

"I have you in my power," Sophy said, gloating and waggling her eyebrows, still playing the part of Roberto.

Mrs. Bagshot choked on a laugh.

"What? You mock me, Madame?" Sophy stiffened and threw Mrs. Bagshot a look of disdain. "I shall force —" she glanced down at the page "— thees Cassandra to wed me tonight, or I will drown her in the river! And her brodder too!"

"Not her brother," Tom interjected. "Her true love."

"You interrupt! But you are correct," she said, checking the book again. "Eet eez ze lover I will drown. I do not permit you to distract me again."

Meekly, Tom promised not to interrupt.

"With mincing steps he crossed the cave," she read, suiting action to words and approaching Tom's chair, *"surveying his fainting prisoner from all sides. 'You shall never escape. No one shall hear your screams. You are mine.'"*

Standing right over him, she thrust the book under his nose.

"It is your line, sir," she whispered.

His raised eyebrow didn't deter her. Grimacing, he cleared his throat. "Never!" he squeaked in falsetto. "You dastardly coward! I'd fight you, if I was a man!"

A curious sound, like a strangled sneeze, escaped Sophy's lips, and she smoothed her face, though her shoulders shook with suppressed laughter. "Much better," she whispered.

His mother chortled, swiping at her eyes with a handkerchief. "I'm like to split my seams, if you two keep this up. But don't stop," she added, seeing Sophy hesitate.

Perching herself on the arm of his chair, she held the book between them. "You can see?"

He nodded. Her arm was close to him, her veins a faint blue line running up her arm from her wrist to the hollow of her elbow. Her hair was as bright and alive as the fire crackling beside them. She was quite beautiful, he realized with a pang, and averted his eyes. He shouldn't stare at her, though her performance was captivating.

"Let me hold the book," he said, lifting it from her hand without touching her fingers. She only had the use of one arm after all, and would soon tire, though the volume was not heavy. And it was easier for him, without her arm intruding in his space.

They kept reading, and Cassandra escaped her bonds, burning through the rope with the candle Roberto unwisely left behind, escaping into the forest. Wading through dense plotting and gothic prose, Tom looked up and saw that his mother's head had fallen back against her chair. She was asleep. Stopping mid-sentence, he blushed like a boy.

"My mother tires early," he offered apologetically. "She falls asleep most evenings while I read, but since tonight's reading is more lively than she's used to, I didn't expect—"

"I've been watching sleep steal over her for the last two pages," Sophy said, but without mockery. "You didn't notice?"

Tom grinned. "I didn't dare give this performance less than my best." Setting the book aside, he watched his mother, lost in sleep. "Do you wish to retire now?" he asked Sophy.

She straightened away from the wing of his chair, where she had been leaning, and frowned, moving her left shoulder in little circles. "After they bring the tea tray. I would like a cup before bed."

He felt his ears grow hot. "Of course. I'm afraid mother forgot to ring for it."

Striding across the room, his hand hovered over the bell beside his mother's chair. No, better not to wake her. She would be embarrassed enough as it was. "I think I'll let her sleep," he said. "If you'll excuse me a moment."

He found Sarah in the hall and asked her to bring up tea. When he returned, Sophy was back on the divan, watching the fire.

"I'm afraid my mother's never gotten used to late evenings," Tom said. "Much of her life was spent rising early and working hard."

"What was her work?" Sophy asked.

Since she seemed disinterested, as if it hardly mattered, he decided to tell her. "Her father was an innkeeper."

She was watching the fire, not him. "I've stayed at inns twice. Both were busy places."

"You travel so little?" he asked.

"I don't travel at all," she said. "I haven't left Cordell Hall in seven years." Seeing his stare of disbelief, she added, "I dine within the neighborhood, of course. And go to Bury St. Edmonds and Newmarket for the shops."

He looked up as Sarah entered the room with the tea tray.

"Don't wake my mother," he commanded. "Set the tray by Miss Rushford. Do you think you are able to pour?" he asked as Sarah withdrew.

"I believe I am up to the task, sir."

"I can do it if your arm pains you," he said, realizing it would be an awkward task for her, one-handed.

"I shall be fine." She lifted the teapot with care, keeping her face and movements smooth. He watched her make up the tea, but she showed no difficulty or discomfort. She was different from the girl who had played Roberto twenty minutes past. She looked very much a lady.

"Do you take sugar?" she asked.

"No."

She brought him a cup, her feet silent on the carpet. "You read very well," she said. "Once you have been properly encouraged. What do you like to read?"

"This and that," he shrugged. "You?"

"My lessons. The books Hen—Henrietta sends me. My older sister." She glanced at the mantel, where he had carelessly left a book. "You are reading Thaddeus of Warsaw?"

"Re-reading it," he admitted. "It's a favorite."

She sipped her tea, inquiring further by lifting her eyebrows.

"I first read it on HMS Leander, in the North Atlantic," he said, remembering.

"You're in the navy?" she frowned. "I thought your family was in trade."

He gave a precise nod. "I am. But I spent a year in the navy. When I was fifteen I sailed with one of my father's partners to Lower Canada. On the voyage home, a party from the Leander boarded and eleven of us were pressed. Ships carrying mast timber, like ours, are supposed to be protected from having their sailors pressed," he explained. "But in practice, the regulations don't stop His Majesty's Navy from taking who they want. The October I was on the Leander there was rioting in Halifax over the press gangs the navy sent into town."

She frowned thoughtfully, setting aside her spoon. "And you are no longer with the navy?"

"No. My father got me out, but it took a year. During that time, the Leander was based out of Halifax. We captured four ships—American merchantmen, carrying goods to France."

"What was it like?" She seemed rather startled.

He shrugged, uncomfortable. "You can see worse in London's slums. The navy might ignore everyone else's laws, but they keep their own. Still, it's the only time in my life I've had to fight to survive." Which was not quite true. There had been those dreadful years at school.

"In the actions against other ships?"

Tom barked a laugh. "That too. No, I was thinking more of crewing the Leander. It's hard work, and the lash rules. Seeing the skin stripped off a man's back isn't a pretty sight. Life on the Leander was very different from my father's ship."

Remembering the tea in his hand, Tom took a sip.

"But you were released?"

"Yes. My father's partner lodged a complaint in Halifax and my father took action on the London end. I was home the following spring. I can't say I regret the experience. Captain Talbot was a fierce man, but a good captain. He forced discipline on me that I had resented from my father. And there's no place like the sea to contemplate God, for there you truly depend upon providence."

At sea, his bitterness had blown away. He had been content with who he was then, an able seaman and part of a hardworking crew. His mates had respected him, not caring who he was. Matters were not so simple off the Leander.

She set down her cup. "What are the colonies like?"

"I didn't spend much time on shore, but I've never forgotten what I saw. You can't imagine so much wild land, such dense and sprawling forests. The St Lawrence River is like its' own sea. I've been back to Lower Canada twice since then. The last time was four years ago, before my father sold out of the shipping business." After his death, Tom had bought back in.

He told her about the cliffs Wolff's army had scaled to surprise Montcalm and the grey stone farms and churches in Quebec. He told her about the fur traders, who paddled tiny boats of birch bark for thousands of miles. He told her about Atlantic storms, and sleeping in a hammock on a crowded ship. When the clock on the mantle chimed, he saw that the candles had burned low and blinked, collecting himself.

"I should have let you go to bed ages ago." His mother would not thank him for tiring Sophy. He had rambled too long under her watchful eyes.

"No, I enjoyed listening. I told you that I've never been anywhere remotely exciting."

"Not for long. Isn't your brother taking you to the metropolis?"

Again at the mention of London, the animation left her face. She dropped her eyes to her lap. "Yes. For the Season, you know."

"I do." Well, not by experience, but he knew something of the path before her. It would take her far away from him. Pushing to his feet, he crossed the room and offered his hand. She rose from the divan and he handed her a candle, resisting the compulsion to let his fingers brush hers. "Goodnight, Miss Rushford."

Her eyes flew to her face. "So formal? I have given you leave to call me Sophy."

He hid a grimace. He wanted to put distance between them. No, to remind himself of the distance already there. "Since you wish it," he said. "You may as well call me Tom, then." She left him with a cryptic smile. Rousing his mother, he summoned Sarah to attend her to bed.

"You shouldn't have let me sleep in front of Miss Rushford!" she fretted.

"Miss Sophy," he corrected. "You were tired, and Miss Sophy understands. Besides, you needn't care what she thinks. It has no relevance to us."

Heaving out of her chair, her joints creaking, she took Tom's arm, patting it affectionately. "I dare say she thinks I'm a silly old woman. She's probably right. But how can anyone not think well of you?"

"You'll give me a swollen head, mother." Damn. She liked Sophy Rushford then, and was plotting for all she was worth.

Tom left his mother at the door of her chambers, with a kiss pressed on her cheek. Then, holding his candle aloft, he made his way downstairs to the library.

He hated this house, so full of sham and pretense. The shelves around him overflowed with handsome volumes in Greek or Latin that he couldn't read. Useless stuff. His years at school had cured him of any desire for a gentrified life. It wasn't real. Pouring himself a brandy, he downed it like cheap gin and slumped in front of the fire, which burned low behind a monstrosity of a screen. He peered at the fire through his empty glass. It looked distorted and strange.

Her injury should have warned him of her dangerous high-spirits, her infectious humor. But he didn't see how he could have foreseen how her face changed when she listened. Mesmerized by her candid grey stare, she had pulled words from him, more words than he had unburdened himself of in a long time. Foolish, when she would be gone from his house tomorrow, or the next day.

He was infatuated with her, but it would pass. He had experienced this fleeting effect before, had seen friends make cakes of themselves before coming to their senses. He knew that if he distanced himself the effect would pass. The important thing was to let the swift fever work its course and not to do anything buffle-headed. Miss Rushford could not be allowed to suspect how she was afflicting him. He would prefer to keep his folly from his mother, but knew she was already speculating on what he and Sophy must have said to each other. They'd been essentially alone for over an hour.

Well, it hardly mattered. Sophy would marry some peer before the Season was out and that was that. He would probably never see her again. It was ridiculous, pathetic even, that he had shared more of his hoarded memories with her than with anyone else.

CHAPTER 13
GUILT

When one was Miss Rushford, one could lay abed as late as one pleased. Sophy didn't. Sleep eluded her, bothered as she was by a guilty conscience.

Unimpressed by the daughter of a viscount, Tom Bagshot seemed to like her person well enough. He had a kind of unflappable charm; whether he was setting her arm or being dragooned into the navy, he faced the world with a smile. A handsome one, if truth be told. He would attract attention, she knew, despite his plain clothes and straightforward manners. And he would lose any respect he had for her, if he discovered the truth.

Kicking aside the twisted sheets, Sophy slid out of her giant bed. She made use of the pot and splashed water on her hands and face. The cold water stung, but it was better than waiting until Sarah carried up a can of hot water.

All night she had lain awake, trying to think how to hide the truth. Jasper would likely arrive today and managing him would be a delicate business. She had to think, and to do that, she needed to move. She was tired of the painted shepherdess on the wall smirking knowingly at her, making her twitchy and cross. Tentatively circling her arm, she decided she would leave off the sling. Though her muscles protested with every inch, the joint worked fine and having just one arm was getting irritating. She tidied her hair and scrubbed her teeth with the toothbrush and soda her hosts had provided, then left to prowl around the house.

Eye-popping, that was the word for it. She had never seen its like. There was an Egyptian salon in black and gold and a ball-room of mirrors and blue silk swathed under dust covers. The long gallery was covered in pictures, all wedged together, with the ceiling a masterwork of plaster and paint. Craning her neck, Sophy counted fourteen cherubs in a single section.

"Up already?"

Sophy spun around. It was Tom, his approaching footsteps muffled by the carpet running the length of the gallery. He was dressed the same as yesterday, in a blue coat and brown trousers, carrying a sheaf of papers in his hand.

"Good morning," she said.

"If you need anything, you must not hesitate to ring," he said. "Were you searching for anything particular?"

"No." Sophy smiled. "I couldn't rest and decided to look around."

"You do not take breakfast in your room today?" he asked.

"I've no appetite this morning. Perhaps later." If her stomach stopped churning, that was.

"I'm afraid my mother has not risen yet," he said. He was edging around her in a wide circle, not quite meeting her eyes, hiding behind his solicitous manners again.

"I am amiably occupied. You have so many remarkable pictures."

Politeness demanded that he offer to show her around. Sophy waited expectantly.

"May I show you the house?" he asked. "Or would you like to see the gardens?" His words were correct, but he thinned his lips as he spoke and glanced impatiently at the papers under his arm.

Of course he must make things difficult. He'd liked her last evening. Why did she have to begin all over again today?

"I should like so much to see both," she said. He blenched and she lowered her eyelashes, hiding her satisfaction at scoring a point. Tom acquiesced with a bow and disappeared to dispose of his papers. Returning, he held out his arm. Letting the hand of her injured arm rest on his forearm, she allowed him to lead her to the next sizable painting, a magnificent portrait. The subject was male, with the mustaches, lace, and curling hair of the seventeenth century.

"This is a picture of—the Marquis of Blaise—by Anthony van Dyck," he said, squinting at the label.

Yesterday he had confided in her. It annoyed her that today he plainly preferred his own company. "It is a handsome portrait," she said, and they walked on. Miss Frensham was a great admirer of Mr. van Dyck and Sophy had seen etchings of his famous works, besides the portrait he had made of two long-ago Rushford brothers hanging in the long gallery at Cordell Hall.

If she had wanted to discomfit Tom, here was revenge indeed, for he stumbled over the subjects of the pictures and could only give the artist if the name was tacked to the frame. Sophy doubted he had ever looked at them before. His color rose as his ignorance grew more apparent, until he was as red as a sunburned farm hand. After traversing half the gallery, Sophy took pity.

"I think you don't really care for pictures," she said and smiled.

He relaxed. "Not a great deal, no."

"Surely you have one favorite?" she said, trying to make it easy for him.

"I don't think so." He considered. "I'm afraid I don't really see them. Which is yours?"

Letting go of his arm, she walked a few steps and sat down on a low settee. "Maybe this one," she said. "The view of Jerusalem."

He joined her on the settee, leaning back and staring at the

JAIMA FIXSEN

painting in question. "It's nice enough, I suppose, but I don't know why you should prefer it to the others."

It was a smaller canvas, with softer colors. Turning her head, she met his eyes and smiled. She needed him in a more malleable state before Jasper came. "For years my governess has been trying to get me to sound less rustic when I look at pictures," she said. "It's no good. I like this one because—see that goatherd in the corner? He looks just like a little boy I once knew. His name was Fred."

Tom laughed and Sophy let her eyes fall to her hands, lightly clasped in her lap.

"So you see, I'll be a dismal failure in London. I can't even be trusted to admire paintings the right way." Her words were teasing, meant to absolve him of his failure and poke fun at the foibles of society. But when she raised her eyes, his warm look smote her, making her hesitate. Earning his friendship only to hoax him . . . she was heartless. He must never be allowed to know.

The thought sent a chill down her arms, and she resolved that in London she would not fail. She would marry before the Season ended, and never see Tom or Suffolk again.

"Well I've never seen Jerusalem, but I've seen goats," Tom said. "And they looked just like these."

"We agree then," Sophy said. "The painting is very well executed." She realized they were sitting very close, the skirt of her habit touching his trousered leg. And again, with just a few words, a spell of confidence and intimacy was cast around them, just like last evening. Well, she had wanted that, hadn't she? Best get it over with.

"I am indebted to you so much already . . ." she began.

"What do you need? Ask." he said.

Yesterday Mrs. Bagshot had assured her she would keep Sophy's accident and her unplanned visit secret. Tom had made no such promise. She needed to extract one, but guilt over her duplicity made her look away. "I know my foolishness can't be

108

kept from Jasper, and of course I will tell my parents the truth. And the servants at Cordell know what has happened." Too many. How would she ever keep this hidden?

"It will be a great embarrassment to me, if my mishap becomes known. . . if the neighbors knew and spoke of it. I am trying not to disgrace Lady Fairchild too badly this Season, and—"

Tom stopped her accelerating speech with a raised hand. "No one will hear it from me or my mother." He gave her a lopsided smile. "Who would we tell? You know my mother and I don't mix in society. We've lived here for nine years and you and I have never met before."

Sophy blushed, ashamed. "I would have liked to have known you."

"Now you are flirting with me," Tom said. Sophy's cheeks flamed hotter, her shoulders rising with indignation, but Tom cut off her outraged reply. "Don't worry. You do it perfectly. You'll be the success of the Season."

Her tension left in a laugh. "Flatterer," she said. "But I will repay your compliment by excusing you from showing me the rest of the house. No doubt you have matters demanding your attention." She smiled, letting him know he was forgiven for preferring business to her company.

"Well, about that . . ." Tom stretched his legs and rotated his neck, relaxing at last. "I don't mind showing you the house and the gardens, so long as you don't expect me to tell you anything about them."

He wasn't going to take her offer?

"It's a deal," said Sophy.

To hell with it, Tom thought, looking sideways at Sophy as she took in the view from the terrace. He may as well enjoy this. She was leaving soon enough, within hours probably. He would spend a few uncomfortable days and nights and then he would forget her. Infatuations always wore off.

She wasn't the loveliest girl he had ever met. Not ugly though; not with that translucent skin, fiery hair and her eyes melting and snapping by turns. She looked merely pretty to the passing eye, her beauty improving on acquaintance. He was not immune to her—he memorized each new expression that crossed her face— but he could not remember being this besotted with a girl who wasn't incomparably beautiful. No, it was the roguish humor that had caught him this time. He couldn't help himself from falling in with each absurdity she came up with. She probably didn't fit easily into her own world.

Her family obviously thought her a sad romp. They must be quite hard on her, he thought, for her to be this anxious about her debut. It was too bad. If they knew how charming her outrageousness could be, they might not censure her so badly. Still, it wasn't his concern.

"You are not always at Chippenstone?" Sophy asked, and he stopped trying to count how many colors were in her hair.

"Hardly ever," he said. "My father chose this house, not me. I keep busy with my work."

She shook her head. "I don't understand how you can not want to always be here. I love Suffolk. It is beautiful."

It was. The land spread away from them, wide and green, burgeoning with new growth and new life. "I've seen many beautiful places," he said. "If I were to fall in love with each of them, where should I be?"

She grinned, abashed. "I don't know. The Canadian colonies? You made them sound quite unforgettable. But that wouldn't do. Your mother would miss you."

"She would indeed." He offered his arm. "As I expect she is right now. She is probably hoping we will join her for breakfast."

Today he wasn't bothered by his mother's ecstatic smile,

seeing the two of them come in arm in arm. His mother would never understand that Sophy, and every girl like her, would always be separate from people of his own class. Even if such a girl were to become his wife, she would be received in society and he would not. He knew society sneered at those upstarts who tried to slip in clinging to their spouse's skirts or coat tails. It was a kind of life he could not contemplate.

In the end, no harm would come of his mother's schemes. He was not the one who would disappoint her. Sophy and her family would do that. She would leave, and they would never see her again. He took a slice of toast, watching Sophy talk to his mother, animated and smiling.

He would enjoy her folly while he could. Her family would soon correct her. This bothered him, more than knowing she was leaving soon, for good. He didn't want this Sophy, who he found so irresistible, becoming someone else.

CHAPTER 14
TACTICAL MANEUVERS

The Honorable Jasper William Rushford was worried, an emotion he hadn't experienced in at least fourteen months. Few things had the power to upset him. Noble, wealthy and blessed with his mother's good looks, he preferred the role of satirical observer to participant in an untidy world.

He tolerated his father, cordially despised his mother and was fond of his two sisters. He seldom saw Henrietta, who was entirely wrapped up with her babies. These infant specimens he could not yet like—they were far too drippy—but he made time for Sophy in his negligent way. He wrote her letters of amusing, sarcastic tidbits and spent most of his time with her when he stopped in at Cordell, though he never stayed long.

Mercy had prompted Jasper's offer to escort Sophy to London. It was a known fact within the family that Lady Fairchild was not a pleasant traveling companion. Used to her comforts, she found even the most luxurious travel arrangements lacking, and did not hesitate to give voice to her complaints. Lord Fairchild made a point of never traveling with his wife, always finding some business constraining him to make his own journey a few days before or after her own.

Jasper had expected no difficulties with the journey. His new curricle was light and fast, and his matched bays, bred at Cordell, were the envy of all his friends. Changing horses regularly, he and Sophy could cover the eighty miles to London at a blistering pace. He was quite prepared to enjoy a few days in Newmarket, followed by his sister's company. Then he had a letter from John, informing him that Miss Sophy had ridden out on Ajax and disappeared.

Surprising his friends, Jasper prepared to leave Newmarket with all speed, but he was intercepted by a second message, telling him that Sophy was found. She had injured her arm, but was recuperating as a guest at Chippenstone. Did he think they should inform Lady Fairchild?

Jasper did not. Sophy would be in enough trouble without his mother hearing about Chippenstone before they arrived. If he broke the news in person, he could deflect some of the blame. A second letter from Sophy, begging him to keep quiet and to collect her from Chippenstone instead, confirmed his decision.

Years before, when Chippenstone fell into the hands of a wealthy merchant, his mother had led the campaign excising the place from the neighborhood. She would not be pleased, having the acquaintance forced on her now. Still, that was a relatively minor trouble. Sophy assured him she was well, so Jasper discarded the notion of setting out immediately. Another day could hardly matter. He stayed for the races as planned, though his mind was elsewhere.

He left Newmarket early, flying along the country roads. Near Cheveley, a washed out road forced him to take a longer route, setting him behind three quarters of an hour, but he nevertheless reached the park gates of Chippenstone well before noon. Surveying the place with a grimace, he imagined again his mother's response when she learned Sophy had stayed under this roof. Bowling down the drive and over the bridge, he stopped the horses in front of the imposing entrance.

"Walk 'em," he said, handing the reins to his tiger. It was churlish to whisk Sophy away after the briefest of thanks, but he knew his mother would expect him to damp any pretensions. And frankly, he doubted his ability to talk civil in front of strangers. The urge to shake Sophy until her teeth rattled had dogged him since the first letter reached him in Newmarket.

As he climbed the steps, the door swung open. Jasper stepped inside, handed his hat to the butler and checked the arrangement of his hair and neckcloth in the mirror on the opposite wall.

"Jasper Rushford. I'm here for Miss —"

"Jasper!" Sophy shrieked from the stairs.

He jerked his head around, surprised by her enthusiastic greeting. Sophy ran to him, catching the lapels of his coat and lifting herself onto her toes to kiss his cheek.

He couldn't help his smile, but he made a show of stepping back and smoothing his coat. "I can see my worries for your health were misguided. You are in working order?" he asked.

"Oh, much better." Taking his hand, she started drawing him up the stairs.

"Good." Jasper cast a helpless glance at the butler. "I suppose my sister intends to present me to her hosts. She's a dreadful hoyden."

Sophy blushed, but kept moving, hurrying him into the drawing room. She curtsied. "Allow me to present my brother, Jasper Rushford."

Jasper bowed, an elegant maneuver for which he was well known.

"Jasper, this is Mrs. Bagshot, and her son Mr. Thomas Bagshot."

The mother rose to her feet and curtsied deeply. The son executed a jerky, mechanical bow that was little more than a nod. Neither spoke.

What a pair of frights, Jasper thought. No wonder Sophy was anxious to escape.

He unsheathed his blinding charm. "Dear sir," he said. "Kind madam. I cannot thank you enough for taking care of my scamp of a sister. I am most indebted to you."

"We did nothing more than any Christian would have done," Bagshot said.

Lord! Pious as well as boring. Jasper began calculating how long it would take to talk himself out of the room.

"He's being modest," Sophy said with an amused glance at the man in question. "Mr. Bagshot set my shoulder and the surgeon said he could not have done it better himself. Mrs. Bagshot has been everything kind, for I am sure I have been a troublesome guest and tedious company."

Mrs. Bagshot took the bait, protesting that she had delighted in Miss Sophy's company. Strangely, the son did not, watching with an impassive face.

"Will you stay for refreshment?" Mrs. Bagshot asked.

Jasper endured a cup of tea, with the overeager mother making most of the conversation. After exchanging pained smiles with the son, Sophy gave up trying to entice words from him and sipped from her cup with downcast eyes. Jasper downed his tea in scalding gulps and rose. "Your servant, Mr. Bagshot," he said, bowing once more.

"Do not feel yourself obliged," Bagshot said. "It was no trouble."

Jasper was turning for the door, Sophy's hand on his arm, when Bagshot thawed, lurching forward.

"You must promise me to be careful, Miss Sophy," he said, extending his hand. "I don't want to hear of you coming to grief again, if I'm not around to put you to rights."

Sophy colored. "I promise," she said.

Bagshot bowed over her hand, then Jasper carefully reclaimed her arm. He'd noticed how hesitantly she'd stirred sugar into her tea, and suspected the shoulder pained her more than she let on. Sighing inwardly, he hustled her down the stairs.

CHAPTER 15
LONDON

You're safe, Sophy thought, relieved and regretful as Chippenstone vanished behind the curving drive. She sighed and leaned into Jasper's arm. Waiting for his arrival, the fear of discovery had nearly overpowered her. Yet all had gone well. Jasper never spoke her name and she had parted on friendly enough terms with the Bagshots, though she had felt an unspoken strain once Jasper joined them. She could not have wished for better, but underneath the heady rush of escape, she felt a lingering dissatisfaction and the temptation to take one more backward glance. Foolish, that. The house was out of sight now.

This caper made child's play of the most daring of her Bottom End pranks, back in her other life. It surprised her that she still had the nerve. Would the Bagshots have been so obliging if she had told them the truth? Likely not. Sophy suppressed a sudden pang.

Don't tempt yourself with that dream, she told herself. May as well wish for wings. Still, her thoughts tripped along familiar ground, to a life where there had never been a Bottom End or a terrifying accident . . . or a Fanny Prescott. When she felt the familiar constriction round her heart, she sank her teeth into her bottom lip.

"That's a curst ugly bonnet," Jasper said. "Where's the one I sent you for Christmas?"

Sophy smiled, happy to be pulled from her thoughts. "In my box, if Dessie remembered to pack it."

They rode a moment in silence, flying round a corner so fast that Sophy's hand flew to the rail beside her.

"I should thank you for allowing me to try my hand at heroics," Jasper said.

She threw him a puzzled glance.

"Come on," Jasper laughed. "Freeing you from those bores?"

Sophy stiffened. "They were very good to me, you know. And they were both more natural with me. I think you overawed them a little."

"I hope so," he said. "Got to curb any pretensions. Dash it, the mater—and Father too, probably—will be blowing steam as it is, without you forcing them to acknowledge these mushrooms. What were you doing anyways, riding Ajax? You've no business on that horse."

Sophy paused before answering, twisting the fingertip of her glove. "Just working out my freaks, I suppose. Thought I'd feel better after a bruising ride. Turns out I was wrong."

"I'll say. How is your shoulder? The truth, now."

She gave a crooked smile. "Sore, when I move it or let my arm hang too long. But it gets better each day."

He slowed the horses to attend to their conversation. "A surgeon saw you? What was his name?"

"Jamieson. He has a surgery in Bury St. Edmonds."

"Never heard of him. Doesn't matter. Father will send for whoever is best."

Sophy jerked her chin. "Surely not. It's not necessary, Jasper."

"Course it is. Don't be wool headed. But you haven't explained your distemper. Why did you need to ride a horse above your weight in wretched weather?"

She returned her gaze to her glove. "I don't know. London, I suppose."

"That makes perfect sense," Jasper snorted. "Your first chance to see the metropolis, a Season . . . No discerning young lady could stomach it."

"Could you stomach it, if you were in my place?"

"That's different," Jasper said. "For females, this is the best option. I'm not saying it will be anything like a good time, letting my mother tow you about, but—"

"It's not just that," Sophy said. "Lord Fairchild is a great deal too kind. I'm not Henrietta."

"Stuff it, Sophy." Jasper said, "Let them do this. Lord knows you deserve the best he can give you."

"We are not the same," Sophy countered.

"I know. All the doors in the world are open to Hen and I, but not you. We all know that. He feels guilty. And so he should." The dark tone in his voice made Sophy look hard at his face. She had broached this topic with him before, but it was not easy.

"How much do you remember of my mother?" she asked.

"Enough." Jasper said. He had told her about indoor games on rainy days, how for months her mother had sat up in the nursery waiting for Henrietta to fall asleep, until she overcame her fear of the imaginary bear that lived in the corner of the stairs. It had been some years though, since they had spoken of Fanny Prescott, and Sophy had developed some rather particular questions.

"Do you ever wonder how it happened?" Her cheeks burned. "I mean, I don't think my mother was a wanton . . ."

"I don't think she was either." Jasper wasn't looking at her, watching his leader's paces. They rattled over a dip in the road, and Sophy lurched sideways, her hand clutching the rail again.

"In a hurry?" she asked.

He smiled from one corner of his mouth. "Not at all. But a man has to maintain his reputation."

Sophy licked her lips. "I don't think, I mean, I've gathered that Lord Fairchild has no other bastards. He doesn't seem especially promiscuous either."

Jasper slanted a glance in her direction. "How would you know if he was? Not the kind of thing anyone would tell you, is it?" He let out a sigh. "But you're right. He isn't. Or not particularly, considering how he and my mother get along. Still, you are the proof it happened."

Sophy hooded her eyes and Jasper turned placating. "It wasn't as sordid as you think, you know. My mother was gone. She left that summer. She and father had the most fearsome rows after Julius died."

Sophy's head jerked up.

"Yes, there were three of us." Jasper said. "Julius was the unnecessary spare, as it turned out."

Sophy recoiled. Jasper was always callous, but seldom harsh. "How—"

"Measles. He was not quite two years old."

"No one has ever spoken of him," Sophy said. "Not in the seven years that I've been at Cordell. I didn't know he existed."

Jasper cocked his head to one side. "Well, we aren't a confiding family, are we? Hold tight." He sprang the horses and they rushed downhill, gathering speed to climb the slope ahead.

"It was a strange summer," Jasper said at last. "Henrietta and I kept wondering where mother was, and when she was coming back. Soon, Miss Prescott always said. But I knew something was wrong, and Miss Prescott was especially kind, taking us outside whenever we wanted, playing games with us even on her free afternoons. Sometimes Father joined us, eating luncheon on the lawn, or rowing us about on the lake. I thought it was wonderful, until one day Miss Prescott was gone. Mother returned a few weeks later, and by then we had a new governess. I was furious

Miss Prescott was gone, and blamed my mother for it, though I suppose it must have been father's doing. Your mother was a kind lady."

"I know." Sophy's voice was gravelly.

Jasper looked at her but said nothing. Grateful for his silence, Sophy let grief wash over her and drain away, her eyes fixed on a distant church spire rising above the surrounding trees.

"Why don't you want to go to London?" Jasper asked.

Sophy shrugged one shoulder, trying to appear offhand. "I always thought Lady Fairchild intended me to be a governess, or a teacher. I thought I had another year or two at Cordell."

"You are happy there?"

"Yes," she said. "It's familiar." It was easy to imagine staying there always, the seasons passing, one after the other, each new year so like the last.

"This is a far better future for you," Jasper said, his eyes fixed on the road. "And though I'm sure father would have done his best to establish you, you'll achieve a much better match with my mother at the helm."

"I know," Sophy said, slumping. "I ought to be grateful. She'll march me into the best marriage she can devise to some man of respectable family and low enough expectations that my portion will compensate for my blood. Or a widower, looking for someone to care for his children. You know how these things work better than I."

"Choose someone old," Jasper said. "Widows have the best time of it."

Sophy laughed. "Have you learned this from the widows of your acquaintance? Henrietta says you know several."

Jasper closed his mouth with a snap. "Henrietta's husband needs to give her a sound spanking."

"Henrietta did all right," Sophy said. "Percy loves her."

"Strange, that," Jasper said.

Fearing she had revealed too much, Sophy turned back to

ruining her gloves.

"I can't tell you what you want to hear," he said, a minute later. "Expecting happiness is a fool's dream. Look at my parents. Their marriage is counted a success! But they will find you a respectable man, one who isn't a brute or a wastrel. You will have a comfortable life, if you reconcile yourself to it."

"Is that what you will do?" Sophy asked.

He gave a lopsided smile. "Yes. But I can't marry someone old. Got to have an heir, you know."

"You are a beast," Sophy said, rolling her eyes.

"Absolutely, but what kind?" Jasper asked, grinning. "I shouldn't mind if you thought I was a lion, or something like that. A toad—now that I couldn't stomach."

BY EARLY EVENING THEY HAD REACHED THE METROPOLIS AND were negotiating the streets of Mile End Town on Whitechapel road.

"Foul, ain't it," Jasper shouted in her ear, his voice barely audible above the clamor of more wagons and carriages than Sophy had ever seen. The streets were choked with hordes of people: grimy urchins begging, their ragged clothing poorly concealing their skeletal limbs; dairymaids walking homeward, pails hanging empty from their yokes; an army of hawkers selling everything from muffins to matches. Jasper was right about the smell. The air was thick with the stink of sewage, unwashed bodies and spoilage.

London seemed endless, street after street: Cheapside, Ludgate, Fleet Street, where the buildings grew more grand.

"Somerset House," Jasper indicated with his whip as he maneuvered the curricle through the traffic on the Strand. Then came Charing Cross and Piccadilly and Mayfair—and their destination, a townhouse on Park Lane, pinched in a tight row with the others. The tall windows looked down on her disapprovingly.

Giving the reins to his tiger, Jasper jumped down and offered his hand to Sophy. The two of them ascended the newly white-washed steps. Jasper sounded the brass knocker on the door.

"Good evening, Mr. Rushford."

"Jenkins," Jasper acknowledged the butler's greeting while handing him his hat, whip and gloves. "I've brought Miss Sophy."

"Will you stay to supper, sir?"

Jasper made a face. "I suppose I must. Have my small portmanteau brought in, will you? I'll need to change."

He took her hand, giving it a reassuring squeeze as they started up the stairs. "Don't worry, brat. I won't leave you to brazen this out on your own."

<hr/>

LORD AND LADY FAIRCHILD WERE WAITING TOGETHER IN THE drawing room, an inauspicious sign. Both of them leapt forward at the sight of her.

"Sophy!" they cried.

Lady Fairchild reached her first. "I have been worried beyond words," she said, taking her into her arms.

"Gently, Georgiana," Lord Fairchild cautioned.

"I'm fine," Sophy said, too stunned by the embrace to notice pain.

"I'll believe that when I hear it from a doctor," he said, with a stern look.

"I'm sorry, sir." Sophy said, trying not to squeak. "I won't do it again."

Lady Fairchild disengaged, busying herself straightening Sophy's dress.

Lord Fairchild grunted. "I'd put you back on leading strings if I thought it would help. Don't ever ride without a groom again, and stay off my horses. There are plenty of suitable mounts for you at Cordell and I'll buy a horse you can ride here."

Sophy's ears pricked, but she was given no chance to speak.

"How did it happen? What did the surgeon say?" Lady Fairchild said, seating Sophy beside her on the sofa. "And what about these Bagshots? Did they treat you well?"

"They were very kind." More than kind, even. She would have liked to know them under her own name.

Lady Fairchild looked skeptical, and brought out three more questions without a pause. Were they well-mannered? Did they see that she had appropriate care? Dared she hope that Sophy had been adequately chaperoned? Sophy faltered, struggling with her answers. Mrs. Bagshot had always been nearby, but she had spent a great deal of time tête-à-tête with Tom. Lady Fairchild would not want to hear that. Noticing her pause, Jasper stepped into the breach.

"Looked like Methodists to me. Bad ton, but honest. You know the type."

Lord Fairchild snorted. Lady Fairchild's exasperated eyes rose to the ceiling. The combined Rushford disdain made Sophy cringe. Tom and his mother deserved better than that.

❧

SOPHY WAS HERE AND SHE APPEARED INTACT, BUT PEACE STILL eluded Lord Fairchild. As the rush of relief subsided, he felt strangely empty. Georgiana embraced Sophy while he remained on the periphery. He wanted to hold Sophy too, but he could not.

So he watched her, still raw from two days of heart wrenching worry. She hardly glanced at him. Her nervous eyes were fixed on his wife, but once Jasper began fielding Georgiana's questions Sophy relaxed. She was probably too tired to fuddle her way through such a detailed interrogation. She ought to be put to bed.

"Really, I don't need another doctor," she said, smiling.

"Don't be absurd," he said, and went himself to speak to Jenkins.

It should please him that Sophy had wriggled her way into the desolate chambers of his wife's heart. The depth of Georgiana's affection still surprised him. She hadn't slept those two anxious days of waiting to hear that Sophy was found. Artful cosmetics failed to conceal the shadows under her eyes, and she had been dreadful with the servants: demanding, short-tempered, constantly countermanding her own orders and icily raging when the wrong thing was done.

That long, sleepless night, before they knew Sophy was found, he had left his library after hours of fruitless pacing and found Georgiana, standing like she was lost halfway up the stairs. Her fingers were knotted together, her knuckles white.

"You must rest," he said, reaching out to cup her elbow.

She blinked, coming back to him. Without thinking, he laid his hand on hers and squeezed. Both of them froze.

They did not touch, not like this. Both of them knew perfectly those prescribed contacts that could not be avoided: bowing over her hand, setting her hand on his arm as he walked her in to dinner, taking her hand as she stepped into or out of her carriage.

A long moment, then she turned her hand in his and squeezed back.

"We will find her," he said.

"I am afraid," she said, dropping her eyes and letting out a long breath.

"As am I."

Her fingers tightened on his again, and he felt the gears inside himself shifting. He looked at his wife, at the faint lines etched around her mouth, her cold, beautiful eyes, the flyaway wisps of her hair. It had been years since he had seen her so upset.

She loved Sophy.

His throat swelled and he turned his face away. Coughed once, hard.

"I need her, William. I cannot lose her," she said.

His own anxiety was intense, but he didn't hesitate. "You shall not."

She attempted a smile, looking up at him through wet eyelashes. The feeling that rose up in him—tenderness? Pity?—threatened to knock him over. But she was looking away again, starting up the stairs, retaining his hand. She did not let him go until they reached her door.

A thousand words choked him. Eight made it out. "You have been wonderful to Sophy. And me."

His cheeks flamed before the words settled. Fearing she suspected his intentions, he bid her good night and strode away down the hall.

He'd been unable to find familiar footing with her since. There was a new wariness between them, even now that Sophy was safely returned.

She was back, that was the main thing. After ordering Jenkins to immediately summon a physician, he returned upstairs. Georgiana was finished with questions, and was now chronicling her plans for the days ahead. They should visit Henrietta of course and see her new baby. They would pay calls to various Suffolk families with whom Sophy was already acquainted, testing the waters. Naturally, there was a great deal of shopping to be done first.

Jasper passed by, walking to the door. "If she asks, tell her I'm changing for dinner," he whispered and drifted out of the room.

Perhaps, like Jasper, he should leave the two of them. He was not needed. They seemed oblivious to his presence. Even so, he settled into a chair close enough to hear them talk, while he mused about the horse he must buy for Sophy.

She should have one spirited enough to challenge her mettle, but well-bred and of a size to keep her safe. It must be an animal with pretty paces, light and swift. One that would draw attention to Sophy's excellent horsemanship. One worthy of belonging to his daughter.

CHAPTER 16
TOWN MOUSE

"Come up! You must see William!" Henrietta, who was not yet dressed for shopping, popped her head into the drawing room, beckoning Sophy and Lady Fairchild. They had waited fifteen minutes for her already. With an exquisite sigh of forbearance, Lady Fairchild rose and followed her daughter. A wasted effort, Sophy decided. Henrietta didn't even notice.

"Look at him!" Henrietta said, throwing wide the nursery door. "Isn't he cunning?"

Sophy doubted there had ever been a fatter baby. He sat in his crib, still as a toad, scowling at the females peering at him. "He's such a jolly little man," Henrietta said, scooping him into her arms.

Little Will, taking exception to his abrupt removal, gave an indignant squawk and yanked his mother's hair. "No, no, sweet," Henrietta said, wincing as she pried apart his sausage fingers. "Mustn't pull mama's hair."

He answered her with a loud belch.

"You are not ready dear," Lady Fairchild said, with a pained look at Henrietta's straggling hair and her rumpled day dress.

"Oh, I won't be but a moment," Henrietta promised. "Here."

Thrusting her red-faced infant into her mother's arms, she flitted out the door. Lady Fairchild drew in a sharp breath. "Good afternoon, William," she said.

"Would you like me to take him, my lady?" asked the nursemaid hovering by the window.

"No," Lady Fairchild said, though she glanced at the door. "Well, what do you think?" she asked Sophy.

Sophy, conquering the spasms of laughter threatening to overtake her replied, "He looks very healthy."

"Indeed." Lady Fairchild surveyed him with a frown. "I suppose he'll grow into those ears. Percy's legacy, no doubt."

"I'm sure he'll turn out very handsome," said Sophy.

This was her first visit to Henrietta's London home since her marriage. It was impossible not to feel the happiness of this house, overflowing the rooms and spilling into the street. And why not? Henrietta ought to reign over a house like this, doting on her children and her helplessly-in-love husband.

If she could have something like this, she wouldn't hesitate to marry whomever Lady Fairchild directed, but experience had taught her that such happiness was rare indeed.

She heard a squeal of laughter, and turned her head to the open nursery door. It was Percy, scholar and aristocrat, galloping into the room with two-year old Laurence on his back.

"Georgiana. Sophy." Greeting them with a nod, he tossed a squealing Laurence onto the bed. He cocked a half-smile at his mother-in-law. "I told Henrietta she wouldn't be ready when you came. You'll have to forgive her, Georgiana. She'll never learn to keep time."

Laurence crawled to the other side of the bed and began thumping his velvet rabbit.

"So what do you think of our boys?" Percy asked.

"Sophy and I were just saying how healthy they are," she replied.

"Mmmmn." Amusement lurked in Percy's eyes. "I'll leave Laurie with you," he said to the nursemaid.

"You have a lovely family," Sophy told him.

"They are rather marvelous, aren't they," he said. "Should I wish you an enjoyable shopping trip, or is today's outing more work than pleasure?"

"A productive afternoon is necessary, but I hope to derive some pleasure from the excursion," Lady Fairchild said, eyeing the door through which Henrietta had vanished. She had progressed to bouncing Little Will on her knee.

"I'll leave you to it then," Percy said, and left with a bow.

"Master William doesn't normally care for jostling, my Lady," said the nursemaid, stepping forward and halting mid step as Lady Fairchild froze her with a stare.

"Really? He seems fine to me," she said. She glanced down at her grandson, a hint of a smile playing around the corners of her mouth. Leaning over to Sophy, she whispered, "I think he and I understand each other." And it seemed they did. Henrietta didn't return for a full half-hour, but in all that time, William frowned silently from his grandmother's knee.

"He's lovely, Hen," Sophy said, upon the errant mother's return.

"Isn't he?" she agreed, bending down beside William. "And will you be good for nursie?" she asked.

He bit his lip and stopped breathing, his face turning red. Henrietta's face crumpled in a worried frown. "Maybe I should stay until he falls asleep."

"Absolutely not," Lady Fairchild said, standing up and holding out little Will to the nursemaid, who stumbled across the room in her haste to obey. "Sophy's wardrobe must be purchased today, and you cannot be seen again in that atrocious jonquil gown I saw you in last week. Burn it. When I saw you at Lady Winward's party, I wished the earth would swallow me up." Despite her dazzling beauty, Henrietta had appalling taste in clothes.

"Very well. We shan't be too long," Henrietta lied to the maid, patting Laurence's head and giving a worried kiss to her beet red baby.

Henrietta abandoned herself to the pleasures of shopping for the first two hours, lingering over a length of tangerine net for so long that a bead of sweat rose on Lady Fairchild's brow. "Come away, dear," she urged. "There's nothing suitable here."

But by late afternoon, the expedition felt as long and exhausting as the peninsular campaign. Henrietta lost interest and Lady Fairchild seized the opportunity to guide her to a smart fawn pelisse and a pale blue gown.

Sophy wished her own outfitting was so easy. She and Lady Fairchild could not agree. Though she felt guilty over her intransigence in the face of Lady Fairchild's generosity, she could not like the clothes Lady Fairchild wanted to choose. They were all perfect debutante clothes in excellent taste—delicate gowns in white and pastel shades that made her look like a corpse.

"It is a beautiful gown, but I will not wear it," Sophy argued. "Look at what it does to me!"

"Yes, but you cannot wear that," Lady Fairchild retorted, gesturing at the bolt of emerald muslin Sophy had chosen. "That color is flashy! We have to tread carefully, given your circumstances."

"Well, I won't show to advantage in that. Unless there are men looking to marry consumptives. And this has too many frills. I'd look like—like Mrs. Bagshot." Sophy said and blushed with shame. Lady Fairchild didn't notice the blush, but she set aside the dress without further protest.

"Mrs. Bagshot . . . from Chippenstone?" Henrietta asked, fingering the dress Sophy had discarded. "How did you meet her?"

"They were good enough to help Sophy when she was thrown

from her horse," Lady Fairchild said, her eyes darting to Madame Foulard, who was bent over, measuring the length for Sophy's skirts.

Henrietta ignored the signal to be silent. "What was the house like? I heard they had the rooms all redone."

"The old Mr. Bagshot did. He spared no expense." Sophy bit her lip. She was recounting facts, not betraying them.

Lady Fairchild sniffed.

"Was it dreadfully vulgar?" Henrietta asked, leaning forward.

"I don't think it would be to either of your tastes," Sophy said quietly, failing to keep her lips in a prim line as she remembered. There was a sparkle in her eye when she added, "My room was quite astonishing. And there was a salon, done in the Egyptian style . . ."

"Hmm?" Madame Foulard looked up, giving a knowing nod. "Quite the mania for Egypt this season. I have some sandals, very popular, that would be just the thing to wear with—"

Lady Fairchild blanched. "We shall stay with slippers. No girl in my charge is venturing out with her toes showing. Don't even think it, Henrietta."

Henrietta pursed her mouth. She would have a pair within a fortnight, Sophy knew.

"How about this?" Lady Fairchild said, holding out another length of silk.

"It's lovely, but I can't wear white," Sophy said.

"Well, what do you propose?" Lady Fairchild snapped. "Packing paper? Corduroy?"

Madame Foulard flinched. "My Lady, I would never bring such things here."

"I want that. Done up like that." Sophy pointed to a bolt of brilliant blue silk lying on a table across the room and a picture in the open magazine before her, while Henrietta made mollifying gestures at Madame Foulard.

Lady Fairchild opened her mouth to protest, but stopped,

looked, then frowned. "I don't know," she said. "Bring it here." Madame's assistant went scurrying across the room for the cloth, bearing it toward Sophy with outstretched arms.

"Hmmn." Lady Fairchild looked from the cloth to the magazine. "Generally, I favor simplicity, but this cut is almost severe. It will look like your father is a nip-farthing, instead of being quite handsome about your portion."

"The excellence of the fabric makes ornament unnecessary," Sophy said.

"It looks perfect with your hair," Henrietta added.

"There is not one girl in a hundred who could support that color, my Lady," inserted Madame Foulard, impatient to make the sale. "You cannot deny it is becoming."

"Very well," Lady Fairchild said. "One of this blue silk and one of the green muslin you liked. But I still want at least one white dress. Put some gold trimming at the neck. That should help."

Madame Foulard nodded, and motioned Sophy to hold out her arms. "Very wise, my Lady."

Madame busied herself with tape and pins. Lady Fairchild sat down on a pretty chair to watch, but stood again almost immediately, frowning and pacing across the room.

"My Lady?" Madame Foulard cocked her head, talking around a mouthful of pins.

"They are such bold colors," Lady Fairchild said. "You must be careful, Sophy. There are some already disposed to dislike you, simply because of what you are. If I let you wear these gowns, your behavior must be impeccable. You cannot afford mistakes. When you are snubbed, you must smile and accept it gracefully, but you must never act as if you expect to be snubbed. Carry yourself proudly, and most people will accord you respect."

"Oh, mama," Henrietta said, but Sophy was nodding, her eyes serious. It was easy to forget, to think she could simply wear what suited her best. Matters would never be so straightforward for her.

"You are right, of course," Lady Fairchild said, settling herself back into her chair with some annoyance. "The colors are brilliant on you. You will have hair plumes dyed to match, Madame?"

Madame nodded vigorously.

Sophy held in a sigh. Her right shoulder ached, but it was the heaviness inside that troubled her. Lady Fairchild, sharp as ever, met her eyes and caught something of it in her face. "Madame," she said severely. "Did I not tell you that Sophy injured her shoulder? Lower your arms, child. You look pale."

"A thousand pardons," Madame said, flustering as she helped Sophy off the stool. "Such stupidity is unforgivable. Sit here, Miss Sophy, and I will have Thérèse bring you biscuits. A fitting is very taxing."

Accepting the offered chair, Sophy agreed with a slight smile. Madame spoke true, but it taxed her in more ways than one.

۞

"How much longer will you stay?" Tom's mother asked over the breakfast table.

"Mmm?" Tom decapitated his egg and looked up.

"I'm happy to have you here of course, but I wondered how long you intend to stay."

He had only intended to visit for a week. Already he'd stayed four extra days, and planned to stay as long as he could stand Chippenstone. He had no desire to be in London, not while she still haunted him.

"Tired of me already?" he teased, scooping runny egg onto his toast. While his mother protested, he folded the toast in half and bit off the corner, before yolk could run too far down his fingers.

It was pathetic, really, he thought, licking his fingers clean. In better moments he could laugh at himself, but moments like this he wanted to stick his head in the horse trough. His mother only made it worse, bringing up Sophy every chance she got. He positively hated that book of hers, *The Wicked Duke*.

Last night, he had suggested starting something new.

"But I'm enjoying it," she said, her eyes all innocence. "I thought you didn't mind it. You certainly seemed to enjoy reading it with Miss Sophy."

He had enjoyed it then. But every evening since, he'd been unable to read it without casting Sophy Rushford in every scene, seeing the flick of her fingers, the turn of her wrist, exactly like a lovesick idiot.

He stabbed a forkful of ham and shoved it into his mouth.

"Hungry?" his mother asked.

He replied with a grunt.

"It's just that you don't seem contented here," his mother continued, recapturing his attention. "I know you prefer London. You needn't put yourself to so much trouble for me."

That forced a bland smile from him. Both of them knew he wasn't staying for her; his visits were always frequent and short.

"Why don't I go with you?"

He nearly choked on his coffee. "What?"

"I thought maybe I'd go with you to London this spring."

"You never go to London," he said, wiping his mouth with his napkin, trying to ignore the burn in his nose.

"Don't you want me to go?"

"Of course I want your company. I drag myself all the way here, just to see you. You surprised me, that's all."

"I might enjoy a change of scene," she said, as if she had been born idle and rich. Tom raised his eyebrows. "Well, why shouldn't I?"

Tom cleared his throat. "I'm not sure London is the best place for me right now, mother."

"Of course it is. There you have your work and the company of your friends. And if you should chance to see—"

"I think it very unlikely," he broke in. "Nor would I wish it."

"Well I wish very much to go to London," she said, folding her hands.

"Do you?" he said, fixing her with a stare. She didn't blink, so he gave up. He didn't want to go to London at all, not with his mother reminding him about her three times a day. But saying that would be admitting defeat. "Very well. We'll go. But I warn you, it's not going to do any good."

Folding up his newspaper, he rose from the table. "Have your maid start packing."

He never was angry with his mother. He was all she had, and she deserved better from him. But just right now, he longed to punch something.

CHAPTER 17
ADVERTISING

The summons came in the evening, from his mother.

"The termagant. Again." Jasper groaned to his friends. He'd invited them to join him at his rooms in St James for supper and cards.

"What does she want this time?" asked Alistair, lounging in the chair beside him.

Jasper frowned at the folded note in his hands, "You may be her nephew, but you have nothing on me. She's my mother."

"Shall you ignore it, Jasper?" asked Boz, a lean man in buff trousers and a claret colored coat, seated at the end of the table.

Jasper smiled, slipping the note into his waistcoat pocket. "Not this time. The favor she demands is not so onerous." Turning to the waiting footman, he said "You may tell my mother I shall present myself in the morning."

Expectant, his friends waited until the footman withdrew.

"Well, what is it?" Boz asked, refilling his glass.

"I'm to go riding with my sister in the morning."

The fourth man, hitherto silent, frowned. "Not Lady Arundel, surely."

Jasper laughed. "No, Andre. Her husband would never let her,

not so soon after her confinement. I meant my half-sister."
Natural sister, the polite name for bastards like Sophy, was a term
he did not use.

Andre's eyebrows rose in surprise, but Boz lapsed into a remi-
niscent smile. "The little one?" Boz had passed one holiday at
Cordell Hall when he and Jasper were still at Cambridge.

"What's she doing in town?" Alistair asked, surprised by Boz's
smile. He too had met Sophy, ages ago, when Lady Fairchild had
gathered her relations to Cordell one Easter. He and Jasper had
captured a grass snake and hid it in one of her cupboards. Her
calm response had been vastly disappointing.

Jasper turned over his hand, inspecting his nails. "Puffing her
off. Why else?"

Boz, his face already rather ruddy, nodded sagely over his port.
"Only reason to bring a young female to town."

"Think your mother will do it?" Alistair asked, still remembering a scrawny red-haired girl hiding from Lady Fairchild's stare.
"Not so easy to puff off a bastard." It surprised him that his Aunt
would trouble himself over the girl, but it had been years since he
had been in England.

Jasper's face turned cold. "Call her my half-sister, or use her
name. I dislike that appellation."

"Of course. My apologies." Alistair waited for Jasper to answer
his question.

Jasper lifted one eyebrow, wearily. "Surely you know better
than to underestimate my mother. She'll have her riveted soon
enough." He proffered the deck of cards. "Cut?"

"Little scrap of a thing, when I saw her last," Alistair said.

"Well, she's grown some," Jasper said. "But she's still up to the
old tricks. Took out one of m'father's prime bits of blood last
week and came to grief." He frowned.

"No lasting hurt?" Boz asked, looking up from his cards with a
worried face.

"Not this time," Jasper grunted. "And damned if there'll be another. Never seen the Pater in such a taking."

"What's she look like?" Andre asked.

"Like my father," Jasper said. "It just about killed my mother, you know."

"Still?" Alistair asked. "Poor girl." Red hair seldom looked well on a woman.

"Oh, she's a rather taking brat," Jasper said. "Boz thought she looked well enough." He glanced at his friend across the table. "If I see you sniffing around her, I'll call you out."

"You don't say?" Alistair settled back in his chair, arranging his cards in a fan. "Then it must be time for me to renew my acquaintance."

Worth looking in, anyways. Fairchild must be giving her an adequate sum. He took a swallow of wine. "I'll join you tomorrow, Jasper, if I may."

"All right," Jasper said. "But lay your card, man, or we'll be here all night."

❦

SOPHY LEANED ON HER DRESSING TABLE, STRAIGHTENING HER brushes. Pale fingers of morning sunlight curled around the edges of the cream silk draperies at her bedroom window. She was dressed for riding; her hat, whip, and gloves ready on the table.

She didn't sleep well in London, too aware of the noise and vibration of so many souls clustered together. The city was busier than an anthill and more crowded. There were always people awake: milkmaids and bakers before dawn; butchers, crossing sweepers and cart men in the day; opera goers, link boys and the watch at night.

"Try to adjust, or the parties will wear you to shreds," Lady Fairchild had urged. She was already half-nocturnal, flitting out in the evenings like a brightly winged moth, then sleeping into the early afternoon. Tonight Sophy would join her for the first time, at the Thorpes' musicale. Already half sick with anticipation, she had another fence to clear first.

This morning she was riding with Lord Fairchild. If she was clever, she would have made more of her shoulder injury to give her an excuse to stay home, but it was a week and a half since that unfortunate business and she wanted to forget it.

Pushing away from the dressing table, Sophy crossed the room, parted the draperies and leaned against the window, resting her forehead against the glass. It was strange, looking down at the tops of people from the third story—costly beaver hats on the few gentlemen venturing out early and worn caps on the rest. The horses hadn't been brought round yet.

Only ladies who were horse mad and keen sporting gentlemen rode in the early morning when the rest of the Polite World was asleep. Sophy supposed she and Lord Fairchild both fit the respective descriptions. There were worse ways to find a husband than riding horses and hobnobbing in the park. What unsettled her was being tied to Lord Fairchild's side for over an hour. What would they possibly say? This was not like their accidental rides in the country, where their paths merged and diverged by chance.

A kitchen boy ran out from a house down the street, momentarily silencing the ragged knife grinder calling out his trade. The man sharpened the knives the boy brought out, accepted his wage with a tug of his cap, and continued down the street, his bass voice rolling ahead of him. Sophy's eyes followed him, catching on a familiar form in a dark green coat.

It was Jasper, trotting up the street on a chestnut she didn't recognize. His companion wasn't familiar either, but he was remarkably handsome and sat well on his horse. Sophy darted to the dressing table, grabbing gloves, whip and hat, ignoring the energizing tonic Lady Fairchild had given her last evening. She was supposed to drink it, but uncorking the bottle had been enough—the vapor of the potion was strong enough to curl her hair. Not that she needed any help with that. Some magic to keep her hair in its pins, maybe.

She left the room with a lighter tread. Riding with Lord Fairchild would be much easier with Jasper along for company. Halfway down the hall, Lady Fairchild stopped her, emerging from her boudoir wrapped in a silk dressing gown. "Sophy! You can't go down yet. At least wait until he's inside."

Lady Fairchild had spent most of yesterday preparing Sophy for this morning's ride, choosing her hat and boots and going over things she might say to the gentlemen she met. It shouldn't surprise her that Lady Fairchild was awake, watching from her window too. This wasn't just any ride. It was important. Sophy's eyes dropped to the carpet. "I beg your pardon ma'am. I thought since it's only Jasper—"

"I won't insist on you receiving him in the drawing room. That is a bit much for your brother, after all. But I won't have you rushing at him as if he were returned from the Orient! Wait a few minutes!"

Beckoning Sophy into her room, Lady Fairchild occupied Sophy for a few minutes, inspecting the color of her cheeks and adjusting the angle of her hat. "Wear the veil when you are outside," she said, referring to the scrap of lace clinging to the brim. Opening a French novel Sophy wasn't allowed to read, Lady Fairchild dismissed her with a wave. Sophy sped down the stairs, smiling to herself. She had Henrietta's copy of the book hidden under her mattress.

"Sophy! You look fine as five pence," Jasper said, coming up the stairs to meet her with a wide smile and outstretched hands.

"Yet this cost a good deal more," she said, taking his hands and offering her cheek with a smile.

He looked her over. "I'm sure it did. How's the shoulder?"

"Never better," she assured him. Glancing past him, she saw that Lord Fairchild was drawing on his gloves, watching them impatiently. He hated having his horses wait. "Sorry to keep you waiting, sir," she said.

As she and Jasper descended the last few steps, Jasper's companion stepped forward and bowed. "Cousin Sophy. So good to see you again."

Cousin? Her eyes flew to Jasper's.

"Alistair," he whispered. "Spent Easter with us years ago. Remember the snake?"

She did, dredging his name out of the wells of memory. "Of course. Mr. Beaumaris. It's been such a long time."

Tired of waiting, Lord Fairchild was making his way to the door. "Come along, Sophy. I've something to show you." Hastening her steps, Sophy followed him outside and stopped so suddenly, Jasper nearly collided with her. She hardly noticed. Her eyes were fixed on the horse.

It was fitted with a side-saddle, but she couldn't believe this beautiful grey mare was for her. Such intelligent eyes, such smooth muscles rippling beneath her glossy coat—surely this horse was meant for a duchess. But there were only the four of them, standing on the steps. Mr. Beaumaris's black was waiting beside Jasper's horse and Lord Fairchild's current favorite, a bay with giant quarters, stood ready. There was no horse for her, besides this one.

"Her paces are faultless," Lord Fairchild said beside her.

Sophy could well believe it. This horse had been formed from clay by a god's hand, before given the breath of life.

"She's yours," Lord Fairchild said, when Sophy remained speechless.

Where had he found her, and what had she cost? Shaking her head, still disbelieving, Sophy said, "I could have ridden Lady Fairchild's horse."

"I'm supposed to ride with you every day, you know," he said. "Do you think I could stand it, with you mounted on that plug?"

Of course. Advertising. That's what this was. Parading her in front of the eligibles and reassuring the squeamish that her father claimed her as his own.

"Seemed a good way to prevent future accidents," Lord Fairchild said, his eyes on the horse.

She ignored that. "What is she called?"

"I thought 'Mischief' might be fitting, but you don't need any encouragement in that direction." He smiled. "What will you call her?"

"Hirondelle," Sophy said immediately. "She looks like she should have wings."

"And like she'd carry you to Africa if you let her run away with you," interjected Mr. Beaumaris, already in his saddle.

"She won't," Jasper said smugly. "Sophy knows what she's about."

Smiling at Jasper's compliment, still incredulous at her good fortune, Sophy accepted a leg up from the groom. Settling into the saddle, she arranged her skirts and dropped the lace veil over her face. Silently, she maneuvered down the street alongside Lord Fairchild, Jasper and Mr. Beaumaris following behind.

Hirondelle was a good name for this horse. She was agile and quick, with a responsive mouth, her steps light, like she would dance if she only had more space. Given free rein, she would fly as far and fast as the swallows for which she was named. Inside the park, Sophy gazed at the open grass, longing to gallop, painfully aware it was one of many things that Must Never Be Done. She would obey for now, but once they were home—

Before the thought could bud, Sophy remembered she wasn't returning to Cordell. Swiftly, she shut her mind to the familiar picture of wide green earth and infinite sky. Wherever she lived, there would be *someplace* to ride.

The morning was damp, with an intermittent wind sweeping

through the row of sentinel trees lining the riding path. Sophy didn't mind it playing with her skirts, but did wish it would stop blowing her veil into her mouth. Spitting it free for the second time, she caught the amused look in Lord Fairchild's eye.

"You look well," he assured her. "The costume suits you." It was designed, Sophy knew, to highlight her resemblance to him. Her brown beaver hat was identical to his, save for its veil of cream lace.

"Want to trade?" she asked, indicating her hat with her whip.

"Not on your life," he laughed. She followed his backward glance to Jasper and Mr. Beaumaris, lagging behind them to greet a party of gentlemen riders. All were dressed in the same fashionable uniform: dark coats, yellow or tan trousers and boots polished to a high gloss. She wasn't sure if the absurdly large peony in the buttonhole of one of them was an attempt to set fashion or a misguided attempt at copying it.

Lord Fairchild cleared his throat. "You should start calling me father in informal situations among the family, you know. It is appropriate, since we want to make your position clear. And it would please me if you did."

"Of course. Father." The word stuck in her throat before she coughed it grudgingly into the silence between them. It was an endearment that would never come naturally to her lips. Given her way, she preferred 'sir.' It was easier not to have to remember where she could be his daughter and where they pretended she was his ward.

A lady in a habit of purple velvet bounced by, trailing a groom. Sophy saw her own frown mirrored by the sour twist of Lord Fairchild's mouth. "Thank God you don't ride like that," he said.

Here was safer ground. Sophy smiled. "I've a better horse. Thank-you," she said fervently.

He snorted. "A crime, if she were to ride Hirondelle. We should wait," he said, looking back again at Jasper. "He will introduce his friends. It's why we're here, after all."

Hirondelle sidled, betraying Sophy's anxiety. Lord Fairchild—
no, her father—lifted an eyebrow. "I'm fine," she lied.

Jasper turned toward them. "Father, may I introduce my
friends to Sophy?"

Lord Fairchild nodded his assent and Jasper nudged his horse
forward, his friends following. "Sophy, may I present Mr. George
DeClerc and Mr. Andre Protheroe. Gentlemen, this is Sophy
Prescott, my father's ward."

"I think you and I have met before," Sophy said to Mr.
DeClerc, who she remembered as Jasper's friend Boz. "But I don't
think I ever heard the name George."

He coughed into his hand. "No, I don't use that handle much.
How are you, Miss Prescott? Jasper says your arm is mending?"

"It is indeed. I am very well." Her nervousness was making
Hirondelle restless, so Sophy let her walk, expecting Mr. DeClerc
to fall in beside her. Instead he held back, answering a question
from Mr. Protheroe, and Sophy ended up ambling beside Mr.
Beaumaris instead.

Unlucky, she sighed. It would have been comfortable, riding
beside the empty headed and amiable Boz. She didn't know what
to do with Mr. Beaumaris, besides try not to stare. He was far too
handsome for her to think of anything to say.

"The hair I recognize," he said, studying her with a raised
eyebrow. It was the kind of glance designed to elicit blushes.
Pressing her lips together—they felt suddenly dry—she conjured
up an airy laugh she was far from feeling. She felt young, gauche,
and eleven years old.

"I wouldn't have expected you to recognize me at all. It's been
ages since you came to Cordell. Except for the snake in my
cupboard, I hardly saw you."

"As I recall, the snake didn't distress you," he smiled. "But
what about the subsequent neglect?"

Sophy turned her eyes to the path ahead, raising her chin.
Females more sophisticated than she had melted for his velvet

brown eyes, she was certain. It was unfair of him to use them on her. "Believe me, I was glad of it. If you and Jasper had troubled with me, I'm sure it would have been only to throw me into the lake."

Alistair laughed. "Maybe so. But if you are ever threatened with such a fate again, you must allow me to defend you."

"I doubt you will be required," she said, scanning the park.

"Pity."

"Since anyone with such ill intent would have to catch me first, I would hardly need you," Sophy added, for good measure.

"True. You're a capital rider. I wasn't sure you could live up to Jasper's boasts."

"He's a good teacher."

"So I see."

She'd applied her whip a little too freely, and now she and Alistair were some distance ahead of the rest of the party. She leaned back in the saddle, so that they would be overtaken. She felt out of her depth bantering with him. "What brings you to town, Mr. Beaumaris?" Sophy asked, filling the silence.

"So formal?" he asked. "We are nearly cousins. You must call me Alistair, because I fully intend to call you Sophy."

Goodness, he was beautiful. Like the corsair in—Oh, stop, Sophy told herself. He must do this to everyone. How could he help it, with those looks? She drew a breath. "I could call you what your mother calls you. I see her letters to Lady Fairchild, you know," she said, unable to entirely suppress the smile that tugged at her mouth.

He was as cool as ever. "And that is?"

"A no-good jackanapes who never writes."

"I'd prefer to hear you say Alistair," he smiled. Sophy looked away again.

"Very well."

The others caught up, but remained just behind them, caught

up in a conversation about Lord Byron's defense of the Luddites. Sophy listened for an opening, but there was none.

"You haven't said it," Alistair said.

He was talking about his name, she realized. "I haven't had occasion to, yet. Are you going to tell me why you came to town?"

"Invalided from Cadiz," he said.

Sophy turned to him in surprise. He didn't look wounded. He sat easily on his horse, managing to look bored and dashing at the same time.

"I hope you are recovering," she stammered.

"Quite nicely, thank-you. I hope to rejoin my regiment before winter." These were rote responses. He must be bored.

"You don't care for London?" she asked.

"No, I like it very much." He was looking past her, to a trio of ornamental ladies walking round a pond. "Excuse me, Sophy. I must speak to some friends." Nodding, touching the brim of his hat, he rode off.

She had been eager to escape his company, but not this way, casually dismissed. Tight-lipped, she turned to Jasper, but he was still engrossed in his own discussion, so she fell in beside Lord Fairchild.

The park grew busier. Her father presented a bewildering array of gentlemen to her, all of them lean and sharing his equine religion. They were carefully polite, probably only for her father and brother's sake. Certainly that was the case with Mr. Beaumaris. He'd dropped her as soon as he'd spied another female. All in all, Sophy was inclined to disagree with Lady Fairchild's assessment of her chances.

❦

ACROSS THE PARK, TOM SWORE. SHE WAS LOVELIER THAN HE remembered. Under her hat, her hair gleamed like a new penny. Beneath a useless wisp of lace, her expression was just as he remembered, impish and imperious by turn as she conversed with the fellow riding beside her. Tom hated him immediately.

Five days he'd been in London. Every morning and afternoon he'd walked the park, hoping for a glimpse of her, certain that sighting her would cure him. Instead, he couldn't help staring at her, warmth spreading from his belly to the tips of his fingers. It felt good to look at her, even with his mind insisting she was trouble. She knew horses, despite her accident, skillfully managing a grey even he could tell was frisky.

Tom watched her companion ride off with a nod. They were all doing that: nodding, smiling, amused no doubt, by their own witty little quips. His usual contempt for her kind had a keener edge today.

As she moved to her father's side, Tom saw the brother, Jasper. Their eyes met and held for an instant before Jasper Rushford looked away, laughing at the jest of the man beside him, pretending not to have seen.

Scowling, Tom looked away, lest his stare draw the attention of the others. His hand clenched around the silver headed walking stick his mother had thrust into his hand as he walked out the door. She had given it to him for Christmas, saying it gave him a distinguished look. He thought it made him look like a fop.

Well, what had he expected? This was what she was here for, to see and be seen, to catch one of them—stupid, useless popinjays who spent their days mixing snuff, tying their cravats into absurd shapes and then giving them names, betting on anything their bored minds could conceive. She would make one of them a fine wife. Hadn't he seen her, directing his servants and pouring out tea? Her preciseness completing that little ritual had told him exactly what she was.

But she was more. He could not forget how she had breathed the air in his gardens and drawn close to his paintings to see the invisible brush strokes making up a wisp of cloud. Or how her absurd acting had amused his mother. When her brother had come for her, she had thrown herself at him with fierce affection. She would be wasted on a husband who did not love her the way she was capable of loving, with such exuberant joy. His own emotion threatened to choke him and he quickened his stride.

He could not banish her from his mind's eye. She was still there, circled by men in sober coats. He did not believe any of them would love her; knew with sinking despair that he did. It hardly mattered. Her brother's hastily averted eyes told him he would never be allowed into her world. What's more, he had promised himself years ago that he would never want to try.

CHAPTER 18
FAMILY

Mrs. Thorpe could be pleased with the attendance at her musicale, Lady Fairchild decided. The rooms were gratifyingly full for an event this early in the season offering such tepid entertainment. The string quartet was good, but she would have hired a soprano. The expense was greater, of course, but so was the drama. Still, this was the right place to test Sophy's wings.

If this evening was a sign of things to come, Sophy would take well. Lady Milford had already congratulated her on her husband's pretty ward, without a hint of irony. The compliment would not persuade her to smooth the path for Lady Milford's impecunious sons, but Lady Fairchild valued the tribute nevertheless.

Sophy was nervous, but hid it well. No one who did not know her intimately would have noticed. Her contributions to conversation throughout dinner had been small, but sparkling. Now she appeared completely focused on the music, but there was tension in her carefully constructed smile. Poor girl. The first party was always the hardest. Reaching over, she laid her hand atop Sophy's own, giving her a reassuring squeeze.

"A definite success," she whispered. True, the minor sensation helped. Her husband had never made a secret of Sophy, but her existence had not been widely known. Her resemblance to William made it unnecessary to speculate on their exact connection, delighting the gossips, who gasped behind their fans and exchanged knowing looks. They had to wonder how she could be so fond of the girl, but Lady Fairchild didn't mind. If well used, the notoriety could help Sophy. If not—well, Lady Fairchild did not intend to fail.

The music ended and they rose to circulate through the rooms.

"We won't stay much longer," Lady Fairchild whispered. "We want people to wonder."

Sophy swallowed. "I'm sure they'll do that, ma'am."

Joining the tide of stiff guests leaving the music room—the pieces had been rather long—Lady Fairchild steered Sophy to the centre of the adjoining salon. It wouldn't do to cower in the corner. Immediately they were accosted by Mr. Franklin. His waistcoat was worse than usual; a blemish on the face of taste, but as he requested an introduction to Sophy, the waistcoat could be overlooked. He conversed with them for some minutes, assessing Sophy in a way that would have made other girls fluster. Sophy, bless her, was cool and polite. Miss Thorpe approached next, and then Lord Finglass. Drawn into conversation about the new production of Hamlet at the Theatre Royal, Lady Fairchild momentarily forgot Sophy, until she realized she was no longer beside her. She'd been drawn aside by Amabel Lowell, who was walking with her to the far side of the room.

"Excuse me," Lady Fairchild said. She could not follow after. It would look as if Sophy couldn't hold her own. But she could not abandon her long to Amabel's company. She was well acquainted with Amabel and her mother, and knew for a certainty the girl had some malicious motive. Swiftly, Lady Fairchild plotted her course around the room. She'd nod to Mr. Greenbough and greet the Allens, then speak to the Dowager Countess of St. Irvin. That would put her in Sophy's vicinity again. It would take some time, but she would be close if she was needed. With any luck, Miss Lowell only intended to drop Sophy in the corner, where she could no longer draw eyes from all across the room.

Sophy and Miss Lowell were still talking when Lady Fairchild halted in front of the Allens. A crimson stain was creeping up Sophy's neck. Where was her courage? Surely a girl who sailed over fences as lightheartedly as Sophy wouldn't quail in the drawing room. Mentally urging her on, Lady Fairchild responded to Mrs. Allen, not hesitating even a heartbeat.

"How fortunate. I shall have to try the vapor baths myself. So far I am untroubled by rheumatism, but if they are as good as you say, they must be efficacious as a preventative measure," she said.

"And so good for the nerves," Mrs. Allen added.

When Miss Lowell swanned off on the arm of Lord Upshaw, Lady Fairchild didn't blink, though Sophy was left standing alone. She was making a valiant attempt at unconcern, but she couldn't be comfortable, with only a few acquaintances present, and those met only this evening. If she could just maintain her poise for a few moments, someone would surely come speak to her. Retreating alone to the ladies withdrawing room or the refreshment table would be admitting defeat before the campaign even started. Sophy held her ground, coolly inspecting the sticks of her fan. Lady Fairchild nearly sighed with relief when Sir Edmund Fowler spotted her and crossed the room. They exchanged pleasantries and a moment later he was offering his arm and conducting her to a vacant sofa. It was a clever bit of work, though Sophy could not know it. Sir Edmund was a widower particularly hard-pressed by the demands of his four children. She would happily see Sophy married to Sir Edmund—if he didn't happen to live in Kent. It was such a distance, after all.

Lady Fairchild knew that once a girl captured the attention of one gentleman, others would follow. She waited until three of them stood around Sophy before gliding in to claim her.

"Forgive me, gentlemen," she said. "I must take Sophy home." With an insincere smile of apology, she whisked Sophy away.

"You handled Miss Lowell very well," she said, once they were in the carriage heading home.

Sophy made a face.

"What did she say?" Lady Fairchild asked.

"Nothing that bears repeating."

"She's rather good at the barbed comment, but you mustn't mind her," Lady Fairchild said. "In a way, it's flattering that she singled you out instead of just ignoring you. She had a very successful Season last year, but everyone knows she's hunting for a title."

"Will she get one?"

"Oh, probably. She's quite beautiful and has a fortune from her mother. But trying to embarrass you only reminds people of her sister. Lady Slade is notorious for the assortment of children she's presented to her husband. Next time you see her, you might want to mention that."

Smiling, Lady Fairchild smoothed her gloves. "It will only get easier. Before you know it, you'll be having the time of your life."

After three more evenings and seven more parties, Lady Fairchild declared that Sophy was looking too tired and that the morning rides must stop. "You'll ruin her looks, dragging her out every day," she said to her husband as they followed Sophy up the stairs. They were all on their way to bed. "Once or twice a week is plenty. You can still ride at the fashionable hour, of course."

"Stand still, rather," Sophy muttered, as her father acquiesced. He was unusually agreeable with his wife lately. He'd even complimented her hair this evening. Of course, he must be greatly indebted to her. Shepherding Sophy through a season was not something he could have asked of her.

Sophy paused at the top of the stairs, watching her father escort his wife to her door and then proceed to his own rooms at the end of the hall. His door closed, leaving her alone with her candle.

She sighed. During the fashionable hour between five and six the park was so jammed with carriages and horses one could hardly move. The morning was less of a show. She suspected it was the parties themselves, not merely the late hours that were dragging her down.

Her maid Betty was waiting for her, ready to unpin her hair and free her from her party dress. She could barely keep her eyes open as Betty unclipped her pearl ear bobs and brushed out her hair.

Lady Fairchild was right, of course. The parties had gotten easier. Her free dances were promptly solicited and she had discovered two or three young ladies interested enough in Jasper and Mr. Beaumaris to pretend friendship with her. Both gentlemen made a point of singling her out in the park and the ballroom. Mr. Beaumaris's attention would have done her more credit if he wasn't simply obliging Lady Fairchild, but it was hard not to enjoy the envious stares of prettier girls, richer girls, and girls with impeccable lineage as he led her into the dance.

"Just go to bed, Betty," Sophy yawned. "I can manage my night dress." Betty might not be so sour natured if she got a decent night's sleep too, instead of waiting up for her every night. If Betty was rested, she might not be so fierce with the hairpins.

Sophy didn't hear her leave; she was feeling her way into the heavy cotton night dress and shuffling to the bed, waiting for her with the covers pulled back. Sliding between the sheets, she stretched her toes, letting herself sink into the mattress.

Mr. Beaumaris's attention might have turned her head, if she didn't know it was all a ploy. He knew perfectly well how handsome he was. It wasn't easy, watching him exercise his considerable charm.

But it was only pretend, and ought not to unsettle her. Clammy hands, stuttering heart—she scolded herself for them often enough, but doubted any girl could be entirely immune to his caressing looks.

Dismissing Mr. Beaumaris, Sophy turned her thoughts to Hirondelle instead, and fell asleep before she and her horse had galloped their first mile. But when she awoke, early in the morning, Mr. Beaumaris was back. Sophy rolled over, thumped her pillow, and screwed her eyes shut.

Overall, she preferred it when he did not join their morning rides. He was not an easy companion. Besides, her father would speak to her when they rode, so long as there were no eligibles floating around. At first, they had talked only generally, of horses or the passers-by. He never probed and was always quick to retreat behind a bland remark. But soon they were talking about more particular matters: Henrietta and her sons, the books Sophy borrowed from the circulating library, and—in surprising detail— her father's fears after the sudden assassination of Spencer Percival, the Prime Minister.

She did not like missing these opportunities so she could traipse from house to house in the evenings. With the sun up now, and the servants creeping through the house, it was impossible to sleep anyway. Sophy climbed out of bed and took out yesterday's riding habit.

Betty heard her digging her boots out of the cupboard. "Just what do you think you're doing?" she asked, hurrying into the room.

"You can help me put this on," Sophy said, gesturing at her habit.

"Not I. My Lady says you are to rest yourself this morning, so you make a good showing at the opera tonight," Betty said, folding her arms below her ample bosom and setting her chin. "Get yourself back into bed."

Sophy gritted her teeth. Opera be damned. She was going

riding. "If you don't help me," she said, slowly and evenly, "I shall have to just go out in what I am already wearing."

"You wouldn't—"

Sophy sat down on the edge of the bed and drew on her stockings. She could feel Betty's eyes, boring through the top of her head, but having her own way felt too good. She laced up her boots. Striding across the room, she laid her hand on the doorknob.

"All right! But I shall tell Lady Fairchild what you've done as soon as she's awake!"

"Please do." With any luck, she would be home before then.

Betty's fingers nipped her as she fastened hooks, ties and buttons, but Sophy didn't care. "Thank-you, Betty," she said, when she was done up at last.

"Hmmph!"

"WHAT ARE YOU DOING?" LORD FAIRCHILD ASKED, WHEN Sophy appeared at the bottom of the stairs. "Aren't you going to the Opera this evening?"

"Aren't you?" He was to accompany them tonight, which was unusual. Most evenings he spent at his club.

He shrugged. "I don't sleep much."

"Neither do I."

"A short ride," he said. "You can rest after." He sent for their horses.

THEY WERE ALONE TODAY UNDER THE LUMPY SLURRY OF A cloudy sky. It was a foul morning. Riding in silence, they traversed the park and climbed to the top of a hill, letting the wind tug at their clothes and their hair.

"Will Lady Fairchild mind?" Sophy asked.

"She might. Think you can bring her round?"

"I'll try. I didn't want to miss our ride. I enjoy them."

He smiled. "So do I. We should have ridden together more often."

Sophy looked at him.

"I mean it," he said. "You're good company."

"Now, maybe," she conceded. "But I expect I'd have bored you at ten."

"No, I have never thought you boring," he said. He waited, but she said nothing, so he turned his horse back down the hill.

Sophy nudged Hirondelle after him. "What did you think?" she asked. He stopped his horse and turned around.

"It's hard to say," he said at last. "For years I had wondered about you, what you were like. Then, to find you so like myself . . . I thought Georgiana was going to choke . . . And you so obviously missed your mother."

Sophy tucked back a strand of hair that whipped across her face. "Do you? Ever miss her?" she asked.

He looked down. "I did. Very much." Gathering his reins in one hand, he straightened the cuffs of his gloves. "I loved her, you know. I would have kept the two of you close by, but that was not what she wanted. I suppose it became too sordid for her, when she found she was with child." He looked up and stopped. She swallowed, afraid of what he might see in her face.

"It was not meant to be," he said. "It was a dream, impossible to keep. It surprised me, you know, that she never married. She was so beautiful." He smiled. "Intelligent too, with a strong will."

"And yet you are surprised?" Sophy said. "I think you have your answer right there."

"Perhaps. What I meant was that I hope she was not lonely."

"How could she be?" Sophy asked, with a shade of belligerence. "You just said I was good company."

"So I did."

They rode in silence. "Do you hate me for it?" he asked.

"Not anymore," she said. Her honesty surprised her and made her cheeks grow warm.

His eyes flashed to her face. "You still miss her."

"Always." Sophy managed a weak smile. Containing her emotions was never this hard when she talked of her mother with Jasper.

Lord Fairchild sighed, turning his eyes away from her to the wet grass before them. "Yes. I'm afraid she is impossible to forget."

They did not speak again until they reached the house. "Don't get me in trouble," he said. "You promised, remember?"

She gave a tiny smile, as tenuous as their new confidence. "Of course."

CHAPTER 19
MEDICINE

Tom found a letter for his mother on the breakfast table. It was from Lord Fairchild. It had gone first to Chippenstone and been forwarded to London, where it arrived late, resting beside his mother's plate. "Read it Tom," she said, passing it eagerly across the table.

He set down his newspaper reluctantly. He had a good idea what the letter would say and knew his mother would be disappointed. He hadn't mentioned sighting Sophy in the park, or being ignored by her brother. He hadn't gone back since. Seeing her hadn't cured him. Besides, he had plenty of work to do and couldn't spend his days idling around the park.

The letter was brief. "Lord Fairchild sends his sincere thanks . . . and hopes to present them again, in person, once he has returned from town." Tom set down the heavy gilt-edged paper and returned to his attention to the Times, avoiding his mother's eyes.

At least now she would stop expecting Miss Rushford to appear at the front door. Skipping past the advertisements, Tom turned to the second page for the foreign news.

His mother gave up on her kippers and set her silverware down with a clang. "What I can't understand—"

"There's nothing to understand, mother."

She only blinked at him.

"Don't look like that. This is exactly what I knew would happen."

"But if you tried—"

"I'm not going to, mother." Tom rose and tucked his newspaper under his arm. "I should be getting along if you don't want me staying at the offices until late."

"But Tom—" she broke off as he bent low to kiss her cheek.

"See you for supper," he said.

It was always busy in the city, the hum of commerce never ceasing. He worked with his door open to the roomful of busy, striving clerks, but again the noise and the bustle could not wholly distract him. His conscience pricked him for being short with his mother and he ended up coming home early for supper. His mother kissed him and tidied his hair, but didn't mention Miss Rushford.

She did mention both of them returning to Chippenstone. He flatly refused. Chippenstone was not the place to find himself again, not with her haunting the rooms.

"If I go anywhere, it should be overseas," he said. "You can't imagine the difficulties I'm having."

His mother blanched. She had stalwartly waved him off before, but that had been when his father was still alive.

"I dare say Stokes can manage it. I'll send him," Tom said, relenting. A sea cure wasn't an option this time.

Instead, he found refuge in the company of his old shipmates. They were good fellows who knew where to go when a man was spoiling for a fight. His evenings with them at riverfront taverns left him with grazed knuckles, a cut lip—and the satisfaction of giving better than he got. When he was squaring up against another man, Tom had no questions about his own worth.

Unfortunately, his cut lip was impossible to hide. His mother accepted his explanation of a brief turn up, hardly worth talking about, with a smooth countenance, but the glove she was knitting ended up with a thumb so twisted there wasn't a person alive who could wear it. The next evening she asked him to take her to the theatre and two evenings after that, she arranged a dinner party—no easy task with her limited acquaintance. Her motives were plain. If he could not have Miss Rushford, she would find him someone else before he did any more damage to his self or his soul. She had never liked boxing. Tom tried to be civil. He would have tried to like the young ladies she trotted out for him too, if they weren't too tall, too shy, and too boring.

"What was wrong with Miss Spencer?" his mother asked, after a rather dreadful evening.

Tom sighed. His sullenness hadn't helped matters. "I'm not fit for company these days." Better if Miss Rushford had been blessed with the sense of a newborn babe and stayed off that cursed horse.

"When will you be?"

"Tomorrow," he promised. "What would you like to do? I could take you to the show at Astley's, we haven't done that yet."

"I'd like that. Will you still have your good manners on Friday?"

"Why?"

She pulled a square of folded paper from her sleeve. "It's from Jeremiah and Lottie Fulham."

"They're still in London?" It had been years since Tom had left England to learn business under Jeremiah Fulham's eye. They hadn't been together long before Tom was pressed into the navy, but Jeremiah had fought hard for Tom's release. His father had always counted him as a friend. They had been neighbors, as well as partners, when Tom had been a child in London. After Tom left the Navy, Jeremiah retired. There had been an occasional exchange of letters, but that had stopped when his father died.

"This is a dinner invitation," he said.

His mother cleared her throat. "I'd like to go, but we won't if you can't—"

He forestalled her with a raised hand. "I can be civil for Jeremiah and Lottie. It will be good to see them again."

"They have their daughter Anna with them. She's been a widow these two years. There will be some other young people. Lottie suggested that after supper the young folk might go to a masquerade."

"In Covent Garden?" Covent Garden masquerades were not for people of character, but Tom knew some people liked to drop in for a lark. Watching for an hour or two was harmless.

"Do you remember Anna?" she asked.

He did. She had employed her two year advantage well when they were small, giving him more than a few bruising pinches. "Mother, if you've raised expectations—"

"All I've done is accept their invitation. I know how you feel about meddling, but you can't go on as you are." She stopped folding pleats into her skirts and smoothed out the burgundy silk with her fingers, remembering her maid's admonitions too late.

Tom sighed. He knew what was coming. But perhaps his mother's solution was best. It was time he acted like a man and not a sulky boy.

"You've always insisted you want to marry your own kind. I understand that. But when will it be? I was old when you were born, Tom. I should like to see you married."

He softened, smiling gently. "All right. I agree to dinner, but I must at least see Anna before you make any more plans."

CHAPTER 20
A DREADFUL SQUEEZE

They always called it Henrietta's ball, which it technically was, since Henrietta and Percy were hosting it at their townhouse on Curzon Street. But since the event was orchestrated for one purpose only—Sophy's come out—calling it Henrietta's ball was a trifle disingenuous. It wasn't as if Henrietta had made any of the decisions. Lady Fairchild had written the guest list, chosen the floral decorations and selected the music. When Henrietta irritably demanded why her mother didn't just host Sophy's debut herself, Lady Fairchild had silenced her with a pointed look.

It was exhausting, Sophy thought, treading this high wire—in the family, but not. Even after she married, there would always be awkwardness and uncertainty.

This ball was grander than anything she had attended before. Nearly every moment of the evening was planned, from the precise moment she was to appear on her father's arm to her first two dance partners. Sophy felt like a clockwork figure, waiting for the hour to strike. She was to enter with Lord Fairchild after the first hour, but before Henrietta and Percy stopped receiving. It was too much, of course, for Sophy to stand in the receiving line beside Henrietta. "Looks like we're trying too hard, dear, and we don't need to," Lady Fairchild said. "You've made such a marvelous start."

Sophy didn't feel marvelous, waiting alone in the library and listening to the party beyond the door. Her courage waned with each passing minute and she still had a quarter of an hour to wait. Sitting would crease her dress, so she walked to the window, parting the curtain with one finger. Because of the branch of candles on the desk behind her, she could see nothing but her own reflection in the windowpane. Letting the curtain fall, she turned back to face the room.

She had no reason to be nervous. This wasn't so different from the other balls.

Her eyes fell on the whisky decanter resting on Percy's desk. Liquid courage, her father called it. She could use some of that. Glancing at the door, she plucked out the stopper and righted one of the tumblers sitting upside down on the tray. The crystal decanter was heavier than she expected. Instead of pouring out a thimbleful, a glug of the golden liquid splashed into the tumbler, swirling around the sides of the glass. She took a long gulp. Halfway through her second swallow, she realized her mistake. It had to be poison. Eyes watering, Sophy rocked back against the desk, forcing empty swallows to rid herself of the stinging vapors curling in the back of her throat and burning through her nose. There was still a finger width of whisky at the bottom of the glass. Impossible to drink it. Could she open the window?

"Whisky isn't a lady's drink," said her father. Sophy jumped, spinning to face the connecting door. "How much have you had?" he asked.

She showed him with her narrowed fingers, unable to speak.

"You ate earlier, right?"

She nodded.

"Not irreparable, then," he said. "Have a biscuit." He pulled a tin out from the desk drawer.

Sophy took a bite, sprinkling crumbs across the blotter.

"Nervous?" he asked.

"Like I'm awaiting the Final Judgement," she said.

He laughed. "Good thing it's you then, and not me." He took the glass from her hand and swallowed the rest, savoring it with a distant smile. "Too good to waste."

He flicked a stray crumb from the corner of her mouth. "You should put on your gloves. It's time."

She tugged them on, grateful they would conceal her damp palms. "Anything amiss?" She turned in a slow circle.

"Nothing," he said, and offered his arm.

Sophy told her shoulders to relax and her neck to lengthen as they traversed the dim corridor and stepped into the brilliantly lit ballroom. It was hard not to stare. She had seen the masses of flowers and the glowing chandeliers before retreating to her hideaway. The magnificence of the room now, filled with guests dressed in the first style of elegance, stunned her. It couldn't be real. It seemed much more likely that the whole scene had been spun out of sugar, ready to crumble at a touch or melt with a splash of water.

They entered the room as the music fell silent, stepping into the open space of the clearing dance floor. Through the parting crowd, Sophy saw Lady Fairchild presiding on the far side of the room, waiting for her to be delivered to her side. Everything was precisely calibrated; she stood beside Lady Fairchild for only a moment before Jasper stepped forward.

"My dance, I think, Sophy?"

Obediently, she transferred her hand from Lord Fairchild's arm to Jasper's so they could promenade around the room before the next set.

"What did your mother do to you?" she asked. "Are you a changeling? You don't even look bored."

Jasper laughed. "She swore she'd leave me alone for a sennight if I did as I was told."

Sophy acknowledged a benign smile from one of Lady Fairchild's friends with a nod, turning again to watch Jasper. "You've stopped riding with us in the mornings. Are your nights so busy?" she asked.

"I haven't wanted to intrude," he said, with his best slippery charm. "Your rapprochement with the pater is so touching."

Sophy looked at him, trying to decide how much he was teasing her. "It's certainly surprising." Lowering her voice, she added, "I asked him about my mother."

Jasper halted, pausing to remove an invisible fleck from the sleeve of his jacket. "Oh? What did he say?" His voice was as diffident as ever, but Sophy felt uneasy.

"It wasn't so much what he said, just that he understood how I still miss her."

"Excellent," Jasper smiled. "Come, it's time to take our places."

He led her into the set, ending the conversation and leaving Sophy trying to unravel the subtext. It was a country dance, a real concession for Jasper, who danced about as regularly as a lunar eclipse. He was surprisingly adept, skipping through the figures without a single misstep, with no signs of shortened breath. Sophy felt her own flush, but she colored at everything. The music stopped; they exchanged courtesies and he steered her to one of the windows to stand in the cooler air.

"Impeccable!" he said.

"Why, thank you," Sophy said, falsely coy.

"I was talking about me. I think I've acquitted myself well enough for this year."

Sophy hid her laugh behind her fan, relieved they were being their usual selves once more. "You would leave me standing by the dowagers with the Misses Matcham?"

"I shall be happy to oblige you if you have any free dances, but I have every expectation of not being needed. Come, she's expecting us. You know that look."

"Better than you. I see it more often."

It was easy to feel confident, floating on Jasper's breeze. If she could keep him with her all evening, she would have no qualms. But Mr. Beaumaris was in position at Lady Fairchild's elbow, waiting for her. Steeling herself for the coming encounter, Sophy reminded herself there was no reason not to treat him exactly the same as Jasper.

"Are you off, now that your duty is done?" Sophy asked.

Jasper gave her a wounded look. "No. I'll stay at least another half-hour, though I risk acquiring a permanent twitch from so much time under my good mother's eye."

"No girl could ask for a better brother," Sophy mocked.

"So long as you know it."

When they reached Lady Fairchild, Jasper bestowed a kiss onto Sophy's hand and greeted his mother with a smile that was more a baring of teeth. "Lovely to see you, Madam," he said, and turned away.

"Good evening, Alistair," Sophy said, taking his arm and returning to the dance floor. At this rate, she would pass the entire evening without speaking to Lady Fairchild, her chaperone. "What did Lady Fairchild promise you in exchange for your kind attention to me?"

"Two bottles of her husband's best smuggled brandy and a promise to wear a crimson turban to Mrs. Goring's Venetian breakfast."

Sophy made a face. "She'd never in her life attend any party of Mrs. Goring's, much less in a turban. Stop bamming me."

"Never. By the by, does Lady Fairchild know you use that term?"

"Of course not." Sophy rolled her eyes. "So are you going to tell me, or not?" She would be more easy with him once they had laid their cards on the table. If only he wasn't capable of that sly look that made her feel so wobbly.

"I think not. Surely the pleasure of your company is motivation enough."

"Don't make fun of me," she said, refusing to return his smile. "When's the last time you danced with a girl fresh out of the school room?"

"Quite possibly never," he said. "Shall we?" And he took her hand, leading her into the forming set.

She didn't know where to look. If she met his eyes, she blushed, and if she looked away, Lady Fairchild would think she was being rude. Maybe she would gradually become accustomed to him, like one did to a hot bath, inch by inch. Just then Alistair smiled and quirked his eyebrow at her, as if he knew the direction of her thoughts. Sophy dropped her eyelids immediately, but her cheeks betrayed her with a scorching flush. If she could just observe him from a distance instead of having to look at him and take his hands all the time, it would be so much easier. Pinning on a bright smile, she swept out every thought except for the steps. They were dancing the cotillion and a misstep would be a disaster.

Mr. Beaumaris was not as tall as he looked, she realized, passing by him as she wove through the dancers. Oh, he was not short, but his posture and bearing made him seem larger than he really was. Not like Tom Bagshot, who slouched in his chair and surprised one with his towering height once he unfolded himself.

The dance ended. With exactly the correct amount of polite nothings, Alistair returned Sophy to Lady Fairchild's side, just in time for her to accept an invitation to dance from Mr. Beadle, one of the widowers on Lady Fairchild's approved list.

Unfortunately, Mr. Beadle's decision to wear side whiskers only exaggerated the egg-like aspects of his round head. As he bounced down the line of dancers, Sophy could think of nothing but Humpty Dumpty. She danced the next set of country dances with Jasper's friend Mr. DeClerc and remembered not to accidentally call him Boz. She stood out the next dance, sipping a glass of lemonade in the crowd of ladies gathered around Lady Fairchild, who occupied the best vantage point in the room.

The Matcham girls, who lived not far from Cordell, exchanged polite greetings with Sophy. Never exactly friends, they were decidedly cooler in town. Eager to escape a silence that was growing uncomfortable, Sophy turned away, expecting to see Lady Fairchild but finding Miss Lowell instead.

"Good evening, Miss Prescott," she smiled.

She must be hunting Jasper. There was no other reason for Miss Lowell to seek her out again to ply her with impertinent questions.

"Do you still enjoy London, Miss Prescott, or has it begun to pall?" She spoke with the faint contempt that young ladies in their second season reserved for yearlings like herself.

"Of course I do, very much," Sophy said. She would not pretend to be fashionable this time. It had only given Miss Lowell more amusement before. "I have been to the Opera since we spoke last and never seen a grander spectacle."

"One's first visit is quite astonishing." Miss Lowell closed her fan and rested it on her lips. "What a shame you were never brought to London before. You told me that you spent your youth at Cordell, but I've forgotten where you spent your childhood."

Sophy's eyes narrowed. "In Herefordshire, with my mother."

"And is your mother from that county?"

"No. She went to Herefordshire solely on my account. Before that, she lived at Cordell. She was governess there. Is there anything else you wish to know?"

Thrown off pace by Sophy's blunt rejoinder, Miss Lowell regained her stride. "Is there anything else interesting about you?"

"Not especially," Sophy said. "Mine isn't a terribly interesting story. Most people know exactly where I spring from, but they have the good manners not to inquire. Of course, I need have no secrets from a particular friend like you."

Sophy opened her fan and turned her eyes towards the dance

floor in time to see Alistair walking towards them. Passing Miss Lowell with a bow, he came to Sophy's side. She couldn't help exulting, just a little. Miss Lowell might be determined to wed a title, but she was surely as susceptible to Alistair's good looks as anyone else.

"Dear coz."

Sophy did not normally like Alistair's lying endearments, but the chagrined look in Miss Lowell's eyes made her gladly accept this one.

"Back again?" she asked.

"I've let the other gentlemen have a turn." Laughing would ruin the game, Sophy knew, but she was sorely tempted. How ridiculous he was.

Miss Lowell looked like she was ready to swallow her tongue. She was not used to being ignored. Sophy decided it was an experience which would greatly improve her character.

"Will you dance?" Alistair asked.

Sophy declined without looking at Lady Fairchild. She was not allowed to waltz.

"May Sophy take a turn around the room with me then?" He spoke to Lady Fairchild this time, not her.

"Dear boy, you needn't ask," Lady Fairchild told him, closing her fan and tapping it against her shoulder.

He smiled and held out his hand. "Come, Sophy."

"My," she said, once they were out of earshot. "What will you order me to do next?"

"Dance this waltz with me."

"Not on your life," she laughed. "Lady Fairchild would skin me alive." His eyebrows flew upward, so she added, "Even though I'm well below the notice of the patronesses of Almack's, she won't have me looking fast, waltzing without their permission. So I won't be doing any waltzing, ever."

"Shame," Alistair said. "You'd make a delightful armful."

She couldn't hide her exasperated look. She was grateful, but wished he knew when to stop.

"Is it odious to you, walking about a ballroom with me?" he asked.

"Not at all," Sophy said. "Being seen on your arm does me great credit. You do tend to draw eyes."

"Flattery, Sophy?"

She made a bald reply. "Yes."

"I will pay you a compliment in return," he laughed. "Contrary to your suspicion—don't deny it, I can read it on your face—I am not paying court to you at my Aunt's behest. You are most charming, tonight more than ever."

Robbed of speech, Sophy looked away, feeling blood rush into her cheeks. No one was close enough to hear. They had moved out of the crowd to the doors opening onto the terrace and the dark garden beyond. Sophy stopped dead. "It's more than my life's worth to leave this room," she said.

"I so admire your frankness," Alistair said. "You don't know how refreshing it is. Do you think I'm a fool? We shan't be missed. My aunt trusts me."

"Should she?" Sophy faltered, as he whisked her outside. The air was cool after the heat of the ballroom, causing goosebumps to rise on her arms. Her heart thumped like she'd just finished one of the jauntier dances.

Alistair laughed. "I like you, Sophy." Drawing her nearer, he lowered his voice. "I like you very much."

It wasn't fair, Sophy thought. She was no match for him. Surely he was about to pinch her on the arm and laugh at her for believing him.

"Are you going to let me kiss you?" he asked.

She could not think.

"Afraid?" he suggested, when she made no reply.

"Of course not," Sophy snapped. Resolutely shutting her eyes, she rose on tiptoe, colliding their lips with bruising force. He retreated a step, laughing and rubbing his lip with his index finger.

"You don't shy away from fences, do you?"

She hoped his lip hurt like blazes. "Don't mock me," she said, turning away to hide her face. The lights and music of the ballroom beckoned her and she moved to flee.

"Wait." Alistair caught her arm. "You misunderstand—" but she didn't stay to hear. Shaking free, she slipped past the French doors and wove through the crowd, out of the ballroom and up the stairs to the family rooms.

She shut herself in a dark room, clenching and unclenching her hands, willing the blood to drain from her face before she had to rejoin Lady Fairchild in the ballroom.

CHAPTER 21
MISBEHAVING

Sophy was still churning with fury and embarrassment the
next morning. She had managed to avoid Alistair the rest
of the evening, ignoring his attempts to catch her eye. By
pretending to fall asleep in the carriage, Sophy had delayed the
inevitable post-mortem with Lady Fairchild, but she would
certainly want to discuss the ball today. Sophy could not speak of
what had happened to anyone, least of all Lady Fairchild. What
would she say if she learned her own nephew had taken her
outside and kind of—almost—kissed her?

He wouldn't have tried such a thing with a respectable female,
she thought angrily. Then reason took hold of her. Of course he
would. He had probably done the same thing with scores of
ladies. Next time, she would introduce his face to her fist.

Next time? What a joke! She'd been so clumsy, he'd never want
to repeat that experience. Which was all to the good, because she
certainly had no intentions of allowing him to ever—*ever*—be
alone with her again.

Summoning a surly Betty, Sophy stalked to Curzon Street
before Lady Fairchild awoke, arriving unconscionably early to call
on Henrietta. Fortunately, Henrietta had no questions. She was

full of her own schemes. Sophy knew Lady Fairchild would not approve of a Covent Garden masquerade, but Henrietta was not so particular.

"As long as we have suitable escorts there will be nothing untoward," she assured Sophy. "And we will be masked, so you needn't worry that anyone will find you out."

It was tempting. Lord and Lady Fairchild were attending a reception at Carlton House this evening, and there of course, they could not bring Sophy.

"It will be easy," Henrietta said. "Tell her you will be here, having dinner with me."

"I don't have a costume."

"Pfftt." Henrietta dismissed this objection. "I have masks and dominos already. Take a look." Henrietta passed Sophy a bandbox containing two masks buried under an assortment of feathers and scraps of ribbon. The long cloaks she spread out on the bed for inspection.

"I'll take the pink," Henrietta said, fingering the thin silk. "Mama always says it is my best color. You can wear the other."

It was a brilliant turquoise blue. Sophy imagined herself whirling through the dances, wonderfully anonymous under her mask. "Percy agrees?"

"Haven't I said so? I'll invite Jasper. He owes me something, after leaving my party early last night."

"All right," Sophy said. With a bounce of excitement, Henrietta threw her arms around Sophy, knocking the bandbox off the bed and waking her sleeping infant. Scooping him from the cradle, she set him on the bed and she and Sophy set to work soothing him, dangling ribbons and bits of finery for him to snatch and drool over.

"You will have a famous time," Henrietta promised. "Wait and see."

. . .

SOPHY RETURNED HOME IN THE AFTERNOON TO CHANGE HER clothes for evening dress, feeding Lady Fairchild a story about a dinner party with Percy and Henrietta. But when she arrived for the masquerade at their house, Sophy was greeted with an unpleasant surprise. Jasper was not there.

"He wouldn't come," Henrietta said, interpreting Sophy's horrified look as one of surprise. "So I recruited Alistair instead."

"Cousin Sophy," Alistair said, urbane as ever. "I'm happy to be of service."

Constructing a reply was impossible. She glared at him instead. "Is Jasper unwell?" she asked, turning back to Henrietta.

"He's sulking over something, the beast," said Henrietta. "It will pass sooner if we ignore him. Don't you think, Percy?"

"You know I don't interfere between you and your brother," Percy said. "Take Sophy upstairs and get ready so we can be off. Did you bring a mask, Beaumaris?"

Henrietta whisked Sophy upstairs. "Isn't it fortunate that Alistair could come? All the ladies will be ready to scratch your eyes out."

Sophy's answering laugh was weak, but Henrietta was too busy to notice, directing her maid to bring a pair of diamond drops for Sophy's ears.

"They're pretty," Sophy said, turning her head before the mirror so the jewels could wink at her.

"Aren't they?" Henrietta allowed her maid to affix her mask and rearrange her curls. The same service was performed for Sophy and then they were both put into their dominos and the strings tied. It was a good disguise, Sophy concluded, with the hood drawn over her hair. She felt bolder under her gold spangled mask, a fortunate circumstance with Alistair in the party. She would do her best to ignore him.

"Perfect!" Henrietta said. "No one will be able to guess who we are. Do you like my pink?" Henrietta twirled, sending her cloak spinning out, revealing the silver net overdress of her gown.

Her mask had paste brilliants in the eye corners to match. It was impossible not to catch some of her enthusiasm.

"You look like you're out to wound hearts," Sophy teased, and Henrietta burst into laughter.

"Maybe just one," she said. Taking Sophy's arm, she led her back down the stairs. "Well? Would you know us?" Henrietta asked, pausing halfway down.

"Yes. You forget your dimple," said Percy. "But I believe I'm more familiar with your features than most."

Henrietta cast Sophy a despairing glance. "Fish for compliments, and what do I get? Mere fingerlings. You'll have to do better, my Lord, if you are to keep me at your side this evening." In grand state, she descended the stairs and attached herself to her husband's arm. Sophy followed more slowly, studying the pattern of the brocade covered walls.

"Still angry?" Alistair whispered, but Sophy pretended not to hear. It was easy enough, in the noisy street. Link boys dodged with frightening speed between the carriages rumbling along the cobbles. Alistair helped her into the carriage, taking the seat beside her despite her frosty glance. No one seemed to notice. The mask had some disadvantages, she realized, but it would make it much harder for him, should he try again to kiss her. She twitched her skirts away from Alistair's well turned legs, annoyed at having to sit beside him. It was a cousin's privilege, but she and Alistair were not related, however convenient it might be for some people to think so.

Arriving at the theatre, Sophy hardly noticed the masquerade. She was busy plotting and avoiding Alistair's eye.

Percy had rented a box on the lowest tier where they could eat their supper and watch the spectacle. Henrietta was already darting avid looks through the crowd. "Is that Lady Saxby? No, it couldn't be. Even she wouldn't damp her skirts like that." Percy nudged Henrietta, throwing a significant glance in Sophy's direction.

As Alistair settled into the chair beside her—positioned far too close for her liking—Sophy turned away from the masquerade to face Percy. "Lord Fairchild was telling me about the debate in parliament on Lord Elgin's removal of the Greek marbles. What is your opinion, my lord?"

Henrietta's head whipped around so she could stare incredulously at Sophy.

"Rather a thorny issue," Percy said, shaking his head. "It's hard to see it as anything but thievery, and yet the local Greeks did not scruple to destroy the stones for lime . . ."

Furious now, Henrietta leaned over to give Sophy a sharp pinch. She was unrepentant. Letting Alistair speculate with Henrietta on the identities of the revelers, she fed Percy questions all through supper. She did not brave a glance in Alistair's direction until dessert. His eyes were resting on her boldly and he wore a smile more amused than deterred. He raised his glass in a silent toast and Sophy returned her eyes to her plate.

When the waiters, dressed like saracens with red turbans and blackened faces, cleared away the plates, Henrietta rose from her chair. "I think it's time we enjoyed ourselves," she said with an accusing glare at Sophy. Percy, still mourning the marbles' unfortunate state of preservation, missed his cue.

"Will you dance, Sophy?" Alistair asked, rising from his chair.

"I'm afraid something's gotten inside my slipper. Do go ahead with Henrietta while I try to wiggle it out," said Sophy.

Henrietta was radiating impatience; he agreed with a smirk. "When you are ready then, Sophy. There will be dancing for hours yet."

Henrietta and Alistair exited the box, appearing moments later on the stage. Sophy watched them find a place in the set, noticing the masquerade at last. The backdrop behind the dancers was painted with a domed palace of crimson and yellow, surrounded by crazily leaning palm trees. Next to the dancers, this exotic scene paled to insignificance. They were garbed in domino cloaks of every hue and gargoyle-featured masks with long curving noses or court dresses of the previous century with face patches and powdered hair. She had never seen a real man in doublet and hose, looking as if he'd stepped out of a portrait frame. A lady in a dress with panniers too wide to pass through a door was somehow dancing the quadrille. How long had she had to practice walking in a frame that size? There was a woman in Roman costume dancing with a harlequin and a man in a Greek tunic with a sheepskin belted over his shoulders. Had he realized that dressing as Paris would be so uncomfortably hot?

"Is that lemonade?" Sophy asked, tilting her head in the direction of a refreshment table. "May I have some?"

"That is punch, which I believe you'd be better without," Percy said. "I'll have the waiter bring you some ratafia, if you would like."

"No, I only fancied lemonade," Sophy said quickly. A beverage was only helpful if it removed Percy from her side long enough for her to slip away. She might be able to hide herself in the corridor or behind the towering potted palms that were gathered in islands around the edges of the pit, conveniently screening some of the boxes. Alistair would come for her soon if she didn't do something. She pinched her lips together in frustration.

"Would you care to dance?" Percy asked. Sophy nodded and they made their way to the stage, joining the other latecomers at the end of the set.

Marking time on the crowded floor, Sophy prepared to seize her chance. When the music ended and the dancers' ordered pattern changed to a mill of confusion, she slipped out of Percy's grasp.

"Sophy?"

He was turning after her, but there were advantages to being small. Dodging behind a corpulent monk, she left the stage and plunged into the pit, where masqueraders sallied to and fro. Some of them were hunting; others were trying to be caught. A corsair raised his quizzing glass at her, startling her with his magnified, goggling eye. Sophy retreated, edging between an Apollo and a Pompadour. Her cloak caught on the lady's stiff lace, tugging back her hood. Sophy kept walking, ignoring the lady's angry cry. She would be safe once she reached her goal.

She was nearing the boxes. A man in a green mask called after her as she passed, but she did not slow her steps. Their own box was empty, of course. She would be able to watch it from her hiding place. The next two boxes she merely glanced at, but as she passed the last, she froze. Tom Bagshot was there. He wore no costume, just a grey domino over his evening clothes and a silver mask pushed onto his forehead. Alerted by her sudden stop, he turned his head.

Alistair was forgotten. The shifting crowd, the grand display; they were gone too. There was only Tom, with a female at his elbow, a dark haired beauty who had to be wearing paint. Nobody had lips as red as that. She laughed, tilting her head confidingly at Tom. A moment late, Tom responded, turning away from Sophy, his mouth shaping itself into a familiar smile.

Sophy was curiously angry. Hadn't that smile belonged to her? She was the one supposed to be making him laugh, sitting in the chair beside him. She took two strides before reason took hold of her. Halting, she closed her hands round the folds of her domino in tight fists.

What was she thinking, staring at him like a lack witted fool? The female beside him saw her, her scarlet mouth curling into a smile of bemusement and scorn. Slowly, Tom followed her eyes back to Sophy. His eyes held hers. Sophy felt herself tremble, cold with despair. Breaking free, she dove into the crowd, weaving her way to the stand of potted palms she had marked. The people closest to her would see her slip behind them, but would they care? It didn't matter. She had to be alone, had to get hold of herself. Hoping fervently, she brushed through the branches and vanished.

CHAPTER 22
GAMES OF CHANCE

H e couldn't imagine why, but Sophy was here and she was alone. Without stopping to consider how this folly had come about, Tom embarked on his own.

"Forgive me. I need to . . ." What? There was nothing he could say, and he was already swinging over the front of the box, plunging into the crowd. All his reasons for avoiding Sophy disappeared, leaving only the question—why not? If he wanted to see her, why shouldn't he? Wandering alone at a masquerade, there was no reason any man could not, he realized with a frown.

She moved quickly. In the press of people, Tom soon lost sight of her bright blue cloak and her flaming hair. The colors hardly stood out in this vivid jungle. He elbowed his way past yet another Turk. A woman dressed as an angel started toward him and then changed her mind.

Where was she? She couldn't have disappeared. There were no doors here into the corridors. Tom moved to the edge of the pit to survey the crowd. He saw an Egyptian princess and a shepherdess, but no slight figure swathed in blue. A Mephistopheles was pursuing a laughing Daphne—despite the leaves woven around her arms he didn't think she would resist as hard as she ought. Mephistopheles' advances seemed quite welcome. No damsels turning into trees tonight . . . Tom turned and looked at the palms behind him. There were three of them, in giant brass urns. He moved closer, and thought he saw movement in the shadows behind them.

He'd found her. But was she alone? Tom thinned his mouth into a hard line, ignoring his sudden qualms. Sidling into the shadow of the nearest plant, he let his eyes wander the crowd. He must wait for the right moment, lest he draw unwelcome attention. Edging under the leaves, he spied a slice of blue through the foliage. Blue, and nothing else. He smiled and began to hum to himself. *Here we go round the mulberry bush* . . .

One last look at the pit. Mephistopheles was the only one who saw him; over Daphne's shoulder he gave Tom a slow wink.

Tom stepped further in, keeping his cloak held tight. "Sophy!" he whispered.

She was hunched down, her head level with the top of the nearest urn, her fingers gripping the edge. Her hood had fallen back and her mask was hanging by its strings, so he was struck by the full force of her furious glare.

"What?" he asked, momentarily baffled.

"What are you doing here?" she asked.

Was she expecting someone else? Impossible. "I came to ask you the same question."

"I'm here with Lord and Lady Arundel. I won't ask after your party. A lady doesn't notice bits of muslin," she said nastily. Tom nearly choked.

"Bits of . . ." A laugh escaped him. "I'm afraid you're mistaken, Sophy. The lady you take for—I suppose you think her my fancy piece?" Sophy didn't answer, so he kept going, his face cracking into a wide grin. "That's Anna Morris, the daughter of a friend of my late father."

Sophy was red as a lobster, but she kept her dignity. "And you walked away from her without a word?"

Tom sucked in a breath through his teeth. He had. There were others in the box; Anna was not alone, but he had treated her exactly as a man might treat a paid companion, dropping her on sight of a new quarry.

"Merciful Lord," Tom breathed. Anna was going to kill him.

"She isn't then?" Sophy asked, interested anew. "She shouldn't be so obvious with her paint. It sends entirely the wrong message."

"Is that what your mother tells you? I thought she had a rather beautiful mouth."

Sophy snorted. "Yes, I saw you hanging on her lips. "

"Well, I was supposed to be," Tom conceded. "And I was, until you gave me the start of my life. What are you doing here alone?" His question came out sharper than he intended. Sophy licked her lips.

"Hiding," she muttered.

"From who?"

"The cousin, Alistair." She cocked her head towards the ball-room, invisible through their leafy screen.

Tom lowered his voice. "Why do you need to hide, Sophy?"

She raised one shoulder in a delicate shrug, sending velvet shadows into the hollows of her collarbones. "I can't explain."

"Has he tried to take liberties?" Tom scowled.

Sophy's face crumpled into a grin. "Hah! You look as fierce as my father."

"Should I be flattered?"

"No." It made no sense that she should be restored to sunny smiles. He wanted to shake her. He repeated his question.

"Did he insult you?"

"Yes, I suppose so." She dropped her eyes. "It was more of an embarrassment than anything else. Every time I look at him I want to run away."

"Your father? Your brother? They did nothing?" The brother was an ineffectual idiot, but surely her father—

"I didn't tell them."

"Why not?"

She wouldn't meet his eyes. "It was nothing really. Please let's not speak of it. Won't you sit down?" She asked as if she were at home in her parents' drawing room, then spoiled the effect by grinning at him.

Already bent over double, it was some relief to settle beside her on the ground. Shielding her dress with her cloak, she slid back a few inches so she could lean against the wall, wrapping her arms around her drawn up knees. Tom copied her, unable to resist her folly. There would be all kinds of trouble if they were found here, never mind that they were hiding like a pair of truant children.

"Did you miss me?" she asked.

"Not at all," he lied. "But it's good to see you."

"Has your mother vanquished her maid yet? And did she finish her book?"

"We lost interest in the story, and I'm afraid it's the other way round with my mother and her maid." He swallowed, saying far too diffidently, "You could call on her, you know."

She stiffened, her neck muscles cording tight. "I can't. My family—"

He scowled. "Would you speak to me at all, if we weren't hiding behind a plant?"

"Of course I would! Lady Fairchild isn't here." Snapping off the tip off a hanging leaf, she shredded it between her fingers.

"Then why did you run from me?"

"I was running already, remember? It is more complicated than you know. Perhaps if I hadn't been so foolish, if my—my family understood—"

"Hasn't anyone told you how injurious honesty can be?"

"Oh, I know," she sighed.

"You must tell me about London," he said, trying to lighten

the cloud that had settled between them. "Looking at you, I would say it suits you very well."

Pink crept into her cheeks. "You think so? And how does it suit you?"

"I live here, remember? I'd say we suit well enough, the city and I."

"Your evening? Has it been enjoyable?"

Tom passed a hand over his forehead. "Not really. I came from a dinner where we were plied with food until I felt like I'd swallowed a nine pounder—cannon shot, you know."

She nodded.

"Then we came here, and I had to wear a stupid mask that itches my forehead abominably, and now I've offended Anna. I'm tempted to take the coward's way out and just go home."

"If only we could!" She froze as soon as the words left her mouth, realizing what she had not meant to say. "I mean . . . What I meant . . . Of course we could not." They were leaning close, like any two conspirators, close enough that he could easily kiss her. There were palm fronds brushing her hair. If he pushed them away and let his own fingers do the brushing, would she permit it or push him away? Or would she turn up her face and offer him her soft, pink mouth? Lord above, but it drew his eyes.

"No, we couldn't," he said. "We ought not to be here either."

She nodded, moistening her lips.

"I should leave first," he said, quickly. "Let you have your sanctuary. Maybe if I return with refreshments, Anna won't be too hard on me." Hah! She was likely to spit him through.

"I'm glad you found me," she said, subdued.

Tom was not a gambler, but he knew when it was time to discard caution and throw the dice. "Will you dance with me? It's a masquerade. You can dance with anyone you like."

"I can. So long as we put our masks on."

"Is that yes?"

She nodded, strangely solemn.

EVERYTHING WAS EASY WITH TOM, AND THERE LAY THE danger. She could never let him find out who she really was.

If only she'd spoken the truth from the first. She wouldn't have needed to run from him then. Speaking to him at all was incredibly foolish, but something about him always drove her to new heights of stupidity: hiding in the shadows like a pair of secret lovers and now agreeing to dance with him. The merest slip of the tongue would destroy her reputation forever.

And yet it felt wonderful, tripping beside him onto the dance floor. She felt as light as a balloon, even without any of the infamous punch. The candlelight struck glints of gold in Tom's light brown hair. In his evening clothes, he seemed to move with unusual grace. And he had abandoned that woman—the one she had hated on sight—only to be with her! It ought to be sung out loud.

Just not by her. She was a deplorable singer. For the first time, she wished she were not.

"Why are you smiling?" he whispered.

"Because you are going to have to go back to Miss Morris—"

"Mrs. Morris," he interrupted. "She's a widow."

Momentarily disconcerted, she began again. "You are going to have to go back to her and I can't even think what she will do to you. I won't be able to stop laughing. Coming after me was the craziest thing."

She didn't ask him why he had done it. She could see the answer, sparkling in his eyes and it made the entire world alive and glittering. If she let herself think, she would know only despair, but now was not the time for thinking. Keeping her hand in his, Tom turned her to face him and moved his free hand to rest at her waist.

"This is a waltz! I'm not allowed to waltz!" she hissed.

"Too late now," Tom said, leading her into a spin. "You do

know the steps, don't you?" he asked, as she faltered, planting a foot squarely on his toe.

"Of course I do!"

"Well then. Who's to know?"

No one will, she thought, talking herself into some measure of calm. No one will know. His hand at her back was warm and sure, reminding her how calmly he had set her shoulder. "How is your foot?" she asked.

"I shall recover," he said. Masked and hooded, there was nothing that betrayed he was not born a gentleman. Perhaps that was his disguise, Sophy thought. Normally he did not take pains to conceal his background. Everyone was pretending tonight, she more than most. She would pretend like this forever, if she could.

The music was fast, the theatre a blur of color. She was nearly breathless. Waltzing was not like other dancing. No wonder some people said it shouldn't be allowed. When he released her, would his hands leave a mark? She didn't think her skin would ever feel the same.

"Can you meet me again?" he asked.

Sophy missed a step. "I wouldn't know how," she said, but her mind was already inventing possibilities. She had wagered everything just for this dance. She couldn't be such a fool to risk all again. And for what? Nothing could ever come of such a meeting. Each time she saw him, the danger of him learning the truth grew. All for this floating, ridiculous feeling, so ephemeral yet impossible to resist.

"Tomorrow afternoon. I'll be at Hookham's library at one o'clock," she said.

His smile thrilled and pierced her. She was certainly mad.

The music swelled in a rapid crescendo, moments away from the finale. "You must leave me after this dance," she whispered.

"I can't leave you alone here."

"Of course you can. How can I possibly get into more trouble than I've agreed to already? You mustn't be seen."

He gave a reluctant nod. "Tomorrow, then. The library." The orchestra stopped and a low rumble of conversation grew in its place. Tom didn't speak. With a courtly grace she hadn't expected, he bowed over her hand and departed into the crowd.

She was not unusual here, wandering without a chaperone. Before the orchestra had played three measures of the next song, a cavalier was soliciting her hand. Still astounded at her own audacity, she allowed him to lead her into the intricate figures of the quadrille. She understood perfectly why Lady Fairchild would never have permitted her here; anonymity bred all kinds of scandal. The cavalier's banter was beyond what she ought to allow, but since he did not know her, what did it matter?

She stood out the next dance, enjoying watching the spectacle nearly as much as being part of it, then accepted a tall man in a swirling domino of midnight blue for another waltz. It was a mistake. His hand at her back was heavy, drawing her uncomfortably close. When he would have steered her out of the ballroom, she twisted her wrist sharply, pulling free and hurrying away. Spying a figure in pink silk, she nudged her way through the crowd, but was stopped by a firm hand laid on her shoulder.

"Sir! You presume—" Spinning round, her words died. This was Alistair, not the man in the blue domino.

"Do I?" he asked. She swallowed, unnerved by his languid voice, the cool eyes under his crimson mask..

"I thought you were someone else."

"Enjoying yourself? I've hardly caught a glimpse of you, except when you've been dancing."

"I like the dancing very much, except for my last partner."

"Percy and I have been a little worried. Some men take license with their partners here. You must stay close by, so we can protect you from any indignity."

Sophy arched her brows. "Oh? *You* will do that for me?"

He didn't flinch at her barb, smoothly leading her past an Arabian sheik and into the corridor. "A masquerade starts as a lark, but the splendor wears off, I assure you. Once you have been to a few of these, the novelty is gone." He set her hand on his arm. "Walk with me?" It was a question, but Sophy did not see how to refuse.

Walking down the corridor, Sophy spied Tom through the open draperies of his box. Mrs. Morris did not look pleased. Sophy averted her eyes, realizing Alistair was speaking.

"You've been avoiding me. I did not mean to offend you."

"How could your behavior be anything but an insult?" Sophy snapped. "You would never have dared to trifle with Henrietta."

"I never wanted to. Why do you assume I am trifling?"

Exasperated, Sophy sighed. "You are more than two and twenty. Must I explain?" Turning her face to the wall, she muttered, only half to herself, "I don't even know how old you are."

"Eight and twenty. What else would you like to know?"

She looked at him, searching his face again. It was a futile attempt. She could not read him. "I don't know. I don't know you at all." He opened his mouth to protest, but she cut him off. "It's true. You saw me once when I was ten and we've ridden in the park and danced a few times together. I don't know about your career, except that you are in the Life Guards, I don't know what you like to eat, whether you are Whig or Tory, or if you like your brothers. Isn't there one of them I haven't even met?"

Did she know Tom? She had seen no more of him than of Alistair. Yet between them, a sympathy had sprung almost immediately. She knew that he loved his mother, worked hard, had little use for society and a friend who was a surgeon. He liked his breakfast eggs runny, preferred a wild landscape to a cultivated one, and disliked his country house. And he liked her better than Mrs. Morris.

A slow smile grew on Alistair's face. "Little Sophy. You'll see I am not so very frightening." They had stopped walking; he lifted her hand to his lips, holding it there for lengthy heartbeats. She could feel his lips through her glove.

"People are staring," she said.

He shrugged, tucking her hand back into the crook of her elbow. "We could go somewhere more private, if you prefer."

"Not likely," Sophy sniffed, and Alistair had to choke back his mirth. Maybe she had gained some ground since the previous evening's ball, but she still felt off-balance with him, like she was fencing with a shorter blade and hard-pressed.

"Beefsteaks. Buttered peas." Seeing her look of incomprehension, he added, "I like to eat them, though after a day in the saddle I'll eat nearly anything. I could tell you the rest, but it would bore you. Now, will you sit with me in the box, or shall we dance?"

"Whatever you wish. I am yours to command," she said. He ignored or else did not hear the echo of bitterness in her voice.

"Dancing it is," he said.

CHAPTER 23
SUBTLETY AND STEALTH

When Sophy arrived at the library, Tom was waiting for her upstairs. He held an open book, like he was skimming the first pages to see if it was worth reading. With a nonchalance she was far from feeling, she moved to survey the shelves. He stalked her as she pulled out titles, replacing them without reading the covers. As he drew nearer, she prayed her wits would not desert her; all night she'd been worrying about what they would say.

He was at the same shelf now, moving past her. When he was directly behind her, he leaned over. "Give up, fair one. There's no escape."

Laughter leaped from her throat, concealing the delicious shivers of his whisper sliding around her neck. She glanced quickly to see if anyone was watching.

"I thought today I might get to play the villain," he explained.

"Who am I then? Cassandra?"

He considered her from bonnet to boot toes. "I'm afraid not. Can't see you in that role. You'll have to try for something else."

She had fretted for nothing. This was all easy smiles. "Should I be offended you can't see me as the heroine?"

"Would you want to be the heroine of that story?"

She liked how he asked questions with his eyebrows. "Probably not," she said.

They were between two shelves, tucked away in the corner. He glanced over her shoulder, making sure they were not being watched. "How long do we have?" he asked.

"Maybe twenty minutes. Then my maid will be back." It hadn't been hard to get rid of Betty; Sophy had dispatched her to purchase Lady Fairchild's bottle of Olympian Dew.

His next smile was not so easy. "I don't know if I should be glad you brought her with you or not. What if she sees us?"

Sophy let out a disgusted hmph. "They'd never let me out of the house without her."

Tom took a book from the shelf. Without looking at her, he asked, "Have you thought how risky this is? Why are we doing it?"

She swallowed. She had no answer, not even for herself. "I don't know. I'm not going to think about it, it only ruins everything."

He seemed less inclined to dismiss the question, so she hastened on. "What happened with Mrs. Morris?"

"Nothing good. My mother is very disappointed. We won't be invited to the Fulham's again for some time."

If only she could draw. Then she could catch and keep his perfect rueful smile. "But otherwise, your mother is well?"

He nodded. "So, do you follow your masquerade with an evening at the Peerless Pool?"

No lady would attempt that, and he knew it. "The masquerade is all I will dare. Lady Fairchild does not know of it. She and I go to the Theatre Royal this evening. Will you be there?"

"Why?"

Again, she shied from the impossible question, arranging her face into a coaxing smile. "To see Mrs. Siddons come out of retirement, of course. And to argue about the merits of the play with me."

"How would we accomplish that? You aren't willing to introduce me to your family," he said dryly.

"We can talk without being nearby. If I touch my fan to my lips, that means I have never seen anything so marvelous," she said.

"And how will I tell you if I don't like it?" he asked.

"You'll look at me through your quizzing glass, letting me know you think the actors ought to be imprisoned and transported."

His smile widened, revealing teeth. "Haven't got one."

She huffed. "I should have known. My brother would have something to say about the careless way you dress, you know."

"I might have something to say in return," he said, a glitter in his eye.

Sophy retreated into silence.

"All right," he said. "I'll play your game."

And he did. He was in the pit that evening, handling a new quizzing glass like it was a dead rat, signaling her that he hated the play above all things. Three days later, she saw him walking in the park. She could not speak to him from Lady Fairchild's barouche, but they exchanged winks. Her yellow sunshade was code telling him she was in dire peril, but capable of handling matters herself. The pink in his buttonhole told her that he was in love—with the leather bound book he carried. He carried it conspicuously as he passed, but she could not make out the title. They met every week at the library, more often if Sophy managed to rid herself of Betty when executing commissions for Lady Fairchild. She wheedled Jenkins into sending her letters to Tom and passing along his replies. She told Tom to address them to Betty.

He sent her one appalling poem, dripping with melodrama that made her laugh aloud. His other letters were frank, summarizing his activities and sharing his thoughts. The honesty in them was sometimes more than she could bear. She wrote as much truth as she dared, telling him about her father and his horses, with a page devoted to Hirondelle, who was her very own. She shared her worries over Jasper's mannerly quarrels with their father and Lady Fairchild, which lately seemed to have a keener edge. She wrote about her triumphant evening at the Castleford's ball and he was good humored enough to joke with her about her success. When Tom sent her a book of travels in the Canadian colonies, she pored over it page by page, imagining him in the middle of each engraved picture. She kept the book under her mattress and had kissed the leather cover more than once.

Alistair was less attentive after the masquerade, much to Lady Fairchild's chagrin. "He added mightily to your consequence," she lamented. He still paid dutiful visits to his aunt and danced with Sophy at every ball, though never more than once. She watched him flirting with a series of worldly ladies, feeling only relief.

The round of entertainments seemed endless. Lord Fairchild refused two gentleman permission to address Sophy and Lady Fairchild predicted that success could not be far off. Sophy scarcely heard, caught up in her own secrets. Her moments of unalloyed happiness with Tom were dwindling; it was harder to meet him and keep her secrets. When they met, the future oppressed him. Perhaps he hoped she would overcome her reluctance to defy her parents. He did not know a real relationship was impossible. He believed in a lie, in a girl who didn't exist.

She always deflected any serious talk, knowing he would soon lose patience with her and their meetings would cease. Until then, she waited, hoping to postpone the day as long as she could.

BUT TOM WAS NOT THE ONE WHO FINISHED THINGS. IT WAS her father, quite unwittingly, on one of their morning rides.

"You know my wife is grown fond of you, Sophy," he said, as they rode at a strict trot down the green roofed alley of Rotten Row. "It would please us both if we could keep you close."

It was a fine morning, and Sophy could enjoy the sunshine now she'd removed the veils from most of her riding hats. She responded carefully. "Lady Fairchild is very good. I hope my marriage will not take me far from her. Or from you, father."

He gave a pleased nod. "What do you think of Alistair?"

Sophy drew Hirondelle to a halt. "As a cousin?"

"As a husband." Lord Fairchild foiled her attempt at ignorance.

Seconds passed before she could speak. "Lady Fairchild's family cannot want him married to me, father. And I do not think he considers me more than a tiresome girl attached to Jasper."

"You do yourself a disservice, surely," he laughed. "If Georgiana no longer regards you as an insult, why should her family? Indeed, she thinks he might have been rather taken with you, though he is no longer so attentive as before. She is determined to promote the match, you know. What happened there?" Suspecting her silence, he added, "Did you rebuff him?"

Sophy looked straight ahead. "I merely informed him he needn't pretend interest in me for Lady Fairchild's sake."

He shook his head. "Men of Alistair Beaumaris's stamp do not pretend affection for girls who are just out, Sophy, not even as a favor to family. If he had an interest, it was genuine. I trust it's not too late for Georgiana to fix matters."

"But father, surely Alistair plans to do better for himself than me!" she said, frightened now. "You've been generous with my portion, but—"

"Alistair is a third son with no fortune," he interrupted. "He is not such a fool to pass up a comfortable living with you."

She felt cold, though the sun was bright on her face.

"As it happens, the two of you could be more than comfortable. Lady Fairchild suggested to me that we could give you Barham for your lifetime." Seeing her uncomprehending look, he added, "It is the house I bought for my second son out of Georgiana's portion. She said it is only fitting that her stepdaughter should have the place, and I agree. You and Alistair would be little more than a stone's throw from Cordell. What could be better?"

She smiled mechanically. "I can't imagine." Her father nudged his mount forward. She followed dutifully. She had never expected Lady Fairchild to contrive so mightily for her future. Or consider her a daughter of any sort.

Her father was blind to her wretchedness. "It is a pretty house," he said. "Not large, but comfortable enough. The land attached to it will give additional income. If you have offended Alistair, I think that can be easily overcome. It will make us very happy to have you settled so close."

She could not refuse such a gift. Impossible as it seemed, the family wanted her. She was not an embarrassment or an unwelcome burden as she had feared for so long. "I don't know what to say."

Alistair had said he liked her. She hoped it was the truth. And as for love, she would have Lady Fairchild's and Jasper's and her father's as well: more than she had expected.

It was time to tell Tom the truth. It would be for the best. Once he knew, he would not love her anymore. Half her problems would be solved.

"Alistair and Jasper are coming to dine this evening," her father said. "Make yourself pretty, and we shall see if we can't catch you a husband you may be proud of."

CHAPTER 24
A FOOL COMES TO NO HARM

J asper was angry with his mother, but he valued self-control. He didn't allow himself the satisfaction of sawing at his beef, relying instead on his usual weapon: finesse.

"I'm afraid you'll catch cold there, madam," he whispered to his mother. She was keeping a discreet but careful watch of Sophy and Alistair, seated further down the table. Throwing Sophy at Alistair was not, he thought, one of her better ideas.

She tilted her head at him. "You think so?" She cut a tiny piece of cauliflower. "My sister Louisa thinks Sophy's portion would be just the thing for Alistair."

Jasper frowned. "Does she indeed?" Sophy's portion was respectable, not grand. "And you think Sophy would take him?"

"Nonsense, Jasper." His mother shot him a dark look. "What young lady would not? He's handsomer than any man ought to be and wins all the ladies' hearts."

"Some might not consider that a recommendation," Jasper observed.

Lady Fairchild smiled behind her wine glass. "I think Sophy would be pleased with a man of Alistair's name and breeding. He is of excellent ton and would make a fine husband. I'd like to keep her close to the family, you know."

"You say it so prettily, mama," Jasper said. "I suppose you'd like to keep Sophy's money in the family too?"

Her answering look was sharp enough to make most people recoil, but Jasper's armor was thick. "Don't be vulgar," she said, a little too loud. Sophy glanced at them with a worried frown.

Jasper waited until Alistair reclaimed her attention. "And what of him? He used to flirt with her, it's true, but you know that means nothing." He peered at them through the candelabra on the table. Alistair always did his best to charm whoever he was seated beside. It was one of the reasons he was so popular.

"Like Sophy herself, you underestimate her appeal," his mother said, dabbing her lips with a napkin. "Alistair would have to be blind not to take an interest. I did not invite him to take a cousin's familiarities with her."

She knew something she was not telling him. He never trusted her, but when she smiled like this he must use extra caution.

"I don't think anyone did," Jasper grunted. He liked Alistair better than any of his cousins, but still . . .

"And there is the matter of Cyril's debts." Lady Fairchild said softly, smiling at her plate.

"What?"

"Cyril. He's proving quite expensive to your uncle, I'm afraid. Alistair's expectations have decreased considerably."

Jasper resisted the urge to grind his teeth. Looking useless, as he chose to do, was one thing; being useless was another matter entirely. He had known for some time that Cyril was the actually useless kind. "Hang Cyril," he said, losing his patience. "Uncle's certainly given him enough rope. How bad is it for Alistair?"

"I told you your Aunt Louisa thinks Sophy's portion would be very suitable."

It was damnably unfair, Jasper thought. Being a third son was bad enough, but to have Cyril blowing through money that would otherwise come to you was the outside of enough.

For the rest of the meal, he watched Sophy and Alistair as assiduously as his mother. Sophy smiled and made a few quips, but when she lapsed into silence her face was solemn. Alistair touched her arm and she reacted like a skittish colt.

"When does my sister arrive?" Lady Fairchild asked more loudly, speaking for everyone's ears now.

"She wrote that we could expect her on Wednesday," Alistair said. "She is anxious to visit with you, Aunt."

"It has been too long since she's come to town," Lady Fairchild said, "It will be such a pleasure to see her." She glanced down the table to her husband.

"Quite so," he said signing to the footman to refill his glass. Jasper concealed a smile. His father hated Aunt Louisa. Across the table the eldest Miss Matcham, invited to even the numbers, piped up that she hoped she should make Lady Ruffington's acquaintance.

"Jasper says you enjoy driving," Alistair said at Sophy's elbow. "Would you honor me with your company sometime this week?"

Jasper did not like the way Sophy's throat constricted. "That would be lovely," she said. "But I much prefer to ride."

"Riding it is, then," he said. "Later this week, so long as the weather holds."

"Sophy isn't deterred by bad weather," Jasper said, nettled. She ought to assert herself. "Take care she doesn't muddy your colors, Alistair." Miss Matcham tittered. She and her sister were hot house blooms; not much good for anything out of doors.

"That wouldn't concern me, coz," Alistair said. "My man is very good at brushing out the dirt."

"You don't object, Father?" Sophy said, casting her eyes up the table.

He gave his answer to Alistair. "So long as you look after her. Can't have her falling again."

Jasper bridled. It wasn't enough that they were dishing her up for Alistair, he had to remind her of her accident too.

"I believe my falling is not an ordinary occurrence, father," Sophy said tightly.

"And I pray it is one that is not repeated, my dear," interjected Lady Fairchild. "I don't think my nerves could stand it."

When the ladies withdrew to the drawing room, Jasper did not linger over the port. "Please give mother my excuses," he told his father. "I'm not feeling quite the thing."

No one believed him, though it was true.

He felt a migraine lurking. It was all his family's fault. They were incapable of leaving a body alone. His mother was cock-a-hoop with her plans for Sophy; if Alistair was going to be her pawn, he despised him too. Even Sophy was grating on his nerves. She was supposed to be his ally, not his parents' creature. It angered him that she had forgiven his father so easily after years of neglect and after what he had done to her mother.

Faugh! His parents were detestable, both of them.

He didn't know why Sophy wasn't turned over in love with Alistair—she must be unique among womankind—but it was clear to him that she wasn't. Nevertheless, she was being maneuvered into marriage by his smiling parents because it was good for her and for the family. It might not have troubled him, if she hadn't told him she'd hoped for more.

Thunder and turf, why didn't they just let Sophy alone? Let her be a spinster if she liked—he'd always give her a home at Cordell. The place was certainly big enough and Sophy wasn't the type to fight domestic battles with the wife he must inevitably take. Perish the thought. He'd probably take Sophy's side, if it came to that.

Pressing a hand to his temples, he blinked away the lights that danced in the dark corners of his vision. Lord, he needed a drink.

"Your hat, sir." Jenkins' voice was calm as ever, but his eyes were troubled. He could always tell when Jasper had a headache coming on. When Jasper was a boy, Jenkins always would find him some dark, cool place to rest undisturbed.

"Thank-you, Jenkins," Jasper said, knowing he wasn't fooled by his smile.

"Forgive me for asking, sir, but does your man look after you right?" Only Jenkins would have presumed to ask.

"He does a bang up job with my boots." But he wasn't good with migraines. Last time he'd waved some odious scent in Jasper's face. Served him right when he had retched all over his shoes.

"I could make up a room for you here, sir." Jenkins lowered his voice. "Lady Fairchild needn't know."

"Ah, Jenkins," Jasper smiled. Dash it, he was fond of the fellow. "You can always divine the source of my troubles. No, I think my removal will serve best."

"Very good, sir." Jenkins correctly handed Jasper his walking stick and held open the door.

Outside, Jasper drank in the cooler air of the street. It was malodorous, but still better than the hot, dead air of his mother's drawing room. Poor Sophy. He did not envy her, stuck beside Alistair with his mother watching expectantly.

Well, there was little he could do if she wasn't going to kick up a dust. Hailing a hackney, he drove round to St. James to have a look in on Boz, who took one look at his friend and decided something must be done. "I know just where to take you," he said. "We'll bring Andre. Fellow's nearly as blue-deviled as you. That aunt of his isn't dying after all."

The three young blades left the exalted streets of Mayfair in another hackney, driving into seedy districts and stopping at a riverside tavern.

"Appalling place," Boz promised. "You'll love it."

Jasper made a face. "Getting cast away and boxing the watch again? We're too old for these pranks."

Boz shot Andre a dismayed look. "There's always the White House."

Jasper shook his head at the mention of this select brothel, assuring Boz his first idea was better.

The Duck and Drake was a weathered tavern favored by seafaring men.

"Pungent," Boz said, bringing a handkerchief to his nose. The public room was nearly empty, but the sour smell of river, sweat and gin was thick enough to stand a knife in. The stink must have sunk into the timbers of the building. Still, the tables looked clean enough. The two serving maids were plump, with clear skin and blushing cheeks, the freshness of youth not yet ground from their faces. An assortment of sailors diced and frowned over tattered cards around rough tables, while two men in plain black suits lounged at the bar, long pipes in hand, blowing out a cloud of smoke.

"Perfect," Andre said, his eyes dancing with delight.

Settling around the table nearest the door, they diced and drank blue ruin, watching the other patrons with interest. Some men left; new ones came; all drank more. One of the serving maids, a pretty blonde, began attending to their table, bending low as she wiped wet rings of gin off the scarred surface. Boz, who received the best view, whistled.

"What's your name?" he asked, slipping his arm around her waist and drawing her in close. A burly, red haired sailor looked up from his dice, but only Jasper noticed. Boz and Andre's attention was all on the girl. She laughed and agreed to join them, sitting on Boz's knee while he signed to the host to bring over a meat pie.

She was good, Jasper thought, watching her charm both Boz and Andre in turn, who were making cakes of themselves. Not surprising, considering how many balls of fire they were swallowing.

Andre was raising his glass in yet another toast. "Your beautiful tits—best I've seen."

"I'll drink to that," Boz agreed.

"Indeed," Jasper said, following. They were magnificent, it could not be denied.

When he set down his glass, the red headed man was standing behind Andre, glowering.

"Yous ain't the only blokes as wants drinks brought to their table."

"Of course not, good man." Andre's eyes were glassy. "There's another one—where is she? Well, the host can serve you."

"An if we don't wants 'im?"

Warily, Jasper tensed in his seat. They were fuddled, all of them, even the girl, who scowled at the intruder. But that man had shoulders like Atlas; none of them were up to his weight.

"I thinks it's time you swells took yourselves off," he said, grabbing Andre's lapels and hoisting him to his feet. Like an eel, the girl darted away, ducking behind the counter.

Over Goliath's shoulder, Jasper saw his friends rising from their seats, anticipatory grins lighting their faces. Boz was standing, slurring protests.

"My good man," Jasper said, stepping forward. "Let's not be too hasty. Five against three? Those aren't fair odds. This calls for a friendly wager. You and your friends are dicing. Let me join you. If your roll beats mine, my friends and I will relinquish all claims to the fair —"

"Kate," Boz supplied.

"Wha's reel-an-quish?"

"We will leave her be."

Goliath shook his head slowly. "You might win. I'm not a Johnny Raw to take worse odds than I've already gots." His eyes flicked at his friends.

"Of course not. But if I win Kate, I'll buy your drinks. How's that?" Lord, let him say yes so they could get out of here.

"Take it," urged Goliath's sharp-eyed friend.

"All right then." Goliath held out a chair for Jasper at his table.

Jasper sat down, Boz and Andre standing behind him, flanking each shoulder. Boz at least seemed to realize they were in something of a fix, but Andre was sulking belligerently.

"You first," Goliath ordered.

Jasper rolled an eight. Higher than he'd wanted, but still a decent chance of being beaten. He glanced at the door, suddenly so far away. The other patrons were gathering around, laying their own bets on the contest. Hopefully they wouldn't stop him and his friends from leaving once the business was concluded.

Goliath threw a five and Jasper nearly groaned. He slapped a guinea onto the table and rose. "My consolations." Kissing his fingers to Kate who was peeking over the top of the bar, he took Andre and Boz's arms and sidestepped towards the door. Goliath and his friends were still staring at the gold piece shining on the table.

"Quickly!" Jasper whispered, hauling his friends out the door. The street was quiet. Not a hackney in sight. Boz swore.

"Leaving so soon?" Goliath and his friends spilled out of the tavern onto the street. "How bout's you and I throw some more?"

"I'm afraid I have no more time, my good man." Jasper did not like to turn and run, but if he stayed, Goliath would fleece him and then mash him to a pulp. He stepped backward and Andre stumbled. Deuce take it.

Goliath advanced. "We'll have a few more throws, right fellows?" They voiced jeering assent.

"Really, I'm afraid it's impossible," Jasper flustered, dragging Andre to his feet. Why hadn't he thought to bring a pistol?

"Hear that mates? He's afraid."

Jasper grimaced. They were not going to walk away from this one.

A tall figure detached himself from the crowd. "Let them go, Jonas. You can't afford any trouble. They won't bother us again."

Hm. His biblical nickname hadn't been far wrong. Goliath-Jonas shook off the man's restraining hand.

"Jonas, I'm warning you."

Goliath-Jonas swore loudly, shoving the man aside with force that should have sent him sprawling. Instead, the man danced nimbly to the side. Before anyone could blink, his fist cannoned into the side of Goliath's head. Goliath fell backwards into the crowd.

The stranger was beside Jasper in an instant, shouldering Andre's other arm. "Move," he commanded.

Boz ran ahead, Jasper and the stranger dragging Andre between them. The shouts of the crowd behind them were drawing attention from the windows leaning over the street. If people were noticing, they might make their escape.

Around the corner deliverance waited in the form of the most run-down hackney Jasper had ever seen. He'd lay odds six to four the thing wouldn't make it to Mayfair.

"Go, or they'll come after you," the stranger said. "You shouldn't flash your blunt around like that."

"What else was I to do, pray?" Jasper grumbled, nodding at the driver and hauling open the door.

"You shouldn't come here. Or if you're chawbacon enough to haunt this district, bring a pistol. You fools haven't even got a sword stick between you."

"I have!" Boz protested, raising his ebony cane and almost hitting Jasper in the face.

The stranger stepped into the lamplight and for the first time Jasper glimpsed his face.

"I know you," he said, but dashed if he could remember where.

"I'm Bagshot," the man said. "Your neighbor."

"Ah." Jasper felt suddenly foolish. He'd seen him once at the park, but had avoided him, because by then his parents had been a fair way to forgetting Sophy's unfortunate accident. He hadn't wanted to bring her more trouble by presenting them with this problem.

"Stay away from here. Not your crowd," Bagshot said.

"Is it yours?" Jasper asked, curious.

Tom's voice was rough. "Yes. I was meeting an old friend."

Jasper pushed Andre inside the coach and stepped aside to allow Bagshot in.

"No, thank you," Bagshot said.

"There's only one, man." Jasper said. "And if we break down, which I'm afraid is very likely, I might have need of your fists again."

"Very well." Bagshot climbed in.

Andre was snoring by the time they reached St. James. "I'll have to help him inside," Jasper said, with an expression of distaste. "You alright, Boz?" Receiving an affirmative, he allowed Boz to walk away down the street.

"Where's your digs?" Jasper asked Tom.

He snorted, not impressed with Jasper's slang. "You can't do it right, you know. It puts people's backs up. I'm not far. I'll take the hackney the rest of the way."

Tempted to ask if the slang bothered him too, Jasper bit his tongue. He had been an ass. This was Bagshot's second favor. He owed the man something. On the pavement, with Andre draped on his shoulder, Jasper turned to the open carriage door. "Bagshot?"

"Yes?" Tom leaned forward, so his face was visible again.

"Please accept my thanks."

"It's nothing to me. I didn't want Jonas to get into trouble. His wife and children need his wage. You can thank me by trying not to be such an ass."

Jasper blinked. Well, he'd thought it himself. "Point taken." He grinned. "May I call on you tomorrow, if I promise not to put up your back?"

Tom frowned, surprised. Jasper pressed on. "Where do you live?" he asked.

"Russell Square, but I'm busy tomorrow." Tom leaned back,

disappearing from sight. "If you want to see me, you can come to my office."

Ah, a test. He probably deserved it. "I shall call on you there, at your convenience," he said. It was too hard to bow, with Andre sliding off him.

"I don't have a card," Tom said and told him the address.

"Goodnight, Mr. Bagshot," Jasper said and ordered the jarvey to drive on.

CHAPTER 25
COMPLICATIONS

I t was all for the best, Sophy told herself, listlessly handing round the tea cups. Sinking onto the love seat beside Alistair, she crumbled a biscuit onto her saucer and watched her tea turn cold.

"You aren't going to drink that," Alistair said, reaching over to take her cup and saucer. "It's stone cold." The cup rattled loudly as he swept it aside and set in on the nearby table. Empty handed, Sophy felt her last barricades were gone.

"What's troubling you?" he asked, leaning forward and lowering his voice. "Not Henrietta's ball still, surely." Seeing fire kindling in her eyes, he rested a large hand on her own. "It does bother you, then?"

Unaccountably, Sophy felt tears threatening at the corners of her eyes. She gave a short nod, looking across the room, but Lord and Lady Fairchild had moved to the opposite corner with Miss Matcham, their heads bent over an open book of engravings resting on the table.

"I'm sorry, Sophy," Alistair said, for once seeming sincere. "I didn't mean to embarrass you. I was pleased. Don't you know that inexperience is exactly what a man looks for in a wife?"

She was speechless, unable to muster the bravado of Henrietta's ball and the masquerade. He was earnest, his eyes assured, with just a hint of lurking amusement.

"You know I'm not trifling," he said. "I promise, next time I kiss you it will be better. You'll like it." He swept his index finger over the back of her hand.

Her mouth went dry. "I don't know what you expect me to say," she said at last.

"Nothing now," he said, smiling. "You haven't met my mother yet."

"I'm to pass muster first?" Sophy asked, sounding waspish.

"I don't anticipate any difficulty. You already belong in this family." She was cornered. Surely that was why she felt so pettish. She ought to be thrilled.

"Why did you stop speaking to me?" she asked.

He shrugged. "To make you jealous of course. It pricks my pride, you know, that it didn't work, but my aunt tells me it will improve my character to have to earn the affections of my wife. I must say, I am quite of the same mind."

He was so glib, she wanted to scream.

Miss Matcham's carriage arrived. Glad for the removal of her unwanted but necessary guest, Lady Fairchild escorted her from the room with a creditable imitation of disappointment. "So soon? You must watch for me in the park. Give my best love to your dear mama."

Taking advantage of Lady Fairchild's brief absence, Sophy disengaged her hand from Alistair's and rose.

"So early, Sophy?" her father asked, crossing the floor towards her.

"I'm afraid if I stay longer I shall be quite overcome," she said. "Early rides and late evenings take their toll."

"I'll escort you upstairs," he said, taking her arm. "Forgive us, Alistair. I'll be back before long."

· · ·

"WHAT IS IT FATHER?" SHE ASKED, ONCE THEY WERE OUT OF earshot.

"Only my good wishes. I'm happy for you, my dear."

In spite of herself, a faltering smile crossed her lips. "I am glad, sir."

At her door, she turned to him, desperate to share some of the truth. "I do not think that I love him."

For a moment he made no reply. "Sophy——" he began.

Her throat burned. "I know you would not want me to marry him if he were not a good choice, but what will I do if I cannot love him?" He would have some answer, some salve for her.

"You are young and sweet-natured. You will learn to love him." He did not meet her eyes.

"Lady Fairchild did not learn to love you," she mumbled.

He smiled, a tight grimace, not exactly amused. "You are more complaisant and know how to content yourself. Nor is Alistair such a fool that he cannot learn from my mistakes."

"Is that the best I can hope for?" Sophy asked.

"Not at all. I hope for much better between the two of you. But if love is not to be, I do not think you will be unhappy. Alistair is an honorable man who will respect you."

"You found love with my mother."

"For a time," he agreed, a little needled. "But you know it was impossible. Love like that usually is. I think it might be the impossibility that makes us feel it at all."

"Yet you both took the chance."

He regarded her sternly. "It was a mistake. Your mother was an innocent lady. If I had not been somewhat broken myself, I should never have done it." He hesitated. "Is there someone you think you love?"

Before she could decide what to answer, he spoke again. "Your mother would not want you to make her choices. Nor would I permit it. You are precious to me and to Lady Fairchild. We want the best for you, and Alistair is the best.

"You have a bit of the dreamer in you, is all. I did my share of dreaming too. But you mustn't hope for something that may be impossible or you will find no peace. I think you will do well with Alistair. He is a handsome man, is he not?"

"Too handsome," Sophy said. "I'll lose my head."

"Isn't that what you wanted?" He gave her a quizzical glance.

"Only if I knew that he loved me back."

Her father sighed. "I cannot promise you happiness. No one can, though Heaven knows I wish I could." He laid a gentle hand on her chin. "I have become a prudent man, but I would lay my money on Alistair. With him I think you can find what you seek." He kissed her forehead and left her at her door.

SHE WAS ALREADY IN BED, IN A CLEAN NIGHTDRESS AND HER braid falling down her back, when Lady Fairchild came into her room.

"I am so pleased, darling! I just had to come congratulate you. You have captivated him!"

"If I haven't, Barham has," Sophy replied. With a house thrown in, of course Alistair would snap her up.

Lady Fairchild's eyes grew wide. "That is not true! Even if it was, he would never be ill-mannered enough to say so." When Sophy's face didn't lighten, she sat down on the bed, clasping her hand affectionately. "I understand why you are afraid. Don't fret. You will have me close by, which is why I knew this match was the best. And you have been wiser than I. Alistair is not sure of your affections and will not take you for granted. He cannot, since the lease to Barham will be in your name." She smiled, a little sad. "Your father will protect your interests better than mine did."

She squeezed Sophy's hand. "It will be well."

Moved, Sophy lifted Lady Fairchild's hand to her cheek. The gesture did not feel strange at all. The emotion behind it had joined them long before. How strange that they had never noticed. Some tightness inside her loosened with the feel of Lady Fairchild's hand, smooth and cool against her cheek.

Lady Fairchild reasoned that Alistair would value her because her heart was not yet won, that affections easily earned were easily scorned. Perhaps she was right. After earning Lady Fairchild's love, she could not cast it aside.

She smiled with trembling lips at the woman who had no reason to love her, but cared for her nonetheless, giving her the house meant for her lost son and choosing to ally her with her own blood. "We shall have to decide what I shall wear when Alistair takes me riding," she said.

"Oh, Sophy." Lady Fairchild brought her other hand to Sophy's face, cupping her cheeks. "I am glad to be your step mama." Dropping her hands, she drew a deep breath. "And yes, we must discuss your clothes. It's a pity you aren't driving. You look so well in your apricot muslin."

CHAPTER 26
COMING CLEAN

Sophy spent the following day with Lady Fairchild and Henrietta. By evening she was fretted to the bone and again retired early. Sleep brought its own counsel. When she rose in the morning, she was resigned to her future. It cut deeply, closing the book on Tom Bagshot, but she would recover with time. She had survived heart-wounds before. The injury from this love—unspoken, brief and fleeting—would not always feel overpowering. She allowed herself two silent tears in front of the mirror after Betty left, then shaped her face into a smile.

"Brighten up," she told herself. "It will get better."

Her father and Jasper were waiting down stairs. She greeted Jasper warmly, grateful she would be able to forget herself with him. Alistair was not with them. She would ride with him in the afternoon before the fashionable world. After that, no one would be too surprised by the announcement of their engagement in the morning papers.

Outwardly calm, Sophy chatted easily on the ride to the park and along Rotten Row, for this morning Jasper seemed to have set aside his quarrel with their father. Lord Fairchild moved off to ride beside one of his cronies, also addicted to horse breeding, leaving her and Jasper alone.

"I ran into an acquaintance of yours the other day," he told her.

"Oh?"

"Tom Bagshot."

Sophy's heart stopped. "Here? In London?" Did Jasper know Tom thought she was a real Rushford?

"Of course in London. Where else should I be?" Jasper's eyes weren't on her. He was lazily scanning the park. "Bagshot said he spends most of his time here. Doesn't go out to Chippenstone much at all." He did not confront her with her crime, but that didn't mean he didn't know. He might enjoy watching her sweat.

"How is he?" Sophy finally asked.

"He looked well enough. Did me a good turn, as it happens. I actually called on him at his office in the city yesterday. Interesting place. Never seen one before. Anyways, I thought I'd speak to the mater. Bagshot and his mother are in town. She and father should pay a call. Only right, after all they did for you."

Swallowing, Sophy nodded, keeping a slantwise gaze on Jasper as they trotted down the tree-lined row.

"Did he mention me?" Sophy ventured at last.

Jasper frowned. "No. I don't think so." Meeting her eyes, he smiled. "Disappointed? Don't be. Both places we met were not ones where I would care to have your name thrown about."

"I'm not disappointed," Sophy said, straightening her spine. "I merely thought it would be natural for him to inquire into my health."

Lady Fairchild would despise her if she knew what she had done. It was a miracle Jasper had not stumbled on the truth already.

"Nice enough fellow," Jasper was saying. "Rather starchy, but a decent sort. Invited him to dine with me tonight."

"You what?" Sophy snapped to attention.

"White's. This evening. Bagshot's joining me. Why?"

"Nothing could be worse!"

Jasper eyed her strangely. "Your mother will hate it," she said, contriving an excuse.

"I don't particularly care. Why let it ruffle your feathers? Don't cut up at me. You seemed to like him well enough."

There was still a little time. She must find Tom, tell him the truth and hope she could beg him to conceal her folly. He would hate her, but with luck he would pity her enough to give her that.

"Where is his office?" she asked. Jasper told her. It was in the city. Betty would never allow her to go there. Even if she could slip away unnoticed, she would still have to find her way there and back; she'd be in nearly as much trouble for wandering into the city unescorted as she would be if Lady Fairchild discovered the truth. There was only one thing to do. She must send Tom a message asking him to meet her someplace else.

"I must go home," she said to Jasper, turning her horse.

"Now?" He looked at her like she had grown a tail.

"Yes. Are you coming?"

"I have to, don't I? What's the matter with you?"

She made some excuse, but he did not look convinced.

Leaving a bewildered and suspicious Jasper in the hall, Sophy dashed upstairs, pausing only to scrawl two quick notes. Tom might be at his office or at home and she could not risk missing him. Jenkins, her reluctant ally, looked askance at her worried face but promised to have the notes delivered. Sophy returned to her room and asked Betty to bring her a walking dress.

"I want to sketch in the park this morning," she said.

"Didn't you just come from there?"

One of these days, she would strangle Betty. For now, she offered up drivel about perfect light and the colors of summer. Betty sent an appealing glance heavenward, but fastened Sophy into a green walking dress and matching spencer and followed her outside, carrying her sketchbook and charcoals with a disgruntled air. They walked to Green Park, where Sophy settled down to wait, watching the park gates for Tom.

"Light not so perfect after all, miss?" Betty said, frowning at Sophy's blank sheet of paper.

"I'm waiting for inspiration," Sophy said, making a few tentative lines, sketching the gate of the park. She tried drawing a passing dandy, then a ragged looking woman hunched dispiritedly beside the gate. The woman was a better choice for her current mood, but neither attempt was any good. She might have made a brilliant caricaturist, but she had no talent for realism. It was a depressing thought.

She was still surveying the park, tapping her charcoal impatiently against the page when Tom appeared at the gate.

"Fetch me a glass of milk, Betty. I've become quite thirsty," Sophy said, returning her gaze to her drawing. There was a herd of dairy cows on the other side of the hill. It would take Betty an age to walk there and bring it back without spilling any.

"I do not think Lady Fairchild would like me leaving you alone," Betty said.

"Would she like you disobeying me?" Sophy asked, raising her eyebrows in her best Lady Fairchild manner. Betty snorted and stumped off.

Tom was carrying a walking stick, swinging it carelessly as he climbed the hill, smiling up at her with an unusually jaunty air. She tried to smile back, but could not.

"Morning Miss Rushford. A fine day."

She didn't feel fine at all, but she nodded, unable to speak. Her carefully rehearsed words deserted her.

"What is it?" he asked, sitting down on the bench beside her. "I was surprised to get your note." He looked so carefree. Blighting his good humor was surely a crime.

"My brother said he called on you," she blurted out.

"Yes, he did." He smiled. "We didn't take to each other right away, but he improves on longer acquaintance. He's bringing me to his club this evening. I think he's trying to make me acceptable to your kind. You know I don't care for that, but I should like to be acceptable to you."

Her throat closed. The stick of charcoal snapped in her hand. "It's no use Tom, however much I might wish it."

"Why not?" he asked, his mouth hardening. "There's no logical reason why you couldn't choose a fellow like me. Anything else is made up prejudice."

"My family wishes me to marry Alistair." This was not going the way she had planned. Alistair wasn't the only reason.

Tom looked away, scowling at the distant city. "Are you engaged to him?"

"Not yet." Not officially.

Neither spoke for some time. "I'm sorry, Tom. You—you must know I have an affection for you," Sophy faltered.

"Then why marry him?"

She pulled free from his gaze, turning blind eyes to the park. "Alistair doesn't matter. That's not the real reason. You might care for me now, but when you know the truth—"

"Care? I'm mad for you—can't you tell?"

She pressed on. "When you know the truth, you will not."

"Almost, I hope you're right. What's come over you today, Sophy? Don't you think I've tried to get you out of my head? You're lodged so tight, I'd have to blow out my brains to get rid of you."

"Don't be absurd," she snapped. "I'm not who you think I am. I'm not a good person. You don't know—"

"I don't believe you. What have you done? It can't be so terrible."

She was angry now, mouth tight, cheeks hot. "You know nothing about me. I was born tainted. I killed the person I loved most."

That silenced him. He stared at her, his eyes wide with horror and disbelief. This wasn't the truth she'd meant to tell him, but she supposed it was a good place to start.

"It wasn't murder," she said with a bitter laugh, "Though at the time I believed I was guilty. I was only ten, you know. I tossed her a chestnut and it stuck in her throat. She turned red, then grey. I could not get it out."

She started at her hands lying limp in her lap. "They brought me to Cordell after that."

This detail caught him by surprise. "Where were you before?"

"Herefordshire. A little village called Bottom End."

"Oh," he said, "I'd forgotten your people do that." It wasn't unusual for the upper classes to send their infants to foster homes when they didn't want to be bothered with their children. "I'm sorry. You must know that it wasn't your fault."

She looked up at him, ashamed of her leaking eyes. "It doesn't matter, though, does it? She still died." She'd be bawling next, and he hadn't yet grasped the truth.

He leaned forward, enclosing her hands in his own. "She must have been like a mother to you. I'm so sorry."

"She was my mother," Sophy sniffed, freeing one hand to swipe at her eyes.

Tom did not hear her. He was staring past her shoulder with a look on his face she didn't understand. Twisting around, Sophy saw Betty standing behind them, scowling and brandishing a glass of milk.

"Here you are, miss." Betty thrust the glass between them, slopping drips onto Sophy's skirt. "There was a boy carrying a glass for his sister," she explained. "I bought this from him instead of walking all the way, since you said you were so thirsty. Who is this gentleman?"

"Mr. Gerald—" Sophy began, choosing a random name from Lady Fairchild's 'acceptable' list.

"Bagshot. Tom Bagshot," Tom interrupted, giving Sophy a severe look.

Sophy took the glass and gulped down the milk, wishing it were poison. Betty and Tom were sizing each other up like strange cats. "Will you return the glass, Betty?" Sophy asked feebly.

"I think we both should, miss. You could use a turn, after sitting for so long. You'll get cramp in your legs." Betty said, full of false solicitude. "Have you finished speaking to Mr. Bagshot?"

She could say no more, not in front of Betty. "Of course," Sophy said, looking around for her charcoals. Only the stub of one was left in her hand. The others had rolled away into the grass.

"Allow me." Tom bent down to retrieve them.

"I don't like your reasons," he whispered as he rose and passed the sticks into her hand. "I'm not giving up."

"Please. You must." But he ignored her, setting his mouth more firmly. Nothing had gone as she had planned. She had failed. Her fingers were thick and clumsy, fumbling with the catch on the charcoal box. She jammed each stick in place and shut the lid with a snap. Taking Tom's offered hand, she rose to her feet and passed the drawing implements to Betty.

"A pleasure to see you, Mr. Bagshot," Sophy said. It was impossible to convey her message within conventional goodbyes. She'd muffed this meeting horribly, going all weepy and telling him about her mother, instead of going to the essential point.

Tom, blast him, seemed almost pleased that Betty had discovered them. He'd won Jasper over; no doubt he planned to do his best with the rest of her family.

"I hope to have the honor of calling on you in the next few days," he said, ignoring her desperate looks. He bowed and walked back down the hill.

When he was gone, Sophy looked sideways at Betty. "I do not want anyone to know about Mr. Bagshot," she said flatly. "What will your silence cost me?"

Betty hugged the drawing tablet close and smirked. "I have

my duty to consider, you know. Lady Fairchild would not like me keeping secrets from her."

Sophy sighed. Betty would be expensive.

They settled on three pounds, a pair of silk stockings and a Chinese fan, with a pound to follow each month for Betty's continued discretion. An exorbitant price, but Sophy didn't plan on giving Betty the extra money. Once Tom knew the truth and she was safely married, it wouldn't matter what Betty had seen.

Returning to Rushford House, they climbed the stairs to Sophy's room. Betty entered first, her nose in the air.

"Here you are," Sophy said, setting the money and trinkets onto the dressing table. Betty seized them with eager fingers, making them disappear like magic.

"I need my blue riding habit," Sophy said. "Please have it ready in five minutes." Alistair would be arriving shortly.

She left. Her room did not feel like her own anymore. The only way to get the truth to Tom was in another letter and she couldn't write that under Betty's eye. Descending to the first floor, she closeted herself in her father's library.

Her mother's garden sketch of Cordell was framed on the wall. Ignoring it as she always did, she moved to the desk and extracted a heavy sheet of gilt edged paper.

Mr. Bagshot— she wrote, then crossed it out.

Tom,

I planned to confess in person, but Betty returned before I could finish. Now I have no choice but to write it down in bald words. I'm sorry, more than I can say.

When I was your guest at Chippenstone, I lied to you. I am not Lord Fairchild's daughter. Not his legitimate one, anyways. Your mother mistook me for the real thing and foolishly, I pretended that I was. The chance to play at being the person I will never be proved too tempting.

There can be no excuse for my deceit; all I can offer in defense is that I began it as a joke, without malice.

You and your mother were most kind to me, which makes my own actions so much worse. Because I admired you, I could not bear for you to know the truth. I should have known it could not be helped.

I ask your forgiveness, but do not expect it. However, there is one favor I must beg. Please conceal my wickedness from my brother Jasper. If my father or Lady Fairchild should hear of it, they would never forgive me. Though I cannot, with justice, claim your compassion, I beg it anyways.

I am so very sorry,
Sophy Prescott

Folding over the paper before she could reread it, she sealed it with a wafer and went to find Jenkins. He was in the pantry, decanting wine.

"Will you deliver this letter for me?" she asked. "To the house in Russell Square?" No matter where Tom spent his afternoon, he would have to return home to change before going out with Jasper. Her letter could not miss him.

Jenkins set down the bottle without making a sound, regarding her solemnly from his deep set eyes. "Is this the last one?"

She nodded, swallowing the lump in her throat. After this message, there would be nothing more to say.

"Then I will do it. You'll do yourself no good my dear, going on as you are. If Mr. Beaumaris should find out, I do not think he would like it."

One side of her mouth lifted and fell. "Probably not. Thank you, Jenkins."

He straightened his cuffs and picked up the bottle again.

"I'm happy to be of service, Miss Sophy. You'd best change. Aren't we expecting your young man this afternoon?"

"Indeed we are."

"You'll look fine indeed on that pretty horse of yours. You'll make us proud."

With Jenkins' tender smile stiffening her resolve, she went to make herself ready. When Alistair collected her, she was quiet and composed. They found his mother in the park, riding in a barouche with a faded looking companion. Her toothy smile made Sophy want to squirm in the saddle, but she imposed an iron self control worthy of her step-mother. They returned to Rushford house in silence, Sophy counting out the minutes remaining.

Exactly as she imagined, Alistair swung off his horse and escorted her up the stairs. Jenkins took their hats and gloves. Sophy walked into the drawing room without looking back, knowing Alistair was behind her.

He cleared his throat. "Will you do me the honor of becoming my wife?"

"Yes." Turning away from the window, she held him off by extending her hand. He planted upon it the requisite kiss. "Thank you, Alistair. If you will allow me to tell Lady Fairchild?"

"Of course."

Sophy climbed the stairs, thinking of summers at Cordell and how the fish she caught felt in her hands when she unpacked them from her basket, laying them on the kitchen table for Cook, eviscerated, limp and staring. She made it to the landing before she had to lean against the wall, biting her knuckle hard to stop herself from crying. She did not let out a sound.

CHAPTER 27
GETTING SCORCHED

Tom arrived home late. It had been a strange day. In the early afternoon, he heard the first rumors of an American declaration of war. His firm had a ship ready to sail, but if war was igniting the Americas it might be better to refit her and send her east. He had chased through the city all afternoon looking for official news, but found none. Nothing more could be done until he knew the truth of the matter.

His thoughts strayed again, as they tended to do. He wondered how his meeting with Sophy would have ended had they not been caught by her maid. With a kiss, he hoped. Tonight he would tell her brother all, so he could pursue her with a clear conscience. Society and her family might censure her, and she had been reared to conform, but he had seen her kick over the traces often enough. Given the chance, wouldn't she choose to follow her heart? She would not suffer. He had money enough to give her all she could want.

Mr. Rushford's hat was lying on the table in the hall when he let himself in the front door. There was a letter too, with Tom's name curling across the front in Sophy's well-trained script. No time to read it now. Had Rushford seen it? For a second Tom debated whether he should turn the letter over. No, he decided. He was finished with concealment. If Sophy would have him, he would take her with or without her family's consent. If she wouldn't . . . Well, with luck it wouldn't come to that.

"How long has Rushford been waiting?" Tom called to his butler from halfway up the stairs.

"Ten minutes, sir," the man said, his face tight with disapproval.

"Tell him I'll be down in five," Tom returned, shocking the butler still more.

In fact, it took seven minutes for him to dress because his valet would not fasten his cravat while he brushed his teeth.

"Impossible, sir!" he gasped. "You'll crease it, or dribble!"

Tom clattered downstairs, knowing his simply knotted cravat would draw no admiring stares, but that it was crisp and neat. He'd allowed his valet to stick a ruby pin in the folds since this was something of an occasion. Following the dictates of the polite world, his linen was spotless white, his coat absurdly snug and a sober black. His tousled, uncombed hair would pass as the popular windblown look. He would concede no more.

Flinging into the library, he found Mr. Rushford turning over the trinkets littering his desk.

"My sincere apologies. I'm afraid I was detained in the city. Rumors of war with the Americans. You may have heard."

Rushford did not look up. "Mmm, yes. I dare say it will come to nothing. Liverpool has repealed the Orders in Council. War shouldn't be necessary now he has decided to mollify them."

"Let us hope," Tom said, less sanguine.

"Something of a traveler, are you?" Rushford set down a stone arrowhead and picked up a fringed leather pouch, turning it over to inspect the intricate beading. "Afraid I can't risk snooping. This one is interesting. What is it?"

"An Indian artifact, from the Canadian colonies," Tom

explained. "They make these to carry the umbilical cords of their children."

Jasper dropped the pouch as if it had caught fire. "Delightful." Rubbing the fingers that had handled the pouch together, he raised his quizzing glass with his unsullied hand and gave Tom a long look.

"Am I bearable?" Tom asked, with a shadowy grin. "Or will I humiliate you utterly?"

"You'll do," Mr. Rushford said. "Though you won't draw any attention, mind. My man has an excellent way with boots. If you like, I can have him send yours the recipe." Tom held back a laugh, sensible of the honor Rushford thought he was bestowing. He guessed the valet would be furious with his master for offering to divulge the secret to perfectly glossed boots.

With light fingers, Rushford affected an infinitesimal adjustment to his own cravat, a rather magnificent example of the nigh-impossible Trone d'Amour. "Shall we?"

Once settled in the carriage, Tom stuffed his hands into the pockets of his greatcoat.

"You don't have to do this, Rushford. My father tried to turn me into a gentleman, but it didn't take. He gave up the second time I ran away from Rugby."

"Didn't know you went there," Rushford said, lifting his eyebrows in surprise. He paused, inspecting his manicured fingers.

"I have no concerns bringing you with me to White's," he lied. "In fact, I should like to nominate you for membership. You would certainly be accepted. My word is good enough that I could nominate an ass and they would take it." He tapped his lip with his quizzing glass. "That might be something to try, you know. I shall have to have an animal sent from Cordell."

"You wouldn't purchase one here?" Tom asked, narrowing his eyes.

"Certainly not. Couldn't vouch for its character then, could I?"

Tom choked on a laugh. "I don't know that I should be flattered by tonight's invitation."

"Dear fellow," Rushford smiled. "I thought we'd agreed between us that I was the ass."

Tom laughed. "Had we? I'd nearly forgotten."

"Rode with my sister today," Rushford said, his fingers idly drumming against the side of the coach. "I expect she'd want to be remembered to you."

"Give her my best regards, Rushford," Tom said. So she had not confided in her brother, nor had her maid exposed her. He should tell Rushford. Better here, in the privacy of the carriage. He could not imagine him receiving the news with perfect equanimity.

"You may as well call me Jasper," Rushford said, taking Tom by surprise.

"I'm honored. You must call me Tom of course."

The hackney jerked to a stop. Too late. Tom disembarked with a rueful glance at the hallowed edifice. His father had never secured an invitation here, but Tom's hopes were not for the connections and prestige he would garner, rubbing shoulders with the upper crust. He thought of the tenderness in Sophy's eyes as she had looked at him that afternoon. Friendship with Jasper would make his suit acceptable. He would wait for a private moment to confide the truth.

"Evening Dawes," Jasper said to the porter. "I've brought my friend Bagshot this evening."

"Very good, sir," the porter said, relieving them of hats and greatcoats. "This way." He ushered them into a salon as rich and heavy as Christmas pudding. Unfortunately, he did not lead them to an empty table.

"I'd like to introduce you to my cousin and my friend," Jasper said, smiling. "Alistair, Andre, allow me to present Tom Bagshot. Alistair Beaumaris is my cousin," he added, gesturing to the dark haired one. "Andre Protheroe, my good friend," he said, indicating the other. "Andre, you have seen Tom before, but I dare say you don't remember."

"Yes I do," Protheroe said. "Foxed or no, I don't forget a leveler like that. Where'd you learn to box?"

"Here and there," said Tom, concealing his chagrin. No doubt Jasper considered this part of the favor, introducing him to society.

He had seen Alistair at the masquerade, and again, whispering into Sophy's ear at the theatre. Jealous sot that he was, he had even made inquiries. Unlike the others (he had ferreted out the background of any man she happened to mention) he hadn't considered Beaumaris a serious threat until Sophy's revelation earlier today. True, Alistair had tried to kiss her, but she'd been furious at him for that. Moreover, Captain Beaumaris was a third son without a fortune. Tom could understand an ambitious marriage—it was what he expected of the Rushfords' ilk—but Alistair Beaumaris was not a brilliant match for Sophy, despite his looks. He'd expected Lady Fairchild to look higher for her daughter.

"Heard anything about the Americans?" Jasper asked as they took their seats.

Mr. Protheroe shrugged. "Haven't asked."

The waiter came and poured. Tom drained his glass, hating Alistair from his sleek black hair to his tasseled boots.

"Are you back to the peninsula soon?" he asked.

"No, I'm selling out and settling down," he said, with a flick of his eyes and a flash of a smile at Jasper. Jasper merely tidied his cuffs.

They ate a surprisingly uninspired meal, subject to the curious looks of the other members who came, singly and in pairs, allowing Jasper to present his friend. Tom was too busy hating Alistair to be gratified by Jasper's introductions. The only bright note was when Lord Harvey stepped into the room. Still tall and whip thin with a fencer's grace, his nose was at an entirely new angle. He locked eyes with Tom, slowly turned scarlet, then spun on his heel and walked out.

"I say," Andre said. "Does Lord Harvey know you?"

"We met at Rugby," Tom replied. "But I'm afraid we were never friends."

When the dishes were removed, Jasper sent for a deck of cards and a bottle of burgundy.

Alistair suggested a game of whist, which wasn't Tom's game. It took only one hand to discover that he had none of the devoted fatalism of his companions and only a fraction of their skill. At least he could afford to lose. Still, he didn't like it.

After three hands, Jasper didn't appear to like it either, tilting his head this way and that, as if to loosen his cravat. Alistair suggested raising the stakes. Tom did not demur, and Jasper's ears turned pink.

Afraid I'll think he's brought me to the vultures to be picked clean, no doubt.

Alistair cleared the table again, smiling wolfishly at Tom. Leaning back in his chair, Tom vowed that guineas were the only things he would ever lose to this fellow. Someday, he might even pity him. For now, he ought to pity Protheroe, forced to partner him across the table.

"You know, I think I may have seen you about town," Alistair said, expertly dealing out the cards.

"It's quite possible," Tom returned, not yielding.

"At the Theatre Royal," Alistair continued, his voice definite. "You were exchanging glances with my cousin."

Jasper laughed. "Not with Sophy?" Tom took a swallow of wine.

"Yes." Alistair laid the last card with unnecessary precision.

Jasper lifted his eyebrows in surprise. "You know, Alistair, warning away Tom is still my prerogative and I assure you it isn't necessary. Sophy knows Tom quite legitimately. He's our neighbor. Did her a service when she was thrown from her horse near

Cordell this spring." His bland tone advised him to dismiss the matter, but Alistair didn't listen.

"Didn't I see you dancing with her at Covent Garden? A grey domino and mask?"

Jasper was immediately attentive.

Tom consulted his cards, playing for time. "It may have been me," he hedged. "All the world seems to have been there. You take a remarkable interest in your cousin."

"I think I have reason. She and I are to be married."

"That's very well, Alistair," said Jasper, making placating motions. "But I don't care to have my sister talked about. If you will kindly—"

But Tom's temper had slipped its leash. He set down his cards. "I understand you hope to marry the lady, but I do not think it will happen."

"Why should it not?" Jasper asked, affronted.

Alistair snorted. "You think to have her instead? Lady Fairchild would never dream of letting you—"

Jasper threw out a warning hand, which they both ignored.

"I am aware my birth is below hers," interrupted Tom, carving out each icy word. "But I do not believe your aspirations are more presumptuous than mine. Do you think Lord Fairchild will accept your meagre competence for Miss Rushford? Family or no—"

Jasper's hands closed into fists. Alistair rose halfway from his chair. It was Protheroe who opened his hands in confusion. "What's this all about? Who is Miss Rushford?"

"I am referring, of course, to Jasper's sister," Tom said in exasperated tones.

Jasper's face bled white. Alistair blinked once, but then a cunning smile stole across his face. "Do you mean Miss Sophy . . . Rushford?"

"Yes," Tom said, truly angry now.

Alistair looked expectantly at Jasper, who swallowed, groping desperately for his quizzing glass. He coughed. "There is no Miss Rushford. She is my—my natural sister. Sophy Prescott."

Silence fell, broken only by the clinking of china from nearby tables and the blood thumping in Tom's ears. He fastened his lips shut. She was a bastard. Not Lady Fairchild's daughter. Probably not even an heiress.

"We've said far too much already," Jasper said. "This is not the place. Cease this discussion now or I'll call you both out."

Tom scarcely heard. She was a half-caste. This is what she had meant to tell him. Without a word, he pushed away from the table. Abandoning his stake, he left the club, not stopping for his greatcoat or his hat. It was cool, out on the street in the dark. Here no man could see his face.

Rugby had nothing on this. Would he be able to wash this shame from his skin? He feared it was tattooed across his forehead. Dupe. Climber. Fool.

"Wait!" It was Jasper, running after him, half-in and half-out of his greatcoat. "Don't leave, Tom."

Turning up his collar, Tom kept walking. Jasper followed at his heels.

"Wait, man. There must be a reason."

Tom froze, glaring at the hand Jasper laid on his arm until it was delicately withdrawn. "I will not make more sport for you, for your cousin, or for your sister. Good night."

"I did not know. I would not have insulted you for the world," Jasper spread his hands wide. "But I must know. Have you been meeting my sister?"

"Oh yes."

Jasper stiffened. "I will trust that in other respects, you have behaved the gentleman?"

"Perfectly," Tom snarled, increasing his pace until Jasper had to trot beside him.

"Did she tell you she was a Rushford?"

"Yes."

Jasper swore. "I don't know what the little fool was thinking, but she wouldn't have meant to embarrass you. She's no end of trouble, but she's not a snob. Think man! Why would she be? She's spent half her life tiptoeing around my mother. She knows exactly where she stands—tolerated on the fringes of our family."

"She's a lying jade!" Tom spat, curling a fist menacingly. "Condescending to my mother with her grand manners! Mocking me like I'm some kind of bloody climber!"

Jasper rocked back on his heels. His mouth hardened as he looked away, brushing the sleeve of his coat. When he spoke, his voice was cold. "It appears we cannot be friends. I suggest we part."

"Agreed. I'm not interested in friendships with useless muck-a-mucks or their lying sisters. Honest folk are good enough for me."

Leaving Jasper fuming, he stormed off down the street, heedless of puddles and filth, anger threatening to explode out his fists. He could not reason or be still, so he walked instead, frightening strangers out of his path.

CHAPTER 28
IN THE BASKET

A hand seized Sophy's shoulder. Plummeting from clouded dreams, she awoke in her own bed.

"What?" she gasped, jerking upright and clutching her bedcovers. Was it fire? Flinching away from the dazzling light beside her, she blinked until her room materialized and the light became a flickering candle, held aloft in Lady Fairchild's sculpted marble hand. Her face made Sophy's heart seize.

"What's wrong?" Sophy croaked.

Lady Fairchild's voice caught. "Is it true? Did you tell them you were my daughter?"

Sinking steadily into trouble's dark waters, Sophy felt cold waves lap over her head. She couldn't breathe.

Lady Fairchild closed her eyes and exhaled. "Heaven help us. You did."

Sophy squirmed but couldn't make a sound. Lady Fairchild's chest rose and fell, each breath louder and deeper.

"I did not teach you to lie and sneak." Her voice was like her best china, splintered into shards. "I can only speculate which of your parents gave you that ability. Nor can I hope to comprehend how you could be so foolish. Such a lie, Sophy! And to such a man! It's a miracle the story hasn't infected all London.

"Alistair swore it was true, but I could not believe him. If he doesn't take you and if the story gets out, no one else will." Swallowing, she seized Sophy's wrist with her free hand. "You must tell me what happened when you met this man."

"Nothing! I swear there was nothing untoward."

Lady Fairchild's shoulders sagged like a tired doll's. She released Sophy's wrist, weaving her fingers between Sophy's own, lifting their joined hands to place a kiss on Sophy's thumb. "Thank God. We can save you yet. Come, we must tell your father."

Wrapping herself in a shawl, Sophy followed Lady Fairchild into the corridor, her bare feet curling away from the cold floor when she stepped between the carpets. Her heart raced like scrambling mouse feet. Her throat felt full of sand.

She followed Lady Fairchild into the library. Her father was waiting for her, turning over a paperweight of Venetian glass in his hands.

"Well?" he asked.

"Not beyond repair," Lady Fairchild said.

"Of course it isn't!" Sophy said, stung. "Tom never even tried to kiss me—not like Alistair."

"And what has he done?" Lord Fairchild demanded, thumping the paperweight onto the desk. Sophy jumped.

"Kissed me," she said, her voice small. "That is all." Unable to meet Lord Fairchild's eyes, she fixed her eyes on the paperweight. Green waves swirled within clear glass flecked with gold. It might have held a genie in its depths, but he was trapped as surely as she.

Lord Fairchild straightened his waistcoat. "Why were you meeting this man?"

"It was a chance meeting at first. Henrietta and Percy took me to a masquerade ball. Alistair came with us. I found Tom by acci-

dent, but seeing him made me so happy, I had to see him again."
She looked up at her father, beseeching. "I met him at the library
when I went to exchange my books, and sometimes saw him from
a distance in the park. That is all."

"You shall not be permitted so much license in the future. Do
I make myself clear?"

"She can have none at all," Lady Fairchild interjected. "Society
is not forgiving. She and Alistair can marry at Cordell, spend the
winter in Suffolk and make an appearance in London next year. If
any rumors have leaked out, they will be forgotten by then."

"You think he will not object?"

Lady Fairchild stared at him coldly. "He is not such a fool."

"Must I—" she had to speak now, before she suffocated. "Must
I marry Alistair?"

They fixed her with identical stares. "Certainly," Lady
Fairchild said.

"But I love Tom. I have considered marriage with Alistair, and
I do not think I can do it." Her careful reasons for obeying were
scorched and gone, leaving only ash. She simply could not.

"Pfft." Lady Fairchild stepped up to Sophy, tucking her shawl
around her shoulders. "Real life is not made of such candy floss. It
is made of duty, family and honor. You cannot be such a child."

Sophy could take no more. Tears spilled down her cheeks. It
was too late now, but if she had spoken the truth, it should have
been possible. It would have made no difference to Tom. He
would have loved his neighbor's bastard as well as the legitimate
daughter of the house. Surely it was her lies, and not her birth,
that were freezing his heart. She could have been happy with
Tom, had she not been such a fool.

"We will explain matters to Alistair," her father said. "Wait
here. He will wish to speak to you himself."

He was at the door, holding it open for his wife when the
words broke free. "No, father. Please. Please don't make me."

He glanced back, but said nothing, continuing out the door.

WILLIAM STOOD WITH HIS HAND ON THE CLOSED DOOR, TRYING not to see his daughter's streaked face. He was not good with teary pleading. The delicate and unpleasant conversation he must have with his wife's nephew would be infinitely worse with Sophy's eyes haunting him. His hand tightened on the knob. For an instant he would have gone back to wrap his arms around her and let her cry out her broken heart. She could whistle away Alistair, if it made her happy.

A choked sound from Georgiana's throat brought his feet back to earth. "What?" he asked. She spun away from him, her nightdress billowing out like a cloud, her ankles flashing as she ran down the hall. He had never seen her run. If anyone had asked, he'd have said she didn't know how.

"Georgiana?" he whispered, already too late. She didn't stop. Hell. Breaking into a run, he followed after, taking the stairs two at a time. In the upstairs corridor, he caught her by the arm.

"Let me go!" she hissed, endeavoring to shake him off.

"Georgiana!" He kept his voice to a whisper, mindful of the sleeping house. The servants mustn't know tonight's business. "What is it?"

Her face was twisted, her skin blotched red. She quivered in his grasp, avoiding his eyes.

"We need a word. Where are you going?" he asked.

"Does it matter?"

"Of course." His wildest guesses would never have predicted distress like this; it covered him like frost pictures creeping over a windowpane, turning him cold. She needed something, but he did not know what. If he tried to help, he was just as likely to set the charges of the mined ground between them.

"You're weak," she spat. "I can see it. You'll let her have that rascal, just to please her. She'll love you then, no doubt."

"You think so? I doubt it." Reason had taken hold of him now.

"I do not foresee approving an alliance with Mr. Bagshot. He hasn't asked my permission for any such thing, so I am disinclined to favor his suit, should marriage be his actual intent."

Hope gleamed in her eyes, quickly concealed. "You think him an adventurer?"

"I see little evidence to the contrary." Sophy was too young and raw to know the difference. Even a plebe like Bagshot knew the proper course to take, if his intentions had been honorable. A quick marriage was probably best. Alistair was a smooth fellow and would know how to turn Sophy's wounded heart in his favor.

"I'm upset too, Georgy," The old name slipped out, but she didn't seem to notice. "Sophy's mistake is serious and unkind to you. But I cannot understand this response. You said yourself we can mend this."

She refused to answer, gathering her skirts. Tightening his hold on her arm, he moved to block her path.

"Let me by," she demanded.

"After you tell me why you are so upset."

"You have no right to my thoughts."

"True. But I ask you to share them, so I may help if I can."

She turned her face aside, her words coming forth haltingly. "It must be Alistair. Without Sophy I have no one. I'll be alone."

She shut her eyes, waiting for him to speak, but he had no words.

Silence was a mistake. Lashed into a fury, Georgiana spat, "You'll give her what she wants. She'll take your heart and walk away with it, just like her mother, that little bi—"

"Stop."

Taking advantage of his shock, she ripped her arm free. "You defend her to me? Still?"

"I am the one you should blame."

"Believe me, I do." Shouldering past him, she swept down the corridor.

"Georgiana." He did not trouble to whisper now. She stopped, but did not turn around. "You needn't worry. I will not see you left alone."

🪶

Sophy refused to show Alistair a tear-stained face. Because she had no handkerchief, she dried her eyes with the sleeve of her nightdress and held the backs of her cold hands to her hot cheeks.

Her father should understand. He had known love. Her mother's painting, hung so he could see it from his desk, made that very plain. If he cared for her he would not be impervious to her pleas.

It was a lovely painting, executed with tenderness and skill, but it was not the real thing. Had her mother known the difference? Had she left her lover determined or despairing? Tonight her father was ordering her into another kind of counterfeit life and giving her no choice at all. Then again, what kind of choice had her mother's been? Sophy turned away from the picture, wondering what had driven her mother. Did she have enough hope of her own?

The door clicked. It was her father, bringing Alistair and Jasper with him, Jasper hanging back like a shadow. She looked Alistair in the eye.

"Did my father tell you why?" He would not wed her if he knew she loved Tom, whatever Lady Fairchild said.

"I did not ask," he said, his cool outplaying her belligerence. "Making sport of the Bourgeois made perfect sense to me. I shall not soon forget his face changing color as he realized the truth. It was rather gratifying."

Of course, Sophy thought numbly. He feared no rival now. She'd been a complete fool, leaving herself open.

"You've framed our difficulty exactly," her father said,

frowning at Alistair and Jasper. "If he is as angry as you say, how can we hope for his silence?"

Alistair smiled faintly. "You worry too much, uncle. Who would he tell? More to the point, who would listen? You may trust me with Sophy's honor. I shall not permit anyone to use her name lightly."

That she could believe. Alistair was known for his marksmanship.

"Obliged to you." Her father looked pleased.

"May I see Sophy alone?" Alistair asked.

Her father wouldn't permit that. Not with her in her nightdress, her toes naked and exposed.

"I've rung a peal over Sophy already, Alistair. She looks tired."

"You mistake my intent, sir," Alistair said. "I wish only to reassure her. This situation might have been avoided, had she not been so apprehensive. I ought to have done more to relieve her anxiety."

They exchanged smiles.

"Five minutes," her father said. "I'll be waiting outside the door. Coming Jasper?"

Jasper followed without a word.

Alistair crossed over to the sofa. "Come sit by me," he commanded.

Sophy obeyed, wondering if she would strangle on his beneficence.

"I've always thought you an endearing little rogue," he said, moving closer and trapping her against the arm of the sofa. "It's all right. I did not act so well either. Better if we had been honest with each other from the first." He gave her plait a little tug, then brushed it over her shoulder.

"Why do you want to marry me?" Sophy said, too frayed to conceal her distress. A tear slipped out of her eye and ran down her nose. "Is it the money?"

"Partly. But there are other ladies I could choose. Of them all, I like you the best Sophy. A man would have to be a fool to tire of you. I have not been wise, perhaps, but I do not think I am a fool."

He had chosen her like he might choose a horse or a hat. She sat, unmoving, as he drew out his handkerchief and wiped the tear off the end of her nose. "Of everyone, I believe I mind this fracas least. You had him well and truly fooled, my dear. It was quite entertaining. I think it will be best though, if you don't entertain me in this way again."

Sophy swiped her nose with the edge of her shawl, scowling bitterly into her lap. "I am so pleased you find it amusing. That makes my heart's breaking all worthwhile."

He raised her chin with his thumb. "Truly Sophy? Is your heart breaking?"

"Can't you tell?" She let her voice rise, trying to hit him with her words. He did not retaliate. Gently he smoothed her hair, shushing her like a young child. "You'll find that hearts can break and mend an astonishing number of times, little one. Sometimes even with the same person. If you give me the pieces, I will do what I can to make you whole.

"Tell me the truth, now," he said. "You never kissed him?"

"I told my father everything. You're the only one who has done that."

"And he was not pleased to learn of it," he chuckled. "I like that color in your cheeks, Sophy. It tempts me to be disagreeable more often."

"I dare say if we marry, we shall find each other very disagreeable," Sophy retorted. "It won't work, Alistair."

"There's no reason it should not. You are too young for your affections to be fixed. This infatuation will pass, and indeed, our marriage will probably be better for your experience. First love is like the measles—a hot rash that one is stronger for surviving. You will not find me a bad husband and you will learn to love me well enough."

"You cannot be certain."

He gave her a flat look. "Nothing is certain." He shifted closer. "But I think I have seen somewhat more of the world than you."

Cornered by the sofa, she could not move away. Alistair set his hand on her cheek, brushing her lower lip with his thumb. She turned her head away, pressing her lips firmly together.

"As you please," Alistair said, dropping his hand. "It is too late for you to have him. Go to bed then. You will feel better once you have watered your pillow. I will see you in the morning."

He was all politeness, escorting her out the door. Sophy did not meet her father's eye and hurried to the stairs. Jasper was nowhere to be seen.

Upstairs, she sat on the edge of her bed, heedless of the cold. She thought and listened, and thought some more. A biddable girl would gratefully accept what Alistair and her family offered, but that wasn't how she was made. Maybe it was because she'd been born of unlawful passion, but whatever the reason, Sophy knew she could not subdue her unruly heart.

When the house was quiet, she began to dress. It was difficult in the dark. She had no idea what color stockings she wore. Her dress and petticoat, fastening up the back, probably took her a half hour. She donned a spencer, bonnet, gloves and her sturdiest boots. Rolling up a second dress and a change of underclothes— they would be a mass of creases, but that was a small concern— she tucked them in an empty bandbox. Toothbrush, hair ribbons, nightdress: she stuffed them in the box along with any gewgaws she could sell.

She tiptoed through the house, unbolted the front door, and let herself outside. There was a chance, albeit a slim one, that her golden future was yet possible. But even if it was not, she would not marry Alistair. It was time she made a life of her own.

Dawn was not far away. Tired folk shambled along, heading to the day's labors. She was barely ahead of the baker's boys and milkmen, busy already with deliveries.

I will be like them, she thought. If this doesn't work, I will be like them and they do not look unhappy. She would have liked to say goodbye to Jasper, and to thank Lady Fairchild, but they would not have understood or allowed her to go.

The sun was up when she reached the building with Tom's offices. She had needed to ask directions numerous times. Though she had driven through the city, she had never walked it before and was more frightened now than when she had left the house. There were so many people, all with very little. Would they make room for her to join their ranks?

Tom's offices were as she had imagined, a plain, solid block of a building, bearing the sign 'Bagshot and Son, Trading' in yellow letters on black. The door was locked and no lights were on, but when she cupped her eyes and put her face against the window, she could see the reception counter and the high desks for a host of clerks behind it. Heedless of the dusty brick, she settled against the building to wait.

CHAPTER 29
BLUE-DEVILED

How long he walked, he did not know. But when Tom let himself in his front door, his eyes fell on the letter waiting for him in the hall.

He had forgotten it entirely. Without thinking, he tore it open. It was too late to be surprised by her confession; he only felt humiliated, remembering her fiancé-cousin's leering face. Damn her. He banged his fist into the table, nearly toppling his waiting candle, which was almost burned to the socket. Snatching up the stub, he stormed into the library, lit himself a fire and poured himself a drink. The letter he threw into the fire; himself he threw into a chair, so he could scowl and nurse his brandy.

He would have woken in his chair in front of a dead fire with an empty glass in his slack hand if not for his valet. Because of Martin, he woke in his own bed, in a nightshirt, even. He could not recall how this miracle had come to pass.

Too sullen to feel embarrassed, as he normally would, Tom told himself Martin had probably enjoyed handling him in such a docile state. The real question was if he would ever be able to get himself out of bed. On the whole, he thought it unlikely. He rolled over and pulled a pillow over his ears.

It didn't prevent him from hearing someone creeping up the stairs, with a tread as heavy as a giant's. "Go away!" he shouted, wincing as his head rang like a clapped bell. "And for heaven's sake, be quiet!"

Hitching the bedcovers over his shoulders, he tried to go back to sleep. Not a squeak came from inside. It was the street noise that hammered his head now. Normally he couldn't sleep without it, but today, each vibration rattled him. Fish sellers, rumbling carriage wheels — damnation! It was impossible for a man to get any peace. His mouth felt like a piece of dusty carpet. Blearily cracking an eye open, he eventually focused on the can of steaming water waiting on his washstand. Muttering that there was no help for it, Tom staggered out of bed.

Pressing a warm cloth on his face helped, as did Martin, materializing wordlessly with a cup of coffee.

"You may as well help me dress," Tom grumbled. He was expected at his office.

"I'll have your breakfast sent up first?"

His stomach rebelled, but he ought to eat something, to at least pretend this was an ordinary day. "Just a roll. And more coffee," he said, setting down the cup and wiping his mouth with the back of his hand, catching the ruffled linen cuff of the nightshirt. Martin winced.

"Your pardon, sir, but I would recommend something more substantial. My last employer, Sir Timothy Blanding— well, he used to dip deeply and often. Took some time, but I learned how to get him going the next morning. If I might suggest the same?"

"You are optimistic, Martin," Tom said. "I'm sure it's nearly noon. But very well." By the time his tray arrived, he was starving, and he made decent work of the plate of cold ham. He thumbed through the morning paper, noting on the second page that the Americans had declared war after all.

Skipping over the society announcements a name stopped him

like a slap. Shaking out the page, he peered more closely, stunned they had acted so fast.

Lord Fairchild announces the engagement of his ward, Sophia Prescott to Captain Alistair Beaumaris, of the 2nd Life Guards.

He tossed the paper aside, spilling his coffee. "Martin!"

His valet appeared in the doorway like a jack-in-the-box. "Yes, sir?"

"I've made a mess. Clear this away, won't you? I should get on my way." He wanted to tear the paper to shreds, to knock out Beaumaris's teeth, to march over to Fairchild house—and what? Heap curses on the Rushfords? Box her ears? Don't be such a fool, he told himself.

Flying out the door, his head pounding like a drum, Tom grimaced against the glare and pulled down the brim of his hat. Not a hackney, he decided. It would do him good to walk, even if it did take an age. There was solace in action. He did not want to examine what lay underneath his seething fury.

It took him a good hour, but Tom arrived at his offices at last, walking through the rows of clerks without a sideways glance. "Mr. Bagshot—" began his secretary, but he kept walking, removing his hat, stripping off his left glove.

"In a moment, Smith. Give me a moment."

Smith dropped his gaze to the sheaf of papers clutched in his hands and backed away. Tom gave a self-disgusted huff. He wasn't fit to speak to others, even after an hour of charging through crowds. Smith didn't deserve his temper.

Letting himself into his private office, he winced and raised a hand to his eyes. Someone had opened the blinds, letting the summer sun pour through the windows. Sharp words gathered in his mouth; already it was warm in the room. By evening the heat would be intolerable. Besides, the light made his head want to split open. He blinked, still shielding his eyes, and realized he was not alone. A woman was sitting in the chair by the window.

It was Sophy.

She was dressed oddly, in a plain brown walking dress, nothing like the fragile confections she wore walking to the library or the dashing habits she wore riding in the park. Her bonnet rested in her lap, made of plain straw, with ribbon to match the dress. It didn't matter that she was dressed like a farmer's daughter; her hair was like fire in the sunlight.

His feet stopped working. Acting on reflex, he grabbed the door frame before his momentum caused him to stumble. "What are you doing here?"

She flinched under his verbal attack but squared her shoulders with her next breath. Tempted to turn on his heel and slam the door, Tom reminded himself that this was his office, his building, his turf. He let the door swing closed, stepping into the room and folding his arms, repeating his question by raising his brows.

"Did you never get my letter?" she asked.

He let out an angry snort. "I did. But not until after I had the pleasure of dining with your brother and learning the truth from him. Your fiancé was also present. Surely they told you?" He watched her turn crimson, glad to see her ashamed.

"Alistair is not my fiancé," she said.

"That's not what I read in the morning paper." What was printed there was practically carved in stone. Freeing himself from her stare, he stalked to his chair and sat down at the desk, letting his hands busy themselves with the papers lying on the blotter. "Was there anything else?"

"I'd almost given you up," she said. "I've been waiting for hours, before your secretary came even."

"Smith did not offer you any refreshment?" His words were polite, but his expression unconcerned as he pretended to read a letter. His eyes darted across the page without seeing the words.

"I was not hungry," she said, becoming angry. "I came to apologize. Which is what I'm trying to do. I wanted to tell you, often. But I never could. I liked you too much and couldn't bear for you to hate me."

He ignored the trembling in her voice and picked up a knife to sharpen his pen. "Lies make me angry. But it is a relief, knowing the girl I loved was mere fiction. With you it always was madness. Happily, truth has cured my infatuation."

He said nothing more, sensing but not seeing her deflate. She waited. He set down the knife, swept aside the shavings and drew out a fresh sheet of paper. At last she rose, tying on her bonnet and saying with awful politeness, "I see it's no use. Please convey my apologies to your mother. Good-bye, Mr. Bagshot."

"Good-bye, Miss—" he stopped, realizing he couldn't remember her real name.

"Prescott," she filled in, pausing at the door. She had a bandbox in her hand that he hadn't noticed before. "I am Miss Prescott. Please, tell me why you despise me. Is it because I am a liar, or because I am a bastard?"

Tom looked up and set down his pen. She was still beautiful, straight and strong as Diana, outlined against the dark wood of his door. He hated her for being beautiful, for making it almost impossible to keep his hands steady and his voice cool. "Both, I imagine," he said, seized with the desire to wound her. "I'm afraid I've never succeeded in divorcing myself from the bourgeois morals of my birth. Good-day."

Her flinch was slight, but unmistakeable. White her face went, leached of all color. She looked sick, her expression stabbing Tom in the gut. She drew a quick breath. "I thought my birth wouldn't matter to you. That to you, I was myself and nothing more. I see now it will never happen. Thank you for reminding me. I will not need to pretend anymore."

She stopped on the threshold and Tom saw that the door had fallen partly open. A crowd of clerks blocked her path, witnesses to this last, dreadful exchange. He could not move, watching helplessly as her simple skirts swayed above her retreating boot heels. At once his employees resumed speaking, their words burying the sound of her footsteps. Still, he felt each one reverberate through him until she must have passed into the street.

Only then did he jump to his feet, rushing outside, dodging through the crowd, straining for a glimpse of her. Twice he thought he sighted her, but was deceived by a similar looking bonnet. She must have started running once she left the building. She was gone.

Drumming an angry rhythm against his right thigh with a closed fist, he returned inside. Smith was saying something, apologizing for not telling him that the lady—the woman—was waiting. Shutting his ears, Tom waved his words aside, dropping bonelessly into his chair, staring like a lost man out the window, aware of each painful breath, each eye rasping blink.

He set his head in his hands, scrubbing his fingers through his hair, as if it could rub away the taint of his words and the thing he had done. He had wanted to hurt her. Well, he certainly had.

Smith's rising voice penetrated his thoughts at last. He looked up to see him bursting through the door, breathless and red-faced, with Jasper Rushford at his heels.

"I told him you were busy, Mr. Bagshot! He would not wait! He shoved past me and—"

Jasper scowled. "This fool would not let me by. Nearly lost my hat trying to go round him. Whether you want to or not, I'll see you, Bagshot. Been looking for you all day. They've turned me away from your house. Twice!"

"What do you want?" Tom groaned. "You can go, Smith." Smith didn't hesitate, vanishing through the door like a wisp.

"I'm looking for Sophy, dammit!" Jasper said, slamming his fist onto the desk. "Where is she?"

"She left. I tried to follow her, but I lost her in the street."

"You dog! You lured her here after all! If you weren't such a commoner I'd call you out! I'll have to beat you purple instead!" Throwing down his cane, Jasper yanked at his gloves.

Tom scowled. "I didn't know she was here! I got here not half an hour ago! She was waiting here alone all day. Ask Smith, if you don't believe me."

"A likely story! Why weren't you here? How would she even know this place?"

"Take a damper," Tom snapped. "Or I'll put your lights out. I wasn't here because I was in bed, dead drunk. And I have no notion how she found this building. I never told her of it!"

Jasper stopped, pinching his lips together. His eyes darted left, right, then back to Tom. "My apologies. I believe it may have been I. Who told her, I mean. Dammit, why didn't you keep her here? Now how am I going to find her?"

"Go home, I expect."

"Confound it!" Jasper crashed both fists onto the desk, knocking over the inkstand. "She's not going back there. That's the problem. First time I came round your house was to ask you to keep mum. Second time my father sent me to find her. She's run away! We thought for certain she was running away with you!"

Was that why she had come? Remembering the bandbox in her hand, he passed a clammy hand over his forehead. "She had a box with her."

"Yes, I know," Jasper said. "And you didn't ask her to elope with you?'

"Of course not!" Tom snapped.

Jasper's face turned a violent purple. "Well, why the hell not? She's bloody in love with you!"

"Hah! She lied to me! Spun me a banbury tale— "

"Flummery," Jasper snorted. "Lord, you're tight-laced for a cit. Who do you think you are? A patroness of Almack's? It was a stupid prank, nothing more! She's just a scrap of a girl. How was she to see her way out? Here she is, not even eighteen, running away from her family and a good marriage to make her own way in the world and you don't even propose to her? You're telling me you've been exchanging letters with her, meeting her at masquerade balls, everything too smoky by half, and you don't even love her? At least if you'd offered her a carte blanche I could kill you! And it'd save me from having to hunt through every quarter of London. Dashed if I know where to find her.

"Anything happens to her, I will kill you. I ought to break your bone box right now. Sophy's sterling. Pluck to the backbone. You, sir, do not deserve her, and you may take that with my compliments!"

Cranking back a fist, Jasper swung, but Tom was quick on his feet. Ducking sideways, the punch grazed him instead of catching him full in the face. Shuffling forward, fists ready, Tom let fly a few jabs, but was blocked by an uppercut of Jasper's.

"Stop this right now!"

Jasper dropped his arms, spinning round like a top. Tempted to throw Jasper a leveler now that his guard was down, Tom froze instead. A lady swept into the room, with all the grace of a queen. "Where is Sophy?" she demanded.

"Not here, mama," Jasper said. "Was, but isn't anymore."

"She did not say where she was going?"

"I'm afraid not," Tom said. "I take it you are Lady Fairchild?" She ignored the last part, refusing to allow an introduction. She looked like a harpy, this woman; an elegant, beautiful, ice-cold harpy, with incongruously swollen eyes. "Come Jasper. We shall continue looking." Without giving him another glance, she glided away.

"She was upset when she left here," Tom said. "It was my fault. I was not kind. Let me help you look."

Poor girls walked the city alone every day. Only the rich and privileged could afford to hedge their women with maids and grooms and chaperones. Common sense told him Sophy was not a helpless flower, yet thinking of her crushed and alone turned his blood cold. Suppose she got lost? Or was robbed? Or ran foul of London's teeming underclass?

"I think you've done enough," Jasper said, departing with a

glare. "No matter what happens, her life is ruined, and you led her into this. Think about that, when you call her a liar."

The room felt very quiet when they had gone. Tom stared at his chair, but kicked it instead of sitting down. Where would she be? He sifted through memories, hoping for some clue. Her family would have found her if she had gone to her sister's. He had seen her at the park and at the library, but she had no reason to go there. She wouldn't go places anyone might recognize her, would she? Not if she were truly determined to cut herself free. She only knew her little neighborhood in Suffolk, and her family's circle in London.

And Herefordshire. Hadn't she said she lived there, once? With the woman who was her mother. Of course.

Tom rushed for the door, forgetting his hat. He must check the departing stagecoaches.

CHAPTER 30

PLAIN SPEAKING

Bertha, her mother's onetime maid, had died three years ago, carried off by a putrid throat. It had been many years since Sophy had heard from the Wilkeses. Still, Bottom End felt like the right place to go. It was a beginning, one that was less frightening than London. There would be people who remembered her there, who might put her in the way of finding work. She could be a teacher, like her mother, or a house-maid, or a milliner's assistant, or — or anything, if need be. No one in Bottom End would have the audacity to write to Lord Fairchild, not if she told them lies. She had been sent to school. Only seen her father twice. No one would probe further than that.

It seemed wrong, putting him in such a light, but it couldn't be helped. And she was a rather good liar. She'd fooled the Bagshots, until it all unravelled. No, she could not face that again. She would tell the truth, that she was estranged from her family. She would not garner any pity, but she would manage.

Lifting her eyes from her gloves, she watched the chickens scratching in the inn yard. The coach would arrive soon. From her handkerchief, she unwrapped the other half of the meat pie she had bought. It was greasy, filled with stringy meat and unidentifiable vegetables, but she had been hungry, and the fragrance of the hot pies had been irresistible. Conscious of her slim purse, she only let herself eat half, intending to save the rest for her supper. But she was hungry now, and tired of waiting.

I will eat and not think about Tom, she thought, breaking off a piece of crust and putting it in her mouth. And she did try.

She tried not to remember his hand clasping hers at the park —only yesterday, but it seemed years ago. She tried not to remember laughing with him, acting in his mother's drawing room. She tried not to remember how happy she felt, when he had looked up at her from the pit at the opera house and winked. Mostly, she tried not to remember what he had said to her last. That one was the hardest of all.

The gravy in the pie was thick and tasteless as paste. She tucked it in her handkerchief and set in on the bench beside her. An inn ought to be an interesting place to wait and watch. With so many people coming and going, there should be plenty to divert her attention. All those hours in Tom's office, she had passed the time watching the street below. She was closer at hand now, not separated by a window. Here, there were chickens, an irate publican bellowing at his lazy ostlers and a rumpled looking man wearing a belcher neckcloth whose chain was missing a watch.

Evading the tipstaffs, no doubt, she thought, glad she had absorbed some of Jasper's worldly wisdom.

Yet none of it was very interesting. Leaning back against the stone wall, she closed her eyes and tilted up her chin to let the sun fall on her face. Sunlight was always reassuring. Next to riding, she liked nothing better than to lie in a quiet place with the sun on her face. She felt a pang, thinking of Hirondelle. How much better it would be if she could fly away on Hirondelle's back to somewhere far and safe and new. Certainly it would be better than lumbering across the country in a late running stagecoach. But there was the matter of the bandbox. She could not ride and carry at the same time. And she would have work enough feeding herself, never mind a horse.

Besides, Hirondelle had been her father's gift. Inside her, a stubborn child's voice piped that she refused to take her.

She heard wheels. It wasn't the stagecoach, only a light chaise, so she closed her eyes again. The chaise stopped and she heard a pair of boots jumping down to the cobbles and crossing the yard. A shadow fell across her face. She opened her eyes.

It was Tom, barely visible with the sun directly behind him. Sophy stiffened, her face falling into an unbecoming squint. Lady Fairchild did not permit squinting, but as Sophy was no longer a lady, she decided she might do it as much as she pleased.

"May I sit?"

"No." Sophy shut her eyes again. In spite of herself, her heart was beating fast. Fool, she scolded herself. But how had he found her? Why had he come? Not, surely, to flay her again with words. Behind her eyelids, hope burst, bright and dazzling. He'd come to apologize, to beg her forgiveness. How long should she make him grovel, before relenting?

Feeling the beginnings of a smile, she turned down the corners of her mouth. The shadow vanished and she frowned in earnest. Peeking under her eyelashes, she saw him calmly buying a ticket for the coach. This wasn't what he was supposed to do! He should be begging her pardon and swearing to love her. She shut her eyes before he could catch her peeking. She ought never to forgive him. What he had said was unpardonable—but was it as bad as lying for weeks?

It was worse, she decided. She had never meant to be insulting. She felt him sit down beside her.

"I did not invite you to sit," she said.

"You don't have to. I don't think rules apply when you're sitting in a dirty inn yard waiting for the stage."

"That's what you think." She glared at him. He ought to be more repentant.

"Going to Herefordshire to visit friends?" he asked.

She didn't answer. "Did you really buy a ticket?"

He nodded.

"Whatever for?"

"I thought I might be needed."

"Good heavens, why?" she asked.

He fiddled with a loose button on the cuff of his coat, taking time with his answer.

"Because you are going, and I hoped I might be of assistance."

Sophy bridled indignantly. "You don't think me capable?"

"Of getting there? Certainly. But what then? What are you going to do?"

"I don't see that it's any of your concern," she said, wishing he would insist that it was. She let her head turn a fraction so she could see his face. Immediately, she wished she hadn't, feeling herself color under his steadfast gaze. She could not read his intent, yet she felt his eyes unearthing every secret of her soul.

"I hope it will be," he said. "Can you forget what I said?"

Her lip trembled. No, she could not. In his anger, he had known precisely how to cripple her. The words smarted still, even under the balm of his steady eyes.

"I knew you would be angry with me," she said. "That was one reason why it was so hard to tell. And I have often wished that my lies were true. It is not pleasant, being what I am."

"I was angry," he said. "I wish you had told me sooner."

"So do I. But seeing your reaction, I think I was right to be afraid."

His mouth twisted into the self-conscious, wry smile she liked best. "What is this?" he said, picking up the bundled half-pie between them. "Were you eating this?" He flipped back the white linen and wrinkled his nose. Breaking off a piece of crust, he tossed it to the nearest chicken. Instantly, the birds gathered at his feet, pecking and flapping their wings.

"Does no one feed them?" he asked, hastily retracting his boots and hurling the remains of the pie to the other end of yard. The chickens followed, a noisy flurry of beaks, scratching feet and feathers. He didn't take his eyes off them as he wiped his fingers with the crumbly handkerchief. "I saw your brother and your stepmother today. You aren't going to marry Beaumaris?"

"I'd rather starve," Sophy said loftily.

Tom rolled his eyes. "Obviously you've never gone hungry. Look at those chickens. People aren't any different." He tilted his head, forestalling her forming retort. "There's no need to be melodramatic. This isn't one of my mother's books. Take me instead."

Never had an offhand remark caused such violent joy, but caution overtook Sophy with her next breath. "Why?" she asked, her voice cracking. "Because I need someone to care for me?" Of course he would offer for her, knowing she was nearly destitute.

"That's part of it, I suppose," Tom said. Under her skirt, Sophy's right hand closed into a fist. "But I'm a selfish man. Mostly, it's because I need you to care for me.

"Will you? If you can forgive me, Sophy, I swear I'll never again be such a clunch. I'm not normally mean, you know. Egad! If you knew how your face has tortured me."

She stopped him with a light touch on his arm. Had she thought the sun warm? It was nothing to the warmth inside her. Her mouth seemed made only for smiles, her feet for nothing but dancing. "You were sorely tried. But I shall accept your promise nevertheless, and absolve myself of all blame," she said. She grinned, but the humor around her mouth was not as catching as the shine in her eyes.

He caught her hand, squeezing it hard. "I'll take that bargain." Pulling her close, he shut his eyes for just a moment, breathing her in, testing the air. Despite all that had passed, it was warm and unshadowed. When he spoke, he whispered, low. "Must we go to Herefordshire, or can I marry you out of hand?"

"No one there is expecting me," Sophy began slowly.

"Good." Without waiting, he picked up her bandbox and brought her to her feet, pulling her to him with the force of a lodestone, crushing the brim of her bonnet. All they achieved was a rough brushing of lips, yet his left behind such a burning tingle Sophy had to touch hers with her fingers, to verify they were still the same shape.

"Hate that hat," said Tom. "You'll have to burn it."

"Kiss me again," she said, tugging at the ribbons.

The bonnet dropped to the ground and rolled away unheeded. Kissing Tom did no good to her hat or her hair, Sophy belatedly realized, but it filled her from top to bottom with rightness and belonging. This is what she'd been seeking. This was the pearl worth trading all she possessed.

"Where are we going?" Sophy asked, when he lifted his head and lowered her heels to the ground, turning her towards his waiting chaise.

"To see your father. You are still underage. So unless you want to go to Gretna, we must have his permission if we are to wed."

Ah. Her practical Tom. "I think our chances are better for Gretna," she said.

Tom took the reins from the waiting ostler and climbed to the seat. "I'll try, nonetheless. It would take us two or three days to reach the border."

Conscious of her glowing lips, Sophy met his eyes. Swallowed. They could not travel all the way to Scotland without kissing, wanting everything that came next, in serious danger of making every scandalous elopement story true. Even here, under the curious eyes of the ostler and the waiting passengers, she wanted to stretch her arms over his shoulders and bring her face to his. The look in his eyes told her he wouldn't mind. Ears scorching, Sophy looked away.

"My mother would be horrified," Tom said. "We'll elope to Scotland if it can't be helped, but I'd rather not. Our marriage will cause hailstorms enough. You deserve better."

"Oh." Primly, Sophy donned her damaged headgear, peeking at him from under the broken brim. "I suppose we must, though I think my father is likely to suffer an apoplexy. There's a good chance Lady Fairchild will have the servants lock me in a cupboard."

Tom looked at her, his eyes grave above his smile. "If you do not want to tell them, it's your choice. I'll not let them take you from me."

"No, we should go," sighed Sophy. If Lady Fairchild had come to question Tom, she must be worried. She could not leave them wondering, or let them find out third-hand. Despite the flint faces they had given her appeals, they did love her. She could not give them obedience, but she must not let them think she did not love them in return. Straightening her back, she folded her hands and hardened her nerve.

"Are you afraid?" Tom asked.

"Terrified. It will hurt them dreadfully. They will not forgive me." She smiled to hide her wobbling lips.

Freeing one hand for an instant, he put his arm round her waist, scooting her right to his side before grasping the reins with both hands again. "You will not regret it. I promise."

CHAPTER 31
RIVETED

The drive to Rushford house passed far too quickly.

"There's always Scotland," Tom said, when she drew her hand back from the door.

"No," she said, pacing back and forth across the step. "You do not think it, but they love me, in their way. I must tell them." It would be easier to tell them after she was back from Scotland. In a month or two, even. Easier, but craven and she was not a coward. She had Tom beside her. Drawing a deep breath, she turned the handle and stepped inside.

Jenkins came into the hall and froze. "What, am I the Medusa?" Sophy asked. "Is my father home?"

"He's in the library," Jenkins said, making heroic attempts to smile. "Would you like me to walk with you?"

"All right," Sophy said, wondering if Jenkins' offer had come to buttress her flagging courage or because she was no longer considered a member of the family. Quickly, she put her hands together to still her trembling fingers. Whatever she lost, she must count it small, for it was no small thing to be loved by Tom.

"And who is the gentleman?" Jenkins asked, trotting along beside them.

"Thomas Henry Bagshot," Tom spoke squarely. "Of Chippenstone, Suffolk."

Never had she seen the house so helter-skelter. Jenkins winced as a kitchen maid stumbled past them in the hallway. A table of Sèvres ornaments was swept bare, the shattered remains littering the floor. Her father's voice rang through the house loud enough to rattle the windows.

"Stop talking at me and find her!" he shouted. Two men in brown tweed coats scrambled out the library door. Spying Sophy, they halted.

Jenkins cleared his throat. "Ah, my Lord . . ."

Sophy took Tom's hand and stepped into the library.

Her father was facing away from them, his hands braced on the top of his desk, his head down. Lady Fairchild and Jasper stood by the mantlepiece. Jasper was holding her hand. Lady Fairchild saw them first. She gasped, ready to fall on Sophy and clasp her like the returned prodigal. Then she saw Tom. Her hand tightened on Jasper's, restraining him.

"William," she said, motioning him to turn around with a nod of her head.

"Sophy!" Instantly he was beside her, seizing her shoulders. "Thank God! Where were you?" Without waiting for an answer, he turned to Tom. "Thank you for finding her. You have my unending gratitude—"

"William," interrupted Lady Fairchild. "You are speaking to Mr. Bagshot."

He stilled, his hand only half extended. "Ah," he said at last. Clapping his hands behind his back, he settled back on his heels, squaring his stance.

"Tom has asked me to marry him," Sophy said. "I have accepted." She meant to sound assured and bold, but her voice was small and feeble, dwarfed by the towering bookcases and her family's outraged eyes. "I want your permission, father."

"You shan't have it," he said. "I've just announced your marriage to Alistair, for God's sake!"

"Engagements are sometimes broken," Tom said. "That's nothing to stop us."

"Nothing?" shrilled Lady Fairchild, breaking her trance. "Our Sophy, married to you? It's deplorable."

"It is no such thing," Sophy said, reddening. "You can't have forgotten I am the bastard daughter of a governess."

Lady Fairchild winced. "We did not raise you for this! If he thinks he will get a penny of your father's money—"

"Don't need it," Tom said. "When my kind marry yours, it's usually the other way round. Now, do I have your permission, or must I drag Sophy to Scotland?"

"Go to your room, Sophy," ordered her father.

She did not move.

"Go to your room, I said!"

Tom took a half step forward. "I do not permit anyone to speak to Sophy in that tone of voice. Would you like to step out of the room, Sophy?"

Not unless he came with her. "I'm sorry. I wanted you to know I was safe. I will be happy." But part of her was tearing inside.

"I cannot permit this," said Lord Fairchild.

"Please." She turned to Lady Fairchild, but she had gone to the window, once more a picture of remote beauty, her jeweled ring scattering the bright sunlight. Sophy drew a shaking breath. This, then, was how it must be. She could not regret her choice.

"Come home, Sophy," her father said.

"No. I'll make my own, with Tom."

"Absolutely not—" he began.

"You cannot stop her," Tom said and followed Sophy out the door.

It had gone faster than expected, but worse than she had feared. Hurrying through the hall, she blinked away the blurring of oak panelling and red damask. Tom was whispering inaudibly in her ear; the shouts in the library seemed far away.

"Just take me away from here," she said.

The sunlight in the street was blinding, her boot heels loud on the stone steps. Tom bent to look in her face, his hand moving to sweep away the wet drops escaping down her cheeks. Then his hand stilled. He straightened, looking back to the doorway.

"Hold up, I said!" Jasper slid to a stop beside them, rather breathless.

"What do you want?" Tom asked sourly.

Jasper ignored Tom, taking Sophy by the shoulders. "You want to marry him?"

Goading, on top of everything else? "I said so, didn't I?" she snapped.

"Don't breathe fire at me," Jasper said. "If you want to marry him, I'll help you get the license. I'd lay a pony Tom doesn't know any bishops."

Turning to Tom, he added, "I don't pretend to understand why she likes you, but evidently, she does. If you are as good to her as she thinks you'll be, I daresay you and I shall rub along tolerably well. But if I see her crying over you again, you and I shall finish that bout we started earlier. You're dashed handy with your fives, but I warn you that I will always be ready, and in practice."

SOPHY SPENT THE NIGHT WITH HENRIETTA AND PERCY, who decided to ignore Lord and Lady Fairchild's fiery demands that Sophy be returned at once. The Arundels brought her to the chapel next morning in a new dress and, more importantly, a new hat.

Jasper was good as his word, or perhaps not, since he perjured himself, swearing to the bishop that Sophy had her father's consent to marry Tom. After the ceremony, Mrs. Bagshot invited the newlyweds and their three guests for breakfast. Jasper and the

Arundels consented to come, though Henrietta could not hide her startled face at the crocodile legged furniture in the Bagshot drawing room.

After breakfast, they waved Sophy and Tom off with bright faces.

"I never even thanked Jasper," Sophy said, as they turned the corner and passed out of sight.

"You can write him a letter. For the first time in my life, I'm anxious to reach Chippenstone." Tom's smile made her stomach flutter. She took his hand, weaving her fingers through his. He leaned back in the seat with a sigh. "Glad I didn't drive," he said.

"I think Jasper and Henrietta don't mind our getting married so much," Sophy ventured. Henrietta had been interested, though not exuberant over the nuptials. It was harder to discern what lay underneath Jasper's charm.

"Said he was happy to put one in his mother's eye," Tom said. He looked thoughtful. "But I don't think that's why he helped us."

"Well, you can't believe everything he says. He likes being outrageous."

Tom laughed. "To be honest, I don't think he likes me above half. But he wants you to be happy. I like him best for that."

Sophy settled her shoulder against Tom's arm, but he went one further, lifting his arm out of the way and wrapping it around her shoulders.

"Ask me to kiss you again," he said.

When they pulled to a stop in front of Chippenstone, Tom realized he'd forgotten to warn his servants.

"You'll see to the horses? And the baggage?" Tom cheerfully asked the goggling stable boy. Picking up his wife, he climbed the front steps and yanked open the door. Kicking it wide, he stepped into the hall. The door slammed shut behind them, bringing his housekeeper at a run. She was in a calico housedress, trailed by two maids with dripping wash rags.

"Mr. Bagshot!" was all she managed, aghast and accusing at once. She recognized the red-haired Miss in his arms, but not her bright eyes and blushing cheeks.

When Tom breezily informed his housekeeper that he had returned with his wife, she only swallowed once and asked them to step into the drawing room—no, that was being cleaned, so perhaps the library—for half an hour while she prepared their rooms.

Tom assured his flummoxed housekeeper that he was certain the rooms were in perfectly good order, ignoring her bloodless face. If anything was lacking he would tend to it himself.

"Sheer nonsense," she grumbled, and sent the maids back to work so she could totter down to the kitchens. What Cook would do about dinner, she hadn't the least notion.

Tom and Sophy didn't notice. He was still carrying her, staggering up the stairs.

"Stop laughing. You'll drop me," Sophy said.

"Can't help it," he wheezed.

"Didn't think you'd be doing this again, did you?" she asked, remembering he had done this once before, when she had arrived injured and soaking wet at his door.

"Wouldn't have wagered a shilling on it. But that doesn't mean I didn't want to," he added with a wink.

He made it to the top of the stairs and started down the hall. His eyes were fixed on her in a way that made her fear he would trip on the carpet. "What is it?" she asked.

"I don't want to miss it," he said.

"Miss what?"

Tom's answering smile was sly. "Your face. You don't fool me. I can tell what you think of my mother's furniture."

Sophy colored hotly. "It is . . ."

"—Impossibly vulgar?" finished Tom.

"I wouldn't have said it, but yes. It doesn't matter. Lady Fairchild will never see it, and no one else will mind." Sophy spoke lightly, but Tom's smile contracted.

"I won't let you be lonely," he promised. "I'll love you so much you won't be able to miss them."

Sophy brushed aside the hair that had fallen across his forehead, tucking the moment away where it would stay bright.

"Are you going to put me down now?" she asked, raising an eyebrow.

"Not a chance." Tom recovered his smile. "You can throw it all out tomorrow if you like, but I'm not missing your face when you see how they furnished the master suite. It's exactly, horribly, incredibly vulgar."

Sophy bit her lip to stifle a laugh. "I hope so."

IN THE END, SOPHY SURPRISED TOM, REFUSING TO ALTER HIS Oriental bedchambers by so much as a hair, claiming she could only belong in this room of decadent splendor. Tom laughed. They both laughed, often.

Mrs. Bagshot managed to contain her happiness for a fortnight before it became too much to bear and she returned to Chippenstone. "Open your presents," she said, pointing Sophy to the pile of boxes unloaded from her coach.

They were expensive and mostly awful, but Sophy wore them with good grace, and determined from then on to always shop with her new mother in law. She even refrained from laughing over the hats privately with Tom. Mostly.

Her mother in law didn't seem to mind. They had been married only three months when she affectionately took Sophy's hand, telling her how glad she was to have her in the family. And though Sophy could not tell her to expect a grandson yet, Mrs. Bagshot was confident that a baby would arrive soon.

Sophy and Tom rode often, though never within sight of Cordell. She ridiculed him shamelessly for his ham-fisted riding, but he said he did not mind being outshone by his wife. He offered to buy her breeding stock but Sophy refused. She could never duplicate her father's stables.

"Do you miss them?" Tom asked, when they reached the boundary of Cordell and wordlessly turned their horses homeward again.

"Yes. But I had to choose between them and you. I needed you most of all. Still do." Her heart was too full for empty spaces.

Henrietta sent regular letters and Jasper visited at Easter. "The pater sends these, and your horse," he said, gesturing at two parcels in brown paper.

"Did he send any word?" Sophy asked.

"Just the presents. Said they were yours anyway."

Sophy untied the first, her heart pounding as she lifted away the paper. She was afraid to hope. The weight of the parcel and the shape argued for it, but after so many years, he had probably forgotten.

"What did he send?" Tom asked, leaning over to look. Sophy was silent, her hand on her lips.

She found her voice at last. "Some things of mine. My mother's sketches." The second parcel was the last one, alone in its frame.

"Where do you think we should put it?" he asked.

"In the nursery," Sophy said. Her mother would have liked that.

Tom was properly speechless, but Jasper was never without words for long. "Blast," he said. "You aren't coming riding with me, are you?"

"I'm afraid not," she said, ending in a squeal, for Tom had seized her. Jasper left the room, smiling, with an ostentatious huff of disgust.

Sophy gave up riding and turned her attentions to the gardens.

She and Tom took turns thinking up hideous names for their child. Sally Bagshot claimed her cup was full, so long as they did not call her granddaughter Clytemnestra.

Summer came and Sophy slept more, embarrassed she was turning so lazy, but still grateful to have her breakfast brought on a tray. Leafing through her letters one morning, her mind fogged with sleep, she did not realize at first that the letter in her hand was not from Henrietta. She stopped reading after the first line and pressed her hand to her mouth.

It would be easy to flip over the sheet of expensive paper and check the sender's name, but the disappointment, if she was wrong—

She kept reading.

Dear Sophy, the letter read.

Preparations are nearly complete for my removal to town again. I shall enjoy London, as I always do, and look forward to seeing Henrietta, Laurence and Little William. It will do him good to spend some time with his grandmama—his nurse is such a hapless creature.

Henrietta tells me that you are expecting an Arrival of your own. I hope you are taking good care of yourself and that your husband has the sense to keep you off a horse. I fear your riding days are over for some time. While I am in town I shall look at finding you a doctor. Choosing a competent physician is most important.

You may not have heard, but Alistair is recently married. She is a handsome widow, with a good fortune. You will be glad, I am sure, to hear he is well settled.

I still tread carefully, for the unpleasantness surrounding your broken engagement is too recent to be entirely forgot and I regret that it must be at least another twelvemonth before I can receive you. Until then, I depend on hearing from you often.

Jasper tells me you are happy, and I am glad to hear it. Please write, for I am anxious for your news.

With affection,
Georgiana

Tom found her, laughing and wiping stray tears from her eyes. "What's wrong?" he asked.

"Nothing," Sophy passed him the letter, the back of her other hand pressed to her mouth to stop her hiccups.

He read it twice, his forehead creasing with suspicion. "Are you upset?" he asked, scooting beside her on the bed.

"Boots!" Sophy pointed at his feet, dismayed on her maid's behalf. Tom dismissed her concerns with a wave.

"Is she elbowing her way back into your life?" he demanded. "I don't know if I'll let her."

Sophy took a last swipe at her streaming eyes. "She can be hard to stop. I'm not upset. I've missed her. She has been as kind to me as she knows how, and you know I love her."

Tom looked affronted.

"Just a very little," she assured him. "You still have the lion's share."

"Well," Tom said, leaning back into the pillows and flinging an arm around his wife, "Lord knows I can't withhold you anything. At least she gave me a year's warning." He kissed her ear, brushing aside her curls, still mussed from sleep. And, because once he had kissed her hair, he had to kiss her face and then her mouth, neither one of them said anything.

A few minutes later, though, Sophy picked up the letter and laughed again.

"At least you can laugh about it," Tom said. "Are you sure? What if she tries to eat me?"

Sophy looked at Tom. "You'll manage," she said. "You listen too much to Jasper. She knows when she's met her match. So do I." And with the light-fingered touch that Tom loved best, she took his face in her hands.

ALSO BY JAIMA FIXSEN

Incognita

Courting Scandal

The Reformer

A Holiday in Bath

The Dark Before Dawn

ABOUT THE AUTHOR

Jaima Fixsen is the author of the popular Fairchild regency romance series. She would rather read than sleep and though all her novels take place in the past, she couldn't live without indoor plumbing or smart phones.

When she isn't writing or child wrangling, she's a snow enthusiast. She lives with her family in Alberta, Canada, and most all just tries to keep up.

Printed in Great Britain
by Amazon

41366393R00158